European Justice

Ray Weaver

European
Justice

Ray Weaver

Sirena Press

For information:

Murmaid Publishing
theMurmaid@tampabay.rr.com

Other books by Ray Weaver:
Tightrope to Justice
Miami Justice

ISBN #   978-0-9819432-8-2

Cover and Book Design
theMurmaid ™
for Sirena Press

Printed in the United States of America

First American Edition

Dedication

I wish to dedicate this novel, European Justice
to my wife, Ellie, who took the words I
wrote on a legal pad and transformed
them into my third novel.

Also a special thanks to my family,
friends and neighbors, my Silver Sneakers
exercise group and LOC Married Couples Club.
Their kindness in purchasing my first two books
and offering their constructive critiques has
given me the inspiration to write this book
and start on a fourth one.

Finally, my gratitude to my editor and publisher,
Nancy Frederich, who in her wisdom and
knowledge continues to give me great advice
and a fantastic cover.

HOPE ALL OF YOU ENJOY MY THIRD NOVEL

Chapter 1

"Phil, get in here quick," Kelley called out to her husband who was in the bathroom adjoining their stateroom, preparing for bed.

"Can't. I'm brushing my teeth."

"Get in here! Now!"

The newly-weds, Kelley and Phil Willis, were on the last night of the Queen Mary II's voyage sailing from New York to England.

He rinsed out his mouth, threw down the toothbrush and rushed to the doorway. "What's so urgent that I can't even finish brushing my teeth?"

In her pajamas, slippers and robe, Kelley was standing in front of the balcony doors. "Look out here," she was pointing outside. "I saw a flash and heard two popping sounds that sounded like pistol shots."

"Kelley, its one o'clock in the morning and you're tired. You're probably just imagining things."

She shot him a look of barely suppressed impatience. "Put your robe on honey. Let's go check it out."

"I thought your undercover days were behind us. But, for you my dear, anything." He put on the plush white terry cloth robe with the ship's insignia the cruise line had provided for each of them. Then, he grabbed a flashlight out of his suitcase. "Lead the way."

Kelley hurried out the stateroom and headed to the end of the corridor. "I'm certain that something happened on the deck above us. Here's the stairs that lead up above."

The majestic 'QM2' as she was nicknamed, was visible from afar with its royal blue hull and snow white upper decks. The Queen Mary II was the most magnificent luxury ocean line ever built. From bow to stern, she provided one of the most modern luxury cruise travel experiences. She had fourteen spacious decks on which to relax and unwind, opulent public areas, extravagant dining rooms, ballrooms, theatres, and lounges...even the only Planetarium at sea.

Kelley was thrilled when she learned that Phil had booked this ship for their honeymoon voyage. Upon their arrival, they found a full bottle of champagne and sugar-iced strawberries waiting for them in their suite. Their balcony stateroom provided full and private access to the ocean breeze

Earlier in the evening, dressed in formal evening attire, Kelley had felt like a queen herself, when she and her husband descended down the sweeping staircase of the two- deck-high Britannia Restaurant, the Queen Mary's main dining room. It looked like the grand dining salon of the ocean's golden age of travel. They had been special quests at the captain's table where they dined on lobster, filet mignon and champagne.

Once outside on the deck above them, Kelley and Phil were able to see the deck chairs, thanks to the full moon that illuminated the area. As most of the passengers had enjoyed the farewell dinner and had retired to their staterooms or the gaming tables, they saw no other passengers. They began searching the deck.

"Bring your flashlight over here," Kelley ordered as she walked toward the railing.

"What am I looking for Kell, a dead body?"

"Could be." As she neared the railing, she thought that she spotted something gleaming on the deck in the moonlight. She walked over and bent down, picking up two shell casings from a gun.

"Look Phil. See I did hear shots. Let's see if we find anything else." She put the casings in her pocket and walked toward two lifeboats that were hanging from the side of the boat.

Phil raced ahead and leaned over the railing looking into the boats. "I think I see something in that one." He pointed to the second boat.

"Can you scramble down there and check it out?"

"I think I can climb down one of the ropes and get inside for a better look."

He grabbed the rope securing the lifeboat to the ship and carefully lowered himself down it using the skills that he had been taught a couple of years earlier in Sarasota at the Wilders Brothers Circus Ranch. He was grateful that his uncle, Jack, had insisted that both he and Kelley learn special skills before they started working as private investigators for him.

"Can you see anything?" Kelley whispered.

"Just a minute."

She watched him inch forward slowly in the life boat, and bend over to look down. "Oh, my God, it's an elderly woman in an evening gown. And she's been shot. I think she's dead."

"Feel for a pulse. But don't touch anything. We don't want to destroy any evidence."

After a few seconds, he said quietly, "She's dead alright. We better get the ship's captain."

"Come on up. But be quiet," she whispered. "We don't want to disturb any passengers that might still be up."

After he was standing beside her, Kelley said, "You stay here. I'll be right back with the captain."

Kelley ran to the elevator, took it to the flight deck and raced up the stairs to the bridge of the ship. She looked inside the door and could see the first mate talking to the purser. She knocked loudly on the door.

The purser opened the door. "Yes, Madam, how can I help you?"

"I need to talk to the captain."

"Please come in. Captain Marcel Giovanni has retired for the night and the deputy captain is in charge."

Kelley walked over to him. "Sir, I need to speak to the captain. I'm Mrs. Willis."

"Yes, I know. We sat together at the farewell dinner tonight. The captain has retired for the night and has left instructions to disturb him only in case of an extreme emergency."

"Believe me. That's what this is."

He caught his breath in frustration and reluctantly went to the phone. "Captain Giovanni, I have Mrs. Willis here. She says that she must speak to you. She said it was an emergency."

Kelley took the phone from him. "Captain, I must talk to you privately at once. It's very important. In fact, it's a matter of life and death."

"Very well, then. Have the purser bring you to my quarters."

She hung up the phone and relayed the captain's orders.

"Follow me then." He led her down to a lower deck and knocked at the captain's door.

He opened the door and gestured for Kelley to enter. "That will be all," he said dismissing the purser. He looked at the distraught woman. "Now, what's so urgent?"

She took a deep breath. "A short time ago, I heard what sounded like gun shots on the deck above our stateroom. Saw a couple of flashes of light too. My husband and I went to the upper deck to investigate. After looking around, my husband found the body of a woman in one of the life boats. We didn't want to alarm any of the other passengers so my husband stayed with the body and I came to get you."

The captain grabbed his coat and started for the door. "You're sure that no one else knows of this?"

"Not as far as I know. My husband is at the scene waiting for us. My husband is an attorney, and we both used to work as private investigators in Florida. Also, I was with a secret service agency there, so we knew that no one should touch anything until the crime crew arrived."

"Take me to the body at once Mrs. Willis."

"Follow me then, sir. I mean Captain."

When they arrived at the scene, they found Phil pacing back and forth on the deck in front of the life boat.

"My God, Kelley. What took you so long?"

"I went to the bridge where I thought the Captain would be. He wasn't there so I had to go to his cabin to get him."

"Where's the body," the Captain whispered.

Phil gestured toward the life boat. "In there. Some elderly lady in a fancy dress. You'll have to climb inside the boat if you want to take a closer look. But the lady is definitely dead."

"I'll take your word for it." The Captain walked over to the phone on the wall. "I'm going to call my chief of security. He'll need to take charge from this point onward. I know that he'll want to examine the body and photograph the crime scene before we move the victim. Then he'll have to alert Scotland Yard so that they meet us when we dock in the morning."

"That sounds like a reasonable plan," Phil replied.

The captain looked at the newlyweds. "Of course, I will rely on your discretion. We cannot let word of this get out. No need to alarm the other passengers."

"Of course," they said in unison.

"We dock in Southampton, about seven in the morning. Please meet me on the bridge about eight."

"Yes sir," Phil replied.

They returned to their stateroom and started to climb into the double bed. Suddenly, she looked over at him and laughed, "Is this a sign of things to come?"

He looked puzzled. "What?"

"You just dropped your robe on the floor."

"Gee Kell. It's after two in the morning." He reached down, picked it up and laid it on a nearby chair. "Look at us; we're starting to sound like an old married couple."

She hung her head and slipped into bed. "Sorry, we've only been married a few days. I have to get used to it."

"Just teasing sweetie." He gave her a big kiss, turned over and went to sleep.

She stayed awake for some time, thinking about the past. Almost three years had passed from the time they first met to the time when they had finally tied the knot.

The first year of their time together was spent working as private investigators to determine who had murdered Kelley's uncle Bill. After that they had parted ways as Phil returned to Syracuse to get his law degree and she had joined the secret service agency that Florida Governor Paul Mathison had formed.

Then, destiny brought Phil and her back together in Miami, Florida, where her last job was as an undercover agent. Phil had returned there for a law case, rejoined Kelley and helped her solve a jewelry robbery. Once more the two of them connected, only now in a romantic way.

Realizing how much she had come to mean to him,

he proposed and she accepted.

They headed back to Syracuse and six months later they were married.

Her thoughts then turned to the fairy tale wedding that they had experienced just days earlier.

Yes. Everything about the wedding and reception afterwards had been perfect and now they were on their way to London, where Phil's law firm had sent him to work on a case. Following this, they would officially start their two week honeymoon in Europe.

Since Phil had not disclosed where they would be going after London, Kelley now wondered what other parts of the continent she would see. She shivered with anticipation as she thought about it. She knew that after the honeymoon, she would resume everyday life.

And she was looking forward to the peace and tranquility.

Chapter 2

It took quite a while for Kelley to get to sleep that evening. She lay awake thinking about the past few hours.

After their formal dinner at the Captain's table, she had said to Phil, "Why don't we change into some casual clothes and go to the 'Golden Lion'?" They're having Karaoke and a talent contest before the regular comedy and magic show."

"Maybe, you would rather spend the rest of the evening in our room. I've got a couple of good novels to read."

Kelley shook her head. "Are you kidding? We need to end this fantastic trip with some fun."

After returning to their room to change, they headed for the "Golden Lion" on deck two, where they took seats at a side table near the stage and ordered a couple of drinks.

The cruise director came out onto the stage, told several jokes, and announced that it was time for the karaoke and talent contest.

"We have available in the back of the stage a variety of costumes for our five performers who signed up earlier in the day for our competition," he announced.

"Our first contestant, Julie will be doing a cheer leading routine to the music 'Stars Spangled Banner'."

Dressed in a tight red, white and blue spandex outfit, Julie performed her act parading up and down, twirling her baton and at the same time singing the words to the song.

Next, an Elvis impersonator, with a black wig and long paste on side burns took his place on stage. He caressed the microphone, wiggled his hips and sang along to "Heart Break Hotel."

Phil leaned over and whispered, "Boy, this really takes guts to get up in front of all these people."

The third performer was a young girl, dressed like Dorothy in the Wizard of Oz. She gave a beautiful and moving rendition of "Over the Rainbow."

Next, was an elderly gentleman who came onto the stage, dressed in a black tuxedo. Sounding like Al Jolson, he belted out "Suwannee" and received a standing ovation from the audience.

Phil leaned over to say something to Kelley. She was no longer sitting in her seat. He looked around the room for her, shrugged his shoulders and decided that she had probably made a quick trip to the ladies room.

The cruise director took his place on the stage once again. "Our last performer will be singing to 'Diamonds are a Girl's Best Friend.'

Ladies and gentlemen, let's hear it for Kelley."

Phil looked up in amazement as his wife, dressed in a long form fitting white gown walked onto the stage. With her blond wig, a fake diamond tiara, necklace, and bracelets, she resembled Marilyn Monroe.

"That's my wife," Phil shouted out.

Moving, grinding and bumping like a stripper, Kelley sang along with the music. Realizing that he had not really heard her sing like this before, Phil decided that she had a terrific voice. And her dancing was not too shabby either.

As she ended the song, Kelley took off the large fake

diamond ring that she was wearing and threw it into the audience, then disappeared behind the curtain.

"That's it ladies and gentlemen; our five acts. Now, I'll call all of our performers back out onto the stage."

The five entered the stage and stood in a row.

"As they step forward, one by one, your shouts and applause will determine our winner."

Each of the first four contestants was given shouts of acceptance and rounds of applause.

When Kelley stepped to the front of the stage, the crowd stood and whistled, screamed and clapped for several minutes.

Phil looked around the room, beaming. "That's my bride."

"It looks like our winner, is Kelley." The emcee walked over to her and presented her with a small silver cup for first place and an envelope. "The cup is for your trophy case, Kelley. But inside this envelope, are two certificates for our monogrammed Queen Mary II terry cloth robes. Unlike the ones in your room, you can keep these and take them home as a reminder of your excellent performance." Turning to the other four contestants, he added, "You will receive complimentary drinks for the rest of the show."

Kelley went backstage; took off her costume and returned to her seat beside Phil.

He leaned over and gave her a kiss. "You never told me that you had such musical talent. And, never in my wildest dreams did I imagine that you could bump and grind like that."

She grinned. "Well, I've have to give you private shows in the future."

When the comedy and magic parts of the show, were over, Kelley stood up. "I'm going to the gift shop to redeem the vouchers for the robes. One large and one medium."

"Good, I'll meet you back in our room."

As Phil took the elevator to their stateroom, he started humming. "Diamonds are a Girl's Best Friend."

Now, Kelley tried in vain to clear her mind and to fall asleep. The rest of the night passed slowly. Consequently, she didn't need an alarm to awaken her. About seven, she wearily turned herself over in bed and looked at her husband. He too, appeared to be wide awake.

"How did you sleep, honey," she asked.

"Not very good." He gave her a quick kiss and slipped out of bed.

"Call room service and order some breakfast while I clean up and finish packing," she said as she got to her feet.

"I see that you already laid out our clothes for today." He picked up the phone. "What time are we supposed to meet with the Captain?"

"Supposed to join him on the bridge about eight."

Shortly after they finished dressing, room service arrived at the door with the bacon, eggs, toast and juice Phil had ordered. They quickly ate and headed for the bridge.

"Good morning, Captain," Kelley said.

Phil shook his hand. "What's going on with the murder investigation this morning?"

"We've already identified the murdered woman. It's Dame Margaret Sinclair. Her daughter, Diana, reported her missing this morning. Seems like Margaret Sinclair never returned to her stateroom after dinner last night with her daughter and secretary, Joyce Dowling. And, from a physical description of her and the clothing that she was wearing, we're certain that it's her.

She's very prominent in the upper circles in London, so New Scotland Yard's Commissioner Andrew Pope, is scheduled to meet us at the dock. He's bringing his people on board to investigate. The main complication at this time is that Scotland Yard has ordered that none of the passengers will be allowed to disembark until they have been questioned and any necessary statements taken."

"That's not going to sit well with most of them," Kelley observed.

The Captain shrugged his shoulders. "Can't be helped. Scotland Yard is in charge at this point."

"Does the daughter have any idea how or why her mother was murdered," Phil asked.

"No. The mother and daughter were returning to England, together with the mother's personal secretary, Joyce Dowling. My security chief questioned both of them already this morning. The last either of the ladies saw Dame Sinclair was at the farewell dinner last night. After dining, Dame Sinclair left the table to walk around the deck and both ladies said that they had not seen her since."

"Did Dame Sinclair know any other people on the ship," Kelley asked.

"Only casual acquaintances that the ladies met during the voyage. I'm going to give the Commissioner my manifest of the passengers on board. He said that the daughter and secretary will be interviewed at length at Scotland Yard and the rest of the passengers will be questioned before they leave the ship. Scotland Yard will remove the body discreetly after they investigate the crime scene."

"Oh, my gosh. I forgot to tell you that I picked up two shell casings from the deck last night," Kelley said.

"Well, I'm certain that Scotland Yard will want to examine those," he said. "I thought you said that you once were private investigators? I'm surprised that you picked up the evidence."

She leveled a calm gaze at him. "I guess that I wasn't thinking very clearly at the time."

"Maybe it's just as well. They could have rolled off the deck and into the ocean," Phil suggested.

"Now follow me and we'll meet the Commissioner. I got a call that his auto was at the dock." The Captain led them down the gangplank and over to a black car.

Standing next to it was a tall and slender gentleman dressed in riding britches and high leather boots.

"Commissioner Pope," the Captain asked.

"Yes. Sorry for my appearance. I was out for an early morning ride at my country house, when I got the call about the murder. Didn't take the time to go back to the house to change. Just had my man drive me to the dock."

"Thank you for responding so quickly. I'm Captain Giovanni." The two shook hands and then the Commissioner asked, "Please fill me in on the details of what has happened the past few hours."

The two talked briefly, and then walked to where Kelley and Phil were standing. The Captain introduced the Commissioner to them. "This is Attorney Phillip Willis and his wife Kelley, American passengers on my ship. They found the deceased in the wee hours of the morning. They both worked as private investigators and Mrs. Willis worked for a Secret Service Agency in Florida."

The Commissioner shook their hands. "I'll need a statement from you about what happened."

"Of course, we understand," Phil answered.

"I'll have my assistant drive you to your hotel, he can take your statements there." He signaled for his assistant, who was standing by the auto. "The Captain said that you have both had experience as private investigators?"

"Yes. That's true." Kelley reached into her pocket and pulled out the two spent shells that she had found on the deck the previous evening. "Oh, Commissioner, I have something here for you. I'm sorry to say, that in the excitement, I picked up these shells from the deck and put them in my pocket."

"I can understand how upset you probably were at the time." The Commissioner motioned for his assistant to take them. "This is my right hand man, Agent Wallace."

Wallace reached into his pocket, pulled out a plastic bag and placed the shells in it.

"Oh, by the way, I know one of your Scotland Yard agents, here in London–James Fleming. I'm sure that you know him," Kelley said to both of the men.

"Yes. Very well," the Commissioner replied. "One of my best young men. You aren't by chance the young female agent that he was sent to America to work with several months back, are you?"

"Yes. That was me. Kelley Ryan. But now, Kelley Willis."

"You know, your backgrounds intrigue me," the Commissioner said. "If you are free tomorrow evening for dinner, I could have my man pick you up at your hotel and bring you to my home. My wife, Robin, will be delighted to meet you. And, maybe, we can get Agent Fleming and his lovely wife, Eva, to join us."

Kelley and Phil looked at each other and nodded in agreement. "That's very kind of you," Phil said. "We would be delighted to accept."

"Now, I have to go talk with the security chief on the ship. Also, I'm bringing a number of my people aboard to help with interviewing the passengers. So I'll be here for the day. In the meantime, I don't see any reason to hold the two of you on board so I'll have Agent Wallace take you and your luggage to your hotel. Where are you staying?"

"At the Windsor."

"Nice hotel, but it has some age you know. Convenient location. I'll have Wallace pick you up there at six tomorrow night. Here is my card in case you need to reach me in the meantime."

In return, Phil reached in his billfold and pulled out his business card. "Here is my mobile phone number. I had it activated for international calls while I'm here."

As the Captain and the Commissioner boarded the ship, Agent Wallace loaded the luggage in the boot and held open the back door of the auto for Kelley and Phil.

"You're staying at the Windsor. Have you been there before?"

"No, sir," Phil answered. "This is our first visit to London. In fact, we're on our honeymoon."

"Well, it shouldn't take too long to take your statements about the murder once we get there. So we Londoners must put out the welcome mat for you. If you aren't pressed for time, I'll take the scenic route to your hotel and show you a bit of the city."

"Bloody nice," Kelley replied.

Phil chuckled at his wife's comment. "I'm so anxious to see Big Ben and St. Paul's Cathedral." Kelley said.

"We'll just take a brief jog around then. I'll call the Windsor and let them know that you are on the way so they can be certain to have your room ready."

He picked up his mobile. "This is Agent Wallace of Scotland Yard. I'm bringing Mr. and Mrs. Willis to your hotel. We should be there within the hour. Please have their suite ready. And by the way, have a bottle of champagne chilled for them. They're on their honeymoon."

For the next hour, Agent Wallace drove them around the heart of the city, pointing out the many famous tourist attractions. Finally, he pulled up in front of the Windsor Hotel. The bell man greeted them and loaded their luggage onto a cart.

They walked inside with Wallace behind them. Phil

approached the front desk. "Mr. and Mrs. Phillip Willis. You should have our reservations."

The man looked in his computer, "Yes sir. Your suite is ready."

The bell man led them to their suite and placed the luggage inside the door.

Phil handed him a generous tip, and turned to the agent, and gestured toward the settee that was placed against one wall of the sitting room. "Please have a seat Agent Wallace and we'll take care of the paperwork now."

On the coffee table in front of them was a bottle of champagne, chilling in a silver bucket.

"Care for a glass of champagne, Agent Wallace?"

"Thank you. No. I'm on duty. But, please feel free to pour some for the missus and yourself."

Phil looked at Kelley and grinned. "I think we'll take care of business first and then enjoy the bubbly later."

Agent Wallace pulled out a legal pad from his briefcase and wrote down their statements about the murder.

"Do you have any opinions as to who may have been the killer," he asked.

"Most definitely it must have been someone in her entourage," Kelly offered.

When he was finished, he had them sign the forms. "I think that concludes our business for today. I'll plan on picking you up tomorrow night at six for your dinner with the Commissioner and his wife."

"Thank you so much for the lovely tour of the city," Kelley said, as they stood up.

"It was a bit quick. But, at least you know where to find the tourist sites if you are staying in the city for a few days."

"We do expect to be here for about a week," Phil answered, shaking his hand.

Agent Wallace smiled. "See you tomorrow. And by the way, thanks for not calling me a bloke. I never cared for that term."

After he left, Kelley asked, "What now dear?"

"I've got to make a phone call to the law office. I need to go over some information with them about our case. Our New York end of it is tied to what they are working on here. Why don't you go to the lobby and inquire about those tour buses that run here every day. Maybe we can line one up for the morning. I won't be long at my phone call."

"Your command is done," she said, and bowed. "While I'm talking to the people at the front desk, I'll ask them if they know of a good restaurant close by for supper."

"Oh, were you going to call your old partner, James?"

"Maybe tomorrow."

Chapter 3

Later that evening, after a delicious dinner and a leisurely stroll around the streets of London, close to their hotel, they returned to their suite.

"That bed will probably feel pretty good," Phil said. "But, first let's open that champagne." He pointed to the bottle still in the ice bucket in the sitting room. The ice had melted but the bottle was still chilled.

He put a towel around the bottle, popped the cork and toasted his bride. "Here's to you and to our first time in London."

After her second glass, Kelley said, "I think that's enough." She walked to the door of the bedroom and looked over at the king size canopy bed. "That bed does look mighty tempting right now."

"You know it's only eight thirty and you're already yawning, Mrs. Willis."

"I know, but we didn't get a whole lot of sleep last night."

"Let's go to bed then, my sweet girl. I'll put some romantic music on the intercom." He took her by the hand and led her to the bed and nestled her in his arms. "You know my love, I'm so glad that you waited to get married until I came along."

"I would have waited forever for you. I always knew

that we were a great team."

After a beautiful love making session, they drifted off into a peaceful slumber.

In the morning, they were awakened by the sound of the phone ringing. Phil reached over and reluctantly answered it.

"Mr. Willis, this is the front desk. I have a courier here with two boxes of papers for you. He said that he is from Manchester Law Firm. May I send him up?"

Phil agreed, rolled over and told Kelley, who was also awake, that a courier was delivering some papers. He got up, put on his robe and walked through the double doors leading to the sitting room. After hearing a brief knock, he opened the door.

The courier standing in front of him had two small boxes and a piece of paper in his hands. "Mr. Willis, I have a delivery for you. I'll need your signature."

Phil stepped back so that the courier could bring the boxes into the sitting room. "Please put the boxes on the desk." Then, he signed the delivery form and gave the man five English pounds as a tip.

After the courier left, Phil opened the boxes and leafed briefly through the papers, then closed them.

Kelley leaned her head out of the bedroom door. "Homework dear?"

"Just some briefs on the upcoming trial that I'm helping the law firm out with. I'll study them later." He followed Kelley back into the bedroom where she gathered up her clothes and headed for the bathroom.

Suddenly, she let out a quick scream. "Damn it!"

Phil ran to the bathroom door and looked in. "You okay?"

"Just trying to figure out how to use this bidet," she answered.

He chuckled and turned away. "Don't ask me to help Kelley. While you're getting dressed, I'll see if I can find the news on the TV."

Later, she went into the sitting room, where she saw Phil, now fully dressed, watching CNN. "Anything interesting happening in the US?"

"No, the stock market went down a few points. But, it's been a roller coaster lately anyway."

"That coffee smells good Phil."

"Yes, I'm glad they had a coffee pot in our room. Help yourself."

She poured a cup and sat down beside him. Suddenly, he stood up, walked to the desk, opened one of the boxes once again and started rifling through the papers.

"I thought you said you were going to do that later."

"Just checking something real quick. And to show you what a good husband you married, I'm going to spend two days showing you around this city."

"The bloody hell you are." She shook her head briefly, with an abrupt laugh. "Phil today is Saturday and tomorrow is Sunday. I know that most law firms are closed."

"My point exactly. Before we left Syracuse, my firm said to enjoy my time in London with my new bride and that's exactly what I intend to do. So, I'm all yours until Monday."

"Excellent. She picked up the menu. "Let's order breakfast from room service. How about an omelet?"

"Wait a minute Kelley. I heard that they had one hell of a breakfast buffet downstairs in the dining room." He picked up the phone and made a call. He hung up and said, "Get ready, girl. We're going downstairs. We may even skip lunch. Got lots to see you know."

"Give me fifteen minutes," she said, heading for the bathroom.

"Hurry. My tummy is growling."

Kelley quickly applied her makeup. Then, as she picked up the hair dryer and started to blow dry her hair, she looked into the mirror, and reflected on the past six months.

After getting engaged, she prepared for her new life as Mrs. Willis. She sold her car to her landlady in Miami and packed up her belongings. Phil rented a car and a U-Haul and drove her and her few possessions to Syracuse. There he helped her move in with his cousin, Sally, who Kelley was going to room with until she and Phil got married.

Sally was twenty-four and as time went on, the two became close friends. Kelley eventually asked Sally to be her maid of honor and Sally's sister, Brenda, to be the bridesmaid.

Before looking around for a job, Kelley decided to fly back to Chicago and talk to her mother about the wedding and her mom's future.

In Chicago, she stayed at a hotel near her mother's retirement home, so that she could spend more time with her. She took her mother, Ann, and her companion, Veronica Miley, out shopping and for lunch as the three discussed the plans for the upcoming wedding. They decided that Kelley and her future mother-in-law, Kaitlin, who lived in Syracuse would make the arrangements for the wedding there.

Kelley's mother and Veronica would fly to Syracuse on the Thursday before the wedding and stay with Phil's parents until the Monday after the wedding.

They all went to a wedding salon and picked out dresses for both Ann and Veronica to wear. Ann had selected an ivory colored tea length lace gown and Veronica picked out a fuchsia colored silk suit.

On the last day of Kelley's stay in Chicago, Veronica suggested that she join them that evening in the retirement home's spacious dining room. "Its Italian night to-night and you'll love the lasagna."

As they sat enjoying their after dinner coffee and dessert, Kelley's cell phone rang. It was Phil. After talking for several minutes, she turned to her mom. "Mom, guess what, Phil found a wonderful retirement home not far from his parent's house and he wants you to move there soon."

Ann looked at her constant and faithful companion, Veronica. "Oh, I don't know dear. I'll have to think it over. I've got a lot of friends here you know."

"Of course. Take all the time you want. But we would love to have you near us. I'll send you pictures of the place and more information when I get back to Syracuse."

"Thank you. I'm just so grateful that you have found such a lovely young man to marry. And his family sounds just wonderful. I talked with his mother on the phone last week and she seems so kind and thoughtful."

"Yes. I think I've found just the right family to marry into. They are very caring. And my Phil is a gift from Heaven."

The next day, Kelley returned to Syracuse, began her quest to find a job there and started to plan for the wedding. Thanks to the reward checks that both she and Phil had received for finding the Wilson's jewels, they had a nice amount of money to spend on the wedding arrangements.

After landing a job at the local high school, teaching journalism and getting settled in with Sally, Kelley was established in her new life. After, she and Phil settled on the date for the wedding, the excitement started to build for both of them. She and Kaitlin began to plan in earnest for the big day.

Finally the big day arrived and Kelley looked stunning. She wore an original "Priscilla of Boston" elegant organza, strapless A-line dress with hand beaded floral designs along the skirt and bodice. With her cathedral length train flowing behind her, she walked proudly down the aisle on the arm of Dexter McLane, her future father-in-law, to the altar, where her Prince Charming was waiting for her, dressed in a tailored Armani tuxedo.

The reception afterwards was held at the local Wentworth Country Club. Cocktails and hors d'oeuvres were served in the entrance hall. The two hundred guests were then led into the opulent banquet room, situated on the second floor, overlooking the golf course, for a sit-down dinner of prime rib, chicken and lobster.

After the main course, with its selection of wines, the best man, who was one of Phil's college chums, gave the first toast. This was followed by one from Sally, the Maid of Honor. Finally, Dexter stood up and toasted his new daughter-in-law as Kaitlin looked on proudly. Kelley's mother Ann, and Ann's companion, Veronica, together with a few friends from work, were the only people present from the bride's side of the family.

Kelley was pleasantly surprised when after the reception Phil told her that her wedding gift was to be a trip on the QM2, to London. Afterwards, they would tour several destinations in Europe, none of which Phil would reveal to her. He said that it was his special surprise.

When they returned from their honeymoon, Phil was going to start restoring the three bedroom Colonial house that they had purchased together shortly before getting married.

Kelley realized that the time was fleeting by and that her hungry husband was waiting for her. She turned off the hair dryer and walked into the sitting room where he was pacing.

"Were you day dreaming in there girl," he asked.
"Just remembering our wedding."

After they enjoyed the generous buffet breakfast at the hotel, Phil decided to show Kelley the city via the famous London double-decker red bus.

"The Commissioner is going to send his assistant to pick us up for dinner later this evening," he said. "So, we've got several hours to work off breakfast and build up an appetite for dinner."

"Lead the way."

Chapter 4

"Let's run upstairs to our room," Kelley said. "I want to change into low heeled shoes in case we decide to do some serious walking when we get off the bus. I might even grab a sweater. And let's get a bottle of water too. There's some in the fridge in the room."

"Good idea. Think I'll grab a jacket and put on my sneakers."

"Got the card for the room," she asked as they left their room, after changing their shoes and grabbing a sweater and jacket.

"Got it. Let's go girl."

Kelley headed toward the end of the hall. "Let's take the steps down. It's only three flights and I've got to keep in shape."

Walking through the hall to the lobby they passed a large crowd gathered around the hotel's four elevators. Entering the lobby, they heard the concierge call out, "Mr. Willis, I have a message for you."

He walked over to him, and opened the note. "It's from the Commissioner. He wants to change the pickup time for dinner to five instead of six; but, that still leaves us plenty of time to sight-see."

Kelley looked at the crowd around the elevators, which appeared to be getting larger. "What's with the elevators," she asked the concierge.

"They're not running. I've called the lift company and the fire department. One of the lifts is stuck between floors. From the screams coming from inside, we think that there are several people trapped in it."

"Anything we can do to help," Phil asked.

"Not unless you can get those people out," the man answered. "Someone called down to the desk from the third floor and said that they could hear the sound of people screaming. God only knows when the lift repair man will show up and when the fire department will arrive."

Phil hesitated, and then looked at Kelley. "Maybe my circus training can come in handy once again. You know that I can't relax when there's a crisis."

"I remember. You just had to climb the Sunshine Skyway Bridge to save the mayor's kid. No challenge seems too big for my hero."

"What about you girl? You got pretty adventurous on high wires after the circus training too."

Kelley shot him a determined gaze. "Let's go up to the fourth floor and see if we can do anything to help."

They ran up the steps and headed to the elevators, where a group of guests had gathered.

Panting, Kelley paused at the top. "Good thing, we put on our running shoes."

Phil looked at a small group standing by the elevators. "No sense in waiting folks. Must be some kind of malfunction. Best to take the stairs."

"We thought we heard screaming from this one." A man pointed to elevator number three.

"We're here to take care of it," Phil answered.

Mumbling, most of the guests walked toward the stairs or went back to their rooms.

Kelley looked up at the lighted numbers above the elevators. "He's right. Its number three that's stuck—see the other ones are stopped higher up."

"Let's see if we can find something to force the doors to open." Looking around, he spotted a door marked "Janitor Closet", walked over to it and tried to open it. It was locked. "Got a hairpin, Kelley?"

"Never go anywhere without one these days." She reached into her hair and pulled out a long one.

After several attempts, Phil got the closet door open, went inside and came out with a huge screwdriver and a big flash light.

"Just be careful. If the elevator doors do open you don't want to take a nose dive," she said.

Wedging the big screwdriver between the doors to the elevator, Phil finally managed to force them open. "There's the car," he said, looking down. "It's stuck about four feet down."

He looked inside the elevator shaft and could see two thick black metal cables in the shaft holding the elevator.

Kelley leaned over and yelled, "Hello, down there." Several screams of "Help" and "Please get us out" were their responses. One voice sounded like that of a small child.

Phil took the flashlight and shone it on the top of the elevator car. "Hey, there's an escape hatch on top."

Kelley peered down. "I know what we can do. I'll carefully climb down the cables, open the trap door and help those people out."

"Be careful not to jolt the car. Maybe, we should wait for the fire department to get here, honey."

"That could take forever. It's time for me to put some of that circus training to use again."

She walked over to the janitor's closet, took a pile of rags from the shelf, wrapped some of them around her hands and dropped the rest on the floor next to the elevator. While Phil shone the flashlight down in the shaft,

Kelley stepped to the edge, reached forward, grabbed hold of one of the cables and slowly lowed herself down to the top of the elevator car.

"Hello. You people in the elevator," she yelled. "I'm up here. Going to get you out."

"Thank God," a voice in the elevator cried out in anguish.

She continued yelling, "Stand over against the wall. There's an escape hatch on the top of your elevator. I'm going to try to unscrew the bolts holding it. Just remain calm."

"Phil, drop that screw driver down to me."

She strained to remove the big bolts holding the escape hatch shut. Finally, she got them unscrewed and pulled on the handle of the escape hatch.

Once it was open, Phil directed the light down in the car as Kelley peered inside. She saw a young woman standing in the corner staring up at her, with a panic-stricken look on her face. She was clutching a small crying girl to her side. Standing next to them was a heavyset woman in a housekeeping uniform.

The older woman called out, "I'm Danielle, the housekeeper. This is little Hallie. And this is Fran, her nanny. Please get us out."

Kelley looked down at the housekeeper. "Do you have a cleaning cart in there?"

"Yes."

"Push it over so that it's underneath the opening. You two ladies put the little girl on top of the cart. I'll try to reach down and grab her by the wrists."

Sobbing, Hallie asked, "Are we going to die?"

"Not on my watch," Kelley answered.

After the two women lifted the little girl onto the cart, Kelley lay down flat on the top of the elevator. She hooked her legs around the cable to secure her body, reached down, grabbed Hallie by the wrists and lifted her out of the elevator.

Once Hallie was on top of the elevator, Kelley turned her back to her. "Put your arms around my neck and hang on sweetie. Just don't look down," she instructed.

Shivering with fear, Hallie clung to her and whispered, "I have to pee."

"Try to hold it honey."

Just then the elevator lurched downward a few inches. Both of the women inside screamed as fear gripped them.

Her heart thumping, Kelley looked down and yelled, "Try not to move, ladies."

With the little girl on her back, she grabbed onto the cables and hoisted both of their bodies upwards toward the floor above them.

Phil had thrown his body flat on the floor at the elevator opening and as soon as Kelley had raised her body up enough for him to reach Hallie; he grabbed her and pulled her to safety. The elevator lurched again.

"My God, maybe the cables are breaking," Kelley whispered.

"Who's left?"

"Just the young nanny and the housekeeper. The housekeeper looks pretty heavy too."

"I'll go get them Kell. I'm stronger than you and can pull them up easier. You come up here with the little girl." He grabbed her by the arm and hoisted her out of the elevator shaft.

He took some of the rags from the pile beside the elevator and put them around his hands. While Kelley shined the flashlight into the shaft for him, Phil worked his way down to the top of the elevator car, leaned over and looked inside.

"Hi. I'm Phil and I'm going to get you two out."

"I'm Danielle and this is Fran," the housekeeper said, as the young nanny just looked up and sobbed.

"Help Fran up onto the cart," Phil instructed Danielle. Fran tensed, panic-stricken, so Danielle grabbed her around the waist and hoisted her onto the cart.

Phil leaned over and gently said, "Raise your arms Fran. I'm going to lift you out."

Acting as if she was almost in a terrified trance, Fran slowly lifted her arms upward. With a swift movement, Phil grabbed her by both wrists and hoisted her out of the elevator car and onto the roof.

"We're only a few feet from the floor above," he said. "I'll lift you up and my wife will grab hold of your arms— reach them up as far as you can."

With a determined effort, he lifted Fran into the air as Kelley lay on the floor above, reached over and grabbed the girl by the wrists. With Phil pushing and Kelley pulling they managed to get Fran out of the elevator shaft and onto the floor above.

"Now, I'll see if I can get the housekeeper up, but she looks mighty heavy. I hope I can manage," Phil said.

Suddenly the stairwell door burst open and four firemen rushed into the hall.

A sweating Kelley turned around. "Thank God. Phil, the cavalry is here!"

The firemen walked over to the elevator and looked down at Phil— his face streaked with oil. He grinned up at them. "The housekeeper is still down there. I was hoping that you could help me get her out."

The fireman looked down at Phil. "You're one brave bloody hero. Climb up here chap and leave it to us."

The elevator car lurched again and dropped about a foot lower in the shaft.

After Phil climbed out of the elevator shaft, firemen unpacked their equipment from a big bag. One of them stepped into a metal basket with a stainless steel cable and a winch attached to it. The other firemen hammered an anchor into the tile floor and hooked the opposite end of the steel cable to it.

They lowered the man and the basket slowly down the shaft until it came to rest on the top of the elevator car. A second fireman lowered himself down the cables, slipped down into the elevator car, and helped the housekeeper stand on top of the cart.

As he pushed the housekeeper from below the other fireman pulled her to the top of the elevator. The fireman inside climbed up and out of the elevator car. Both of them helped the housekeeper climb inside the basket. They yelled "Okay" to the two firemen standing above; the basket with the housekeeper inside was slowly raised to the upper floor. After she was out of the basket, they lowered it again, and one by one, the other firemen were pulled up.

Once everyone was safely standing on the fourth floor, the women hugged each other. As Phil turned to shake hands with the firemen, the group heard a loud snapping sound. The cables on the elevator broke and the elevator suddenly plunged down to the basement with a loud crash. Then silence.

"Man, that was close," one of the firemen said. "If you hadn't gotten this little tyke and her companion out before we got here. Well, who knows?"

Hallie and her nanny hugged Kelley and Phil. "You saved us. Thank you."

"Who are you people, the nanny asked, wiping her tears from her face.

"Just some guests of the hotel. I'm Phil and this is my wife, Kelley."

"You two are really heroes," Danielle said, wiping her eyes as the manager of the hotel rushed up.

"Thank you my dear American guests. My concierge said that you were coming up here to help. We consider your stay with us a blessing."

"Yes. Thank you." Fran turned to Hallie. "It's time for

your nap."

"I still have to pee," Hallie responded.

Fran took her by the hand and they headed down the hall to their room. The firemen forced the elevator doors shut and put a strip of yellow tape in front of them.

When they got back down to the lobby, the firemen placed yellow tape in front of all the elevators doors. The manager posted a sign that read "Lifts out of Order—Awaiting Repair."

"Thank goodness, this older hotel only has six floors," Kelley said.

"Right. Well, what do you want to do now Sweetie? We still have several hours before the Commissioner's man is going to pick us up for dinner."

"I think that we should go to our room and wash up a bit. Thank God for these walking shoes. I'm ready to do some real sightseeing. I've had enough excitement for this morning. Now I've got to pee."

"Me too."

Chapter 5

"Look," Phil said as they entered the lobby after their tour. "The desk clerk is motioning to us."

They walked over. "Oh Mr. and Mrs. Willis, we have a slight problem here. Since all of our lifts are down and will require some time for repair, the hotel owner, Jeffrey Windsor, has decided to transfer all of the guests to other hotels for their own safety. Because of the inconvenience of having to move, there will be no charge for your short stay here. And we will, of course, absorb any difference in the room price between here and your new hotel."

"Agent Wallace from Scotland Yard is scheduled to pick us up here at five," Phil said.

"Of course. If you and your wife would be so kind to return to your room and pack, we'll get you moved to your next location in due time. By the way, Mr. Windsor said to tell you that he would be calling on you shortly."

Back in their suite, Phil said, "Why don't you take a shower first and I'll follow you. I'll lay out my clothes and start packing. We can put your cosmetics and my shaving stuff in the carry-on bags."

He had just started to lay his clothes out on the bed, when they heard a brisk knock on the door. They walked into the sitting room and Kelley opened the door. A distinguished looking middle-aged gentleman was standing in the hallway.

"Good afternoon. I'm Jeffrey Windsor, owner of the hotel. May I come in for a few moments?"

"Of course," Kelley backed up. "The desk clerk said that you would be stopping by. Please have a seat." She motioned to the settee on the opposite side of the sitting room.

He walked across the room and sat down. Kelley followed him and sat beside him while Phil sat in the nearby chair.

"I can only stay for a few minutes," Windsor said. "I've come to personally thank both of you for your assistance during our lift crisis. I was told by the hotel manager that you risked your lives to save the three people trapped in the lift."

Phil leaned forward in his chair. "We're glad that we were able to be of some help, Mr. Windsor."

"I'm just thankful that no one was injured. This incident, however, has confirmed what I've been thinking recently. Although this hotel looks grand and is very prestigious, it's showing its age and needs some serious overhauling. It was built by my great grandfather and the management of it has passed over the years to my grandfather, father and me. Although the lifts are inspected regularly and were supposed to be up to code; apparently something was amiss there. I have decided to close the hotel for at least six months and give it a partial restoration."

Kelley nodded. "I'm certain that this beautiful old girl still has some life in her."

"I would like, however, to offer you a free week's stay in any of our suites, once our restoration is complete. I shall see that you get a voucher for it. Also I am going to try to get you a commendation from the mayor for your heroism."

"Thanks, very kind of you," Phil replied. "I don't know when we'll be returning to London after this trip. However, if we do, we would be delighted to take advantage of your offer."

"The bellboy will be up later to remove your bags and forward them on to your next destination. The desk clerk will inform you of your new hotel." Windsor stood and shook hands with them. "Now, I need to return to the lobby and supervise the moving of my other guests."

After Windsor left, Phil said, "We've got a date for dinner, Kelley."

Later, dressed in a black crepe pant suit and high heeled black shoes, she stood waiting for Phil to finish dressing. He put on navy blue slacks, an open necked white dress shirt and a light grey sport coat.

"I think we're ready for our evening out, Mrs. Willis. The hotel manager said for us to just leave our luggage on the bed and the bell boy will take care of it."

"I packed my cosmetics in my carry on. Did the hotel manager say where they are moving us?"

"No. He said the clerk would call me later on my cell. They'll transport the baggage for us. All we have to do is head to the new hotel when we're finished with dinner at the Commissioner's house."

"Sounds like a workable plan to me." Kelley looked at her watch. "Agent Wallace will probably be downstairs for us soon."

"I noticed a nice bar adjoining the lobby. Let's stop by there and have a cocktail. We'll tell the desk clerk where we are. By the way, Kelley, I'm glad you put good name tags on our luggage for our stay in Europe."

As they left the room and started for the stairwell, a soft voice called out, "Mr. and Mrs. Willis. So glad I caught you before you went out. It's me. Danielle, the housekeeper. I wanted to thank you for saving my life."

"Actually, the fire department rescued you. But it's

nice to see you smiling and that's all that counts." Phil shook her hand.

Kelley gave Danielle a hug. "What's going to happen to you now that the hotel is closing?"

"Oh, I have a new job lined up. I'll be okay."

As they opened the door to the stairway, Danielle gave them a brief wave, "Take care, me Luvs."

They entered the almost empty bar off the hotel lobby. "Two gin and tonics, my good man," Phil said to the bartender as they both sat down on the bars tools.

"You're the bloke what saved those people in the lift, aren't you," the bartender said. "The story about you is on the Telly you know. But you aren't the big news. Prince Harry and his new girl friend are back in town."

"Now, that's really news," Kelley laughed

As they sipped their drinks, a tall young man wearing a grey business suit approached them. "Excuse me. I overheard the bartender say that you were the two who rescued the ladies from the lift earlier today. I'm Moss Jenner, from the London Post."

"Oh, that's the local gossip magazine here in the UK. I've read it," Kelley said.

Phil glared at the man. "What can we do for you?"

"Would you care to give me your names and a brief statement about what happened here earlier? Perhaps, I could even get a photo to go with the story?"

"Thanks. But no thanks," Phil answered. "We're here on our honeymoon and would like to enjoy some privacy."

"Yes. We've had enough excitement lately," Kelley added. "I'm sure that your readers would be more interested in hearing about Prince Harry's latest conquest. But, you do print spicy articles in your paper."

"We do try to give our readers what they want, Luv."

Phil stood up. "Then, I'm certain that they wouldn't

be interested in us. Now, if you will excuse us I think that I see our driver standing in the lobby."

He took Kelley's arm and led her out to where Agent Wallace stood at the reception desk.

"Looking for us Agent Wallace?" Phil asked.

"Yes sir. Please follow me. The car is right out front."

They walked outside the hotel and followed Wallace to a black car parked nearby. Wallace opened the back door and gestured for them to get in.

"My God. This is a Bentley," Phil exclaimed.

"Are you familiar with Bentleys, sir?"

"My stepfather, who lives in New York, is a car buff. He owns a restored Morgan. Took me to several car shows where I learned all about autos. My favorite is a Corvette convertible with bucket seats. But my wife favors motorcycles or her Toyota Rav4."

"Well, sir, this is the Commissioner's own personal vehicle. Uses it only for special occasions. He must think a lot of you to have me pick you up in it. Now sit back and I'll show you a few more highlights of the city."

"By the way Agent Wallace, did the desk clerk mention anything about where we and our luggage are headed after the dinner at the Commissioner's?" Kelley asked.

"Yes, madam. It's all taken care of."

"By the way, did you ever discover who murdered Dame Sinclair?"

He smiled. "We linked the shell casings you found on the deck to a gun owned by Joyce Dowling, the personal secretary. She became furious when she found out that, after all her years of dedicated service, Dame Sinclair was going to dismiss her and hire a younger person."

Chapter 6

Following a short trip through the streets of London, Agent Wallace drove the Bentley between two old stone pillars that marked the entrance way to a plush estate located just outside the city.

He followed the tree lined driveway, entered the enclosed courtyard of what appeared to be a small mcdieval castle, drove around the circular driveway and stopped the Bentley in front of the regal home.

Its exterior was made of limestone and had a gray slate roof with spires extending above it. The front of the castle had a rampart like balcony. At one side of the main structure was a carriage house that appeared to have been converted into a garage.

"Wow! This is more than a home. This is a castle," Kelley exclaimed.

"That it is. Been in Commissioner Pope's family for centuries I've been told. Well, this is as far as I take you folks," he said as he helped them out of the automobile. "I hope that before you leave London, you will take the time to visit our New Scotland Yard."

"We'll try," Phil shook his hand. "Your mini tour was great, especially seeing the Wimbledon Tennis facility. Thanks for taking us for that brief look-a-round."

"My pleasure. You have to come back for the Open."

Agent Wallace led them up the stone entrance way to the double bronze doors and knocked on the huge ancient door knocker. "I'll leave you here. I'm sure that we'll see each other again before you leave."

Just then the massive doors slowly opened and a tall, thin elderly man, dressed in a butler's uniform, stood in the doorway. "Mr. and Mrs. Willis, I presume. The Commissioner and his Missus are expecting you."

He stepped back so that they could enter through the limestone arched doorway. Once inside Kelley stood in awe, trying to take in the magnificent scene in front of her.

A spiral stairway, flanked by massive support columns lead to the upper floors of the castle. The floor was made of old flagstone and the walls of the hallway were covered in huge pictures of what she assumed were the Commissioner's ancestors.

A ten-foot tall grandfather mahogany clock started to chime the half hour.

"You're right on time," the butler said. "Commissioner Pope appreciates promptness. He's working in his study. Please follow me."

He led them down the hall, opened a set of tall wooden doors and announced. "Mr. and Mrs. Willis, sir."

The Commissioner walked over and shook their hands warmly. "Glad you could make it. My wife, Birdie, is waiting for us in the living room."

As they walked out of the study and down the hall, Kelley was busy, once again, observing the décor of the castle. Three monstrous crystal chandeliers lined the hall and large portraits filled the walls.

They entered the gigantic living room with floor to ceiling windows overlooking an English garden beyond. Two large overstuffed sofas flanked the fireplace with a large coffee table in between them. Chairs in flowered patterns of lavender and pink were scattered about the room in small groups that seemed designed to invite casual chats. Next to them were massive old oak tables with piles of books on them.

Standing next to the stone fireplace that reached to the ceiling, was a tiny lady in her early sixties with silver hair, wearing a lavender colored tea length gown. Kelley thought she looked like Queen Elizabeth.

The Commissioner walked over and put his arm around her waist, protectively. "This is my wife, Robin. But, I've always called her Birdie. Sweetheart, I want you to meet my lovely young friends from the States. This is Phillip Willis and his charming bride, Kelley. They are the young couple that was involved in the murder on the Queen Mary II the other day."

"So glad to meet you, my dears," Birdie said as she extended her hand. "Now, have a seat." She pointed to one of the comfy looking sofas in front of the fireplace. "I'll have Nora bring in our drinks and appetizers."

As they sat down, Birdie walked to the wall and rang a small bell with an embroidered silk pull rope.

Soon thereafter, a petite middle-aged woman wearing a white lace apron with a white lace cap perched on top of her head entered the room, pushing an ornate wooden tea cart. "I made some small cucumber and salmon sandwiches, Madam. I know you would want something light with your drinks."

"Thank you Nora. You can serve our guests. Andrew, would you be kind enough to mix the martinis?"

"Yes my love." The Commissioner went over to the bar, mixed the drinks and handed one to Kelley and Phil as Nora served the small sandwiches on tiny porcelain dishes decorated with pink and lavender flowers.

After serving them, Nora said, "If that will be all, Madam, I shall return to the kitchen and finish the dinner."

Mrs. Pope waved her hand. "Yes, that will be all."

Birdie looked fondly at Nora as she left the room. "Nora has been with us for over twenty years and is one of the most sought after cooks in all of London. Our guests are always trying to steal her from us. Even the Prime Minister's wife was after her."

"We'll look forward to her dinner then, thank you. And what a beautiful living room you have, Mrs. Pope."

"Please, call me Birdie. All my friends do. As you can see lavender is my favorite color. I had the decorator put shades of it in every room." She sat down on the sofa that was opposite from where Phil and Kelley were seated.

The Commissioner handed his wife her drink and sat down beside her. He picked up a coaster from a small rack and carefully placed it in front of him on the table, then placed his drink on it.

Kelley looked at Phil. He winked back at her. They both knew that although the Commissioner ran Scotland Yard that his little wife, Birdie, was in charge at home.

"Birdie, these young people are on their honeymoon."

"That sounds so romantic."

"And speaking of romantic," Kelley said, "I can't believe how extraordinary your beautiful home is. It's like a small castle."

"That's exactly what it is. Andrew's ancestors built it years ago. It has had the electric and plumbing updated over the years. And we put in a new and modern kitchen several years ago." Birdie replied.

The Commissioner nodded. "Yes, but it still requires a tremendous amount of money to keep it up. I'm afraid that we shall have to start tours of it to make do once I'm retired."

Birdie patted him on the hand. "Time enough to worry about that later, my love."

Nora appeared in the doorway. "Dinner is ready,

Madam."

The Commissioner stood up and offered his arm to Kelley. "If you would be so kind to accompany me, we'll head for the dining room."

Kelley took his arm as Phil stood up and extended his to Birdie.

They walked down the hall to the dining room. Kelley could see that this room had been redone in the past few years. The lower half of the walls were covered in distressed oak paneling but the upper half was wall papered in lovely garden scenes of green, lavender and pink.

The table was set for four with an exquisite lace tablecloth; the china featured the Pope family crest and was edged in gold as were the crystal glasses. The large centerpiece was greenery accented with fresh flowers in different shades of Birdie's favorite colors.

"This room is breath taking," Kelley commented as the Commissioner pulled out a chair for her.

"One can do wonders with a good decorator," Birdie said.

"Also takes a lot of money," the Commissioner mumbled.

Kelley and Phil looked at each other and chuckled as Nora entered the room with a large white soup tureen.

"I do hope that you like lobster bisque," Birdie said.

"We love it," Phil commented as he sat back in his chair and watched Nora ladle two big spoonfuls into the bowl set in front of him.

The soup was followed by a lovely Caesar salad and the main course was Beef Wellington. Between serving the courses, Nora kept filling the wine glasses with several selections of wine.

"This is simply delicious," Kelley said as she sat back in her chair and wiped her mouth politely with her napkin. "You know, Birdie, I'm going to try to get Nora to go back to the States with us."

"Don't you dare. She's mine."

Kelley laughed. "Just teasing."

"I hope you saved room for Nora's special dessert. She makes the most delicious plum pudding topped with brandy," the Commissioner said. "This special three course meal is featured at many five star restaurants in London."

Nora cleared the dirty dishes and brought in the dessert on a cart.

"Well, I definitely have room for that plum pudding," Phil said as he looked at the dark and rich looking speckled canon ball that was topped with flaming brandy. Nora cut a slice for each of them and served it with together with cups of hot coffee.

When they were finished, the Commissioner pushed back his chair. "Now, I'll give you a quick tour of the place. Then, we'll retire to the drawing room for a nice glass of port and I'll tell you young people why I have invited you here this evening."

"If you will excuse me, I'll leave you to visit while I do some packing. I'm leaving for the countryside tomorrow to visit my mother," Birdie said. "It was so nice meeting you and I do hope that you will come back again."

"The dinner was just delicious," Kelley replied. "And we enjoyed meeting you and seeing your lovely home."

As Birdie left the room, the Commissioner looked lovingly after her. "Birdie has been the love of my life. We have been married for over forty years. Now let me give you a brief tour of the rest of the castle."

After viewing the upper floors and the gardens, the Commissioner led Kelley and Phil to the study and motioned for them to have a seat on the brown leather settee. He walked over to the bar and poured three generous glasses of port.

"I can't believe this house. You must be very proud of it." Kelley said, as she took the glass from him. "How many rooms does it actually have?"

"Eight bedrooms with adjoining baths on the second floor. Living room, library, dining room and kitchen on the first floor. And of course this drawing room which serves as both my study and office. Then, let's see, a wine cellar and a cold cellar for vegetables in the basement. Servant quarters are on the third floor."

"I remember seeing a garage at the side of the drive. How many cars does it hold," Phil asked.

"Oh, that's the old carriage house. I converted it to a four car garage. My prize possession is that Bentley I sent Wallace to pick you up in. I've had that for years. Use it for our Sunday rides into the country. It belonged to my father. Only Wallace and I drive it."

"I noticed the lovely turrets on either side of the house, when we drove up. Do you use them for anything," Kelley asked.

"My great grandfather had them added to the castle years ago. The servants said that he used to sit up there and read late in the evenings while he waited for my grandfather to come home from clubbing in London. He was quite a party boy, they say. Now-a-days, we just use the turrets to store old paintings and furniture."

"This is quite a place to keep up. It must cost a fortune to just heat it." Phil said as he sipped his port.

"Yes. That's why I am thinking of turning it into a tourist attraction or selling it to the county government. It would make a nice museum. After the first of the year, I plan to retire from Scotland Yard and Birdie will give up her volunteering job at the hospital.

We want to just settle back into an easy life. Maybe move to the countryside to be with Birdie's mom, who's in her nineties now. Maybe, I shall even start writing a history of the early days of Scotland Yard."

Kelley smiled. "That sounds like a lovely plan. But will you be happy living in the country after all the excitement of Scotland Yard?"

"I believe so. I'm becoming somewhat of a museum piece myself. The sign on our building says 'New Scotland Yard' and I think they are ready for some changes in management too. The board is supposed to name a new Commissioner in less than a month."

The Commissioner leaned forward. "Now, I must get to the real reason why I asked you here this evening."

A brisk knock was heard at the study door. It opened and the butler entered. "Sir, a gentleman is here to see Mr. and Mrs. Willis."

Kelley looked up, jumped to her feet, ran to the man who appeared in the doorway and threw her arms around him. "Look whose here Phil!"

Chapter 7

The grandfather clock in the hall chimed the hour as the Commissioner stood up. "You're early, Agent Fleming."

James Barrett Fleming II grinned. "Made all the lights sir."

He gave Kelley a big hug and a kiss and twirled her around. "My Luv, you look simply smashing. Marriage seems to agree with you. And what a glow!"

Kelley smiled and they embraced again as Phil walked toward them. "May I interrupt you two and introduce myself. I'm Phil Willis and that's my wife you're hugging."

James pushed Kelley gently aside as he shook Phil's hand. "So you're the bloke that Kelley always talked so much about when we were partners at the Secret Service Agency in Florida. Well, you're one lucky fellow to get this gal."

"I know that. And I'm glad to finally meet you James. Sorry that you couldn't come to the States for our wedding."

"Unfortunately, I was tied up with a case here. Besides my wife, Eva, is getting close to the delivery date with the twins. Her doctor didn't want her flying over the pond."

Kelley took his arm. "We understand. How's she doing now?"

"Just fine. The delivery date is soon."

"Why not have a seat and a glass of port while you continue your reminiscing," the Commissioner interjected.

"I'd like that sir," James replied as he led Kelley and Phil over to the leather settee as the Commissioner refilled the drinks and made one for James.

James sat down on the settee between Kelley and Phil. "Before we go any further, I have to tell you about the surprise that the Commissioner and I have arranged for you. When he told me that your hotel was closing and that you were scheduled to go to another hotel, Eva and I decided that you must stay with us for the duration of your time in jolly Old England. We called the Windsor Hotel and Agent Wallace is picking up your bags there and taking them to my house as we speak."

Kelley looked questioningly at Phil. "That's very generous of you. But Eva is close to delivery you said. Are you sure it won't be an imposition?"

"Not at all. Everything is all ready for the babies and Eva insisted that you stay with us, so that we can all get to know each other better. Say no more. Everything is arranged. I brought my SUV and will take you home with me after we talk over some business with the Commissioner."

"Talk over some business," Phil asked.

"Yes," the Commissioner sat down on a near-by chair and sipped his port. "You see I have Fleming working on some cold cases and I was hoping that perhaps your wife could take a look at one of them and give him a few suggestions. You know a fresh eye is always good when reviewing this sort of things."

"How long do you expect this to take sir," Phil asked.

"Well, how long are you planning to be in the city to help that law firm you are consulting with?"

"We planned on being in London for at least a week and then moving on. This is sort of a combined work vacation and a honeymoon for us."

The Commissioner thought for a while. "That should be ample time for Mrs. Willis to help Agent Fleming get some real insight into a special situation."

"What is that," a very much interested Kelley asked, sitting on the edge of her seat. Her investigative blood was now flowing.

"Ten years ago a bloke from Essex was bilking elderly women out of their savings. We thought we had a good lead on him. Suddenly, the bloody bastard disappeared. Now, he has raised his ghastly head and is starting his scams all over again."

"And I've been trying to track down all possible leads on him," James added.

"What's he doing now," Kelley asked.

"This character is not like Michael Caine in the movie, *Dirty Rotten Scoundrels*," James replied. "He doesn't fleece the rich people on the French Rivera. He goes into our small towns and preys on ladies whose husbands have just passed away. He takes advantage of their fragile emotional state and talks them out of their savings or the life insurance money that they just received from the death of the husband. Then he just disappears into thin air. Eventually he resurfaces; sometimes even in the same town."

"And recently, he went a bit too far and bilked my very own sister, Victoria out of her savings," the Commissioner added. "So I need you to go over the case with James, Kelley. I know your background and maybe your undercover experience will help us."

Kelley jumped to her feet, started to pace the floor and rubbed her hands. Phil had not seen her so excited about anything other than the wedding in months. He could see that her face was transformed. Her energy forces had definitely been thrown into gear.

"Maybe you have been looking for him in the wrong places," she suggested after thinking for a few minutes.

"What do you mean by that, Luv," James asked.

"You say that you have been looking all over for the man. But, maybe he's really a she and is living right out in the open," she answered. "When Phil and I trained with the circus a couple of years ago, we learned how a woman could easily disguise herself as a man."

"Right." Phil chimed in. "And a man could easily disguise himself and pass for a woman, like Dustin Hoffman in the movie, *Tootsie*."

James nodded. "You could be right. While we were busy looking for a man; maybe, we should have been looking for a woman."

The Commissioner stood up. "That sounds like it could be a possibility. Perhaps, you can spend a few days helping James with the case Mrs. Willis."

"I would love to if it's okay with my husband."

Phil shot her a hard assessing look, and then nodded slowly. "It's okay with me, if it's only for a few days. Just so you realize, Kelley, that as soon as I'm finished with the Manchester Law Firm here, we'll be moving on. I've already made our future travel arrangements."

With a lightning reflex, Kelley smiled and nodded in agreement. "A few days might just be enough time for the two of us to crack the case."

"And of course, you'll both be staying with Eva and me," James added.

"Sounds like it's all settled then," the Commissioner said. "Now, I have to be going upstairs. It's almost Birdie's bedtime and she will be looking for her nightcap—a brandy. Good luck, Mr. Willis with the Manchester firm. Hope you resolve the case."

"Thank you, sir. And thank you for the lovely dinner." He shook the Commissioner's hand.

The Commissioner turned to Kelley, "Now, the two of you keep me informed. Fleming, call me tomorrow evening and give me an update."

"Yes sir. Thank you."

The Commissioner gave Kelley a hug and offered a brief salute to James. "My butler will show you all out. And thank you for a very interesting evening." He turned to the sideboard, poured a brandy into a sniffer and headed for the study door. "My Birdie awaits me now."

As they left the Commissioner's house, James took Kelley by the arm. "You know, Luv, you've got my juices flowing on this case now. We just might be starting on a positive roll."

Chapter 8

After exiting the Commissioner's house, James helped Kelley and Phil into his small SUV. "I got a call from Eva earlier. She said that Agent Wallace already delivered your luggage to our house in Greenwich."

"How far is it to your house, James," Kelley asked.

"Only about twenty minutes, Luv. Eva and I wanted to buy a place in a quiet suburb. Better for raising the children, you know. Good schools and all that."

A light shower began as they pulled up to the two story modern brick house with a small English garden in front, enclosed by a white picket fence.

James hit the button on the garage door remote and drove into the attached garage. He helped Kelley out of the car, and Phil followed as they entered the house through the door that led to the kitchen and the adjoining spacious family room with a wood burning fireplace.

Inside the kitchen door, James stopped to take off his shoes. "No need for you two to take yours off," he said. "We just got into the habit to save on cleaning the family room carpet."

They looked at each other, bent down and took off their shoes.

"Eva prepared the guest room for you yesterday and Agent Wallace took your luggage upstairs for her when he arrived tonight. I assume that you are pretty tired after your long day so I'll just take you to your room now, if that's okay. Tomorrow, we'll chit, chat.

You can meet Eva in the morning. I'm certain that she's probably sleeping by now. She may have even taken one of the sleeping pills that the doctor prescribed. She's had a bit of a problem sleeping lately and I don't want to disturb her."

Kelley and Phil carried their shoes in their hands as they followed James up the stairs and down the hall to the guest room.

James opened the door to the room, and whispered. "You'll find soap and towels in the adjoining bathroom."

Kelley looked at the lovely king size, four poster bed, topped with a homey looking quilt of apple green and yellow. The windows were draped with matching tied back curtains. In the front of the window was a small desk with two chairs beside it. Their carry-on luggage was placed on the chairs and on the floor were their large suit cases.

"This room is so cozy," she said, as she kissed James on the cheek.

"Yes. Eva does have good decorating skills. Wait until you see the nursery that she prepared for the twins."

Phil shook James's hand. "Thank you for putting us up, old chap."

"My pleasure. Have a good sleep and I will see you in the morning." James quietly closed the bedroom door behind him.

Kelley opened her suitcase and removed her nightgown. After taking her cosmetic bag out of the carry on, she headed for the bathroom, while Phil unpacked his bag and turned down the bed.

When she emerged from the bathroom, Phil took his turn and they were soon in bed. As had quickly become her habit, Kelley took her place on the left side of the bed while Phil took his on the right.

"Man. Does this bed ever feel good," he said.

"Maybe it has one of those memory foam mattresses." She snuggled deeper into it and pulled the down comforter and the quilt over both of them.

Phil leaned over and tenderly kissed her good-night.

The following morning, Phil awoke, opened one eye and looked at the clock sitting on the night stand. He refocused his eyes and looked again. It was after eight a.m. He sat up, shook Kelley and whispered, "Are you awake honey?"

She slowly opened her eyes. "I think I am now. What time is it?"

"After eight."

"Thank goodness it's Sunday." She climbed slowly out of bed. "I'm going to head downstairs and see what the Flemings are up to."

As she was putting her robe on, they heard a knock on the bedroom door. She opened it and saw James standing there. He was all dressed. "Eva and I are off to early church services. We attend Christ's Church nearby. We wanted to know if you wanted to accompany us."

"We attend Catholic church. Do you know if there's one nearby?"

"Yes. As a matter of fact, there's one right across the street from our church. I know that they have an early mass. You can accompany us and we'll drop you off there. Right now, Eva is having her morning tea and she put on a pot of coffee for you. Won't you join us?"

"Give us about twenty minutes and we'll be down," Kelley answered.

"Take a left at the bottom of the back steps and you'll find us both in the kitchen. And oh yes, Kelley, I got some of those mini donuts that you like."

"That sounds heavenly."

After James left the room, Kelley looked out the window. "The weather is misty again. Better dress appropriately."

"Will do," Phil answered. "Say, I'm anxious to meet Eva, aren't you."

They hurried downstairs, where in the daylight they could see the modern looking kitchen with its stainless steel appliances, modern oak cabinets, tile floors and adjoining family room. Next, they noticed the tall young woman with straight blonde hair standing at the stove with her back to them.

When she turned around, both Kelley's and Phil's eyes immediately drifted to her stomach. The apron that she was wearing over it did little to conceal its huge size.

James walked over to Eva, put his arm around her shoulders and said, "Dear, meet the Willis's, Kelley and Phil."

Eva wiped her hands on the apron, walked over to Kelley and took her hands in hers. "Hi there. We've visited on the phone several times and James talks constantly about you. I feel like I know you both already"

"The same here. When are the babies due?"

Eva patted her stomach. "We think on Wednesday. We're just waiting for word from the doctor. He's planning to take the babies by C-section."

James smiled, "Two girls you know. We've been busy going through lists of names on the computer trying to select just the perfect ones for our little ones."

Eva pointed to the large oak kitchen table with six matching chairs surrounding it. "Now sit. We have time for tea or coffee before we leave for church."

"Both our church service and your mass start and end about the same time, so we'll just drop you off and pick you up afterwards," James said. "Our service always lasts a little longer than the mass at St. Joseph's. But we're not going to bible study today."

"You'll love St. Joseph's, very small and friendly.

We've been there a couple of times for our friends' weddings and such," Eva added, as she passed a tray of mini donuts and raspberry scones. "We just love this little town and all the friends that we have made here."

James picked up a scone and took a big bite out of it. "And, I'll give you a little tour of the town this afternoon, while Eva naps."

"Smashing," Kelley giggled and grabbed for a donut.

"We appreciate your having us," Phil said. "But, I hope that it isn't too much for Eva in her condition."

"Not at all," Eva responded. "We try to keep everything as simple and stress free as possible. I've taken a leave of absence from my teaching job. So we're not rushed at all these days."

James grinned at his wife. "And Eva has planned an all-American lunch for you today. Hamburgers and hot dogs on the barbeque. Potato salad and ice tea."

Kelley looked up and smiled. "That sounds so good. We had so much rich food on the ship."

"And the Commissioner's dinner last night was a bit heavy too," Phil added.

After church, James drove to the house and parked the car in the driveway. They exited and walked through the stone path in the colorful garden to the front of the house.

Along the way, Kelley stopped and bent over to smell the roses. "I just love this English rose garden. It must be a lot of work for you Eva."

"No. I just love working in it."

Phil looked up at the sharp sloped tile roof. "That roof seems like it has a really steep angle to it."

James nodded. "That's to help the snow slide to the ground in our British winters."

"I like those large over size windows in front," Kelley said.

"Yes. There are big ones in the back also," Eva replied.

"They let the light flow through the house."

James walked up the stairs leading to the metal front door, with a beveled glass insert and glass side lights. He opened it with his key and stepped aside so that the others could enter before him.

Kelley stood and admired the entrance hall with its grand oak circular stairway that led to the second floor. On the right was a small study with floor to ceiling bookcases. On the left was a large guest closet.

After removing their shoes, they walked down the hallway to the kitchen and family room, passing a formal dining room with a small chandelier hanging above the oak dining room table.

"We chose not to have a living room," Eva said. "I prefer the open look of the family room, attached to the kitchen."

"Well, I certainly think that you have an attractive home," Kelley said.

"Yes. I'm just thankful that we have a good sized basement and attic," Eva said, "so that James can store everything. And four bedrooms turned out to be a good choice so that we have room for the babies and guests too."

At lunch time, they sat outside on the back wooden deck which opened off the family room and kitchen and enjoyed their meal.

"This is a great back yard," Phil said, looking at the manicured lawn outlined with colorful flower beds and tall shady trees that stretched out before them.

"Yes. We thought it would be lovely for the children. Enough room for a sandbox and a nice swing set," Eva said.

"But no pets, Luv," James frowned at her, his dark brows drawn together. "They're a lot of work, you know."

Following lunch, James drove Kelley and Phil around the small town, showing them the local sites, while Eva took her nap.

When they returned home, James said, "Hope you enjoyed the tour."

"Your town is just charming," Kelley responded.

That evening, James took everyone out to the local pub for fish and chips. When they got back to the house, Eva served hot apple pie with ice cream for dessert.

Afterwards, James started a fire in the family room fireplace. He poured Kelley, Phil and himself a glass of sherry, while Eva drank a cup of hot tea. Then each couple brought the other one up to date on what had transpired in their lives the past few months.

Finally, after some time, James said, "Here's the plan for tomorrow, if it's okay with you two. I leave for work about eight-thirty and I would like for you to join me at Scotland Yard, Kelley. Phil, we can drop you off at the Manchester Law office on our way."

"That sounds like a good idea. I have a lot of things that I need to go over with their lawyers. So I expect to spend the whole day there."

"Good. We'll call you when we are ready to leave Scotland Yard in the evening."

James got up, walked over to his briefcase that was lying on a near-by chair, opened it and pulled out two cell phones. "The Commissioner gave me a top of the line cell phone from the Yard for each of you to use while you're here. I've already programmed in the numbers to my private line, Scotland Yard and the house for you. Feel free to add any others that you might need. It also takes photos."

Phil took one of the phones and looked at it. "Thanks. I appreciate it. It's nice to know that I can contact Kelley anytime if I need to."

"Yes. Thanks," Kelley started to yawn. "Excuse me; I guess I'm not used to the time change yet. I think I'm about ready to turn in."

James stood up. "Good idea. The doctor said that Eva should get plenty of rest. She probably won't get a lot for the first few days after the babies come home."

Kelley got up and put her arm around Eva. "I still worry that we will be too much of a burden on you. But, I want you to know that I'm willing to do whatever I can to help with the babies while I'm here."

Eva nodded. "Thank you. I just might have to take you up on that."

They all headed upstairs to their respective rooms. Inside their bedroom, Kelley asked, "Well, what you think of my friends, the Flemings?"

"They're wonderful. Very warm and friendly."

"I hope that you won't expect me to keep our house as clean and neat as Eva does."

"No. And did you notice James' back yard? Not a blade of grass out of place. Was he that neat and proper when you worked with him in the States?"

"Oh, yes."

Once they were resting comfortably in bed, Kelley whispered, "Ask someone at the law firm tomorrow, for a nice fancy place to take the Flemings tomorrow night for dinner. We should take them to someplace chic before the delivery. She won't be able to go out for a while after the babies are here."

"Good idea. I think that James mentioned that they're planning on the delivery on either Wednesday or Thursday."

"Just think, in a few days they'll have twin babies."

"Girls. Did Eva say what they were going to call them?"

"I believe that they were still thinking about it."

Chapter 9

When Kelley and Phil entered the kitchen the next morning, they found James sitting at the table, sipping a cup of tea and reading the morning newspaper. "Morning you two. No need for the brolly today. The paper says no chance of rain."

"That's good news," Phil replied.

James motioned to the counter behind him. "I made a pot of coffee. I know that you Americans prefer that to tea."

"Thanks." Kelley poured two cups and carried them to the table while Phil pulled out a chair and sat down.

"Didn't know what you chaps usually ate in the morning. So I put out some cereal and juice. Bagels and scones too." He pointed to the items on the table. "Help yourself. Eva won't be joining us this morning. She needs all the rest she can get for the next couple of days. I'll take her up a tray before we leave."

"Is she feeling okay," Kelley asked, concerned.

"Just had a little trouble sleeping again last night. She can't seem to find a comfortable position and the little ones keep kicking. Active little buggers."

Kelley grabbed a bagel and handed one to Phil. He poured himself a bowl of cereal and added the milk.

After they finished breakfast, James stood up and

pulled a tray out of the cupboard. He put tea, cereal, a raspberry scone and the newspaper on it. "I'm going to take this up to Eva and tell her that we've leaving for the day. She has her phone close at hand in case she needs to reach me. Join you in a few minutes."

Kelley took the last sip of her coffee. "Before you go up to Eva, James, we wanted to tell you that we would like to take the two of you out to eat at a nice restaurant tonight. Something real fancy."

"No need for that," he replied. "I can pick up some takeaway food on our way home from the office."

"No. We insist," Phil added. "Might be the last chance for Eva to get out for a while."

"I'm sure Eva will appreciate that."

After James left the room, Kelley packaged up the remainder of the bagels and scones. Phil took the dishes to the sink, rinsed them and placed them in the dishwasher.

James returned to the kitchen with his briefcase in hand. He placed it on the table, opened it and pulled out a folder and handed it to Phil. "Here is my schedule for the next few days. Kelley will probably be with me most of the time. And you can reach either of us with your mobile."

James zipped up his briefcase. "Well, if you two are ready to depart so am I. I usually leave about eight thirty and try to be in the office before nine. We'll drop you off at the Manchester Law Firm on our way in, Phil. Sorry we only have the one auto. Eva always walked to her school, which is only a couple of blocks away. But, we'll have to get another car soon for her."

"I'm certain I'll manage just fine. If I need to come home before you're done, I can always take a taxi."

"Give us a call when you're done for the day. But, in case you want to take the bus home, the bus stop is right around the corner from you. Just take Number 84 to Greenwich. Let's you off just a block from our house."

"Great. For the next few days, we're in your hands James," Kelley replied.

After dropping Phil off, James and Kelley headed toward the offices of New Scotland Yard.

"You never told me much about Scotland Yard, itself," Kelley said as they drove though the streets of the city. "Why is it called Scotland Yard?"

"The Yard has become a symbol for law and order since it was established in 1829, on a plot of land called 'Great Scotland Yard.' One story was that the land had been set aside to build a London residence for the Kings of Scotland. The other story was that it was named after a former land owner."

Kelley looked amazed. "It was established that long ago?"

"Yes. For over one hundred and eighty years, Scotland Yard has been the headquarters of the Metropolitan Police Service. It's responsible for policing Greater London."

"I know that it's recognized around the world."

James continued, "New Scotland Yard occupies a twenty-story office block along Broadway and Victoria streets in Westminster, just a few hundred feet from the Houses of Parliament."

He pulled into the rear entrance, underground employee parking garage on 4 Whitehead Place. "Most of the offices are in the Norman Shaw Building on 10 Broadway, but I've been assigned here."

As they exited the car, James continued, "Before we enter my office, I want you to know that we're not usually in such a mess. We're undergoing a face lift presently.

Everyone that works here will be given new state of the art computers. Also going to get new wiring, cables and new furnishings. Should be smashing once it is done. But for now, you have to overlook the untidiness. I'll take you around to the front entrance so you can get a good look at the place."

He escorted Kelley through the doors at the front entrance.

She noticed an eternal flame burning in the lobby. "What's that for?"

"It commemorates the members of the Service who died on duty or in the War. See those illuminated Rolls of Honor over there—the pages are turned daily. Sometimes we have ceremonies here—like the annual Remembrance Day Service conducted by the chaplain."

James led Kelley down the hall to his office. Upon entering, he introduced her to a heavy-set, middle-aged woman seated at a desk.

"Kelley, this is Maggie, my assistant. Maggie, this is Kelley Ryan Willis, the young lady that I told you about. As per the Commissioner's orders, she'll be working with me for the next several days."

Maggie stood up, walked around the desk and extended her hand.

"Glad to meet you Mrs. Willis."

"Please, call me Kelley."

Maggie turned back to her desk and picked up an identification badge that was attached to a neck ribbon. "You'll need to wear this at all times."

As Kelley put the badge around her neck, James said to Maggie, "Kelley will be working closely with me while she is here. So, I'll keep an eye on her."

Maggie sat back down at her desk. "And I need to inform you, Agent Fleming, that the cafeteria is closed for the week for the remodeling as well as most of this building. The majority of the staff here is being housed in the Central Communications Complex down the street."

"Doesn't sound like you'll get the big tour then, Kelley," James said.

"I'm very disappointed. I had hoped to meet Q, Agent 007, and Miss Money Penny today."

"Just so you won't be totally disappointed," Maggie said, "maybe Agent Fleming can take you over to the Communications Complex later on."

"That sounds very interesting."

James nodded. "Yes. Years ago, they replaced the old information room, map room and telegraph office. It's now fully computerized and electronically linked to the international Telex Network and National Computer. It's the call center for all emergency calls to our Metropolitan Police District."

"It handles over a million and a half calls a year," Maggie added. "And be sure to take her to see the Special Operations Room. She doesn't want to miss that—it's our nerve center."

"Right. As you will discover Kelley, we guard London, as well as its suburbs, the Queen, and Buckingham Palace all from Scotland Yard. Now, let me direct you to your desk."

He led her to the back of the room and pointed to a desk with a computer on it. "You can use this station, next to me, while you're here. The Commissioner specifically said that he wanted you to work on his sister Victoria's case. He is most anxious to find out who bilked her out of her savings. We've got a few leads. And we want to be ready in case this person strikes again."

He pulled a folder from his bottom drawer and handed it to her. "Look this information over and see if you can discover anything new. I'll have Maggie bring us some tea and coffee about ten. In the meantime, let's both get to work."

Kelley opened the folder and found two computer discs in it. One was marked 'Victoria Pope' and the other was marked 'Cold Case' and was dated ten years previous.

Kelley put Victoria Pope's disc in her computer. It revealed that Victoria lived outside of London in the small town of Essex. She studied the file carefully, and then reviewed the cold case file on the other disc. Deep in thought, she chewed her lower lip as she noted the similarities between the two cases on a note pad.

An hour and a half later, James walked up to her. "Here's your coffee. Sorry no bagels. How's your investigation going?"

"Pretty well. I discovered a lot of similarities between Victoria's case and the old ones. Any chance that I could get a car to use?"

"Where are you headed?"

"I'd like to go out to Essex and check out where the Commissioner's sister lives. Maybe, even interview her."

"I think I can get you a loaner. Do you think that you can handle driving on the opposite side of the road?"

With a toss of her head, she answered, "I'm certain I can handle it."

"I'm going to leave at noon. Want to run home and check on Eva. I'll have a car waiting for you to use out front. I'll put a map in it and mark the directions to Essex on it for you."

"Sounds good."

Chapter 10

After James headed home to check on Eva, Kelley decided that it was time to start some good old USA investigating by first looking around the town of Essex where Victoria Pope lived and then visiting Victoria herself.

Thanks to the map that James had given her, she had little trouble finding her way.

Once she reached the downtown area of Essex, she pulled into a parking spot on the main street. Now I know why these Brits drive such small cars, she thought. They barely fit into the undersized parking spaces.

She looked at her watch—one p.m. As she fumbled in her purse for a coin for the parking meter, she glanced in the back of the auto and saw a sign thrown on the back seat. It read 'Scotland Yard-Official Business.' That works for me, she thought. Forget the meter. She placed the sign in the front window on the passenger side.

Kelley exited the car, locked the door and headed down the street. She passed a drugstore, hardware store, an old fashion dime store, several dress shops and a furniture store. Finally on the corner at the end of the street, she approached a single story yellow wooden building with a sign in front that read 'The Essex Theatre.'

A sign on the front door was worded: 'Closed. Ticket office open daily at 7 p.m. Shows at 8 p.m. except for

Sunday. Deliveries at the side entrance.'

Kelley walked around to the door at the side of the building. A sign on the wall read 'Deliveries' and faded yellow lettering on the black door, read 'Stage Entrance.'

She knocked, waited a while and knocked again. Just as she turned to walk away, the door opened. A tall, weathered, thin old man, holding a lighted cigarette in his hand, yelled out, "Tryouts tomorrow."

Kelley ran back to him. "Just have a quick question for you, my good man."

"Make it quick. I'm leaving for the day."

"Is your theatre open for business?"

"Yes. We just finished one production. But, like I said, auditions for the next play start tomorrow."

Kelley put on her sexy smile. "Any chance I can have a few minutes of your time. I'm looking for some play-bills that would feature your various actors."

The old man stepped back. "I'm Duncan. I run the place. Come on in. I think I've got several in my office."

Kelley followed him down the hall to his office which was not only dark but also appeared to be quite dingy.

Duncan rifled through a stack on the desk and hand-ed her a playbill.

Kelley looked at it. It was for the play presently clos-ing. "Any chance of getting some old ones sir?"

"My God girl. Okay." He whipped around, opened the rusty file cabinet behind him and pulled out some pa-pers. "Here are some old playbills."

Then, looking at one of them, he said. "This play was made up of all women—dressed as men. And here are a couple of photos of the women without their makeup."

As he handed them to her, he laughed. "I just can't see you as a man. No sir, just can't see it."

Kelley grinned. "Thank you."

Walking behind her, Duncan chuckled to himself as they went down the hall to the exit door. "No, sir. Just can't see you as a..."

Kelley returned to her car, opened her briefcase that was on the front seat and put the playbills inside it. I'll show these and the photos to Victoria. She just might recognize someone. She picked up her cell phone and called Victoria.

After a few rings, Victoria Pope answered. Kelley introduced herself and explained to her who she was and that the Commissioner had asked her to investigate Victoria's case. After agreeing to see her, Victoria gave her directions to her home.

On her way, she took the time to look around the town of Essex briefly. Just off the main street, were blocks and blocks of townhouses. Several of them had signs; "Flat for Let." Guess that means "For Rent" in England, she decided.

She knocked on the door of Victoria's small flat that was one of four units in a single one-story beige stucco building. After a few seconds, the door was opened by an elderly woman.

Based on the Commissioner's appearance, Kelley had expected his sister would be tall and slender. Instead, Victoria was less than five feet tall. With her white curly hair and horn rimmed glasses she reminded her of a librarian.

Kelley introduced herself and flashed the Scotland Yard identification badge.

"So glad to meet you. Please come in." She led her into the sitting room that had an old braided rug on the floor and was filled with furniture that was showing its age.

Victoria pointed to a flowery chintz covered sofa placed near the fireplace which had wood burning briskly in it. "Please have a seat here miss. It's a bit damp outside today. Would you care for a spot of tea with some cucumber sandwiches and crumpets?"

"Please, call me Kelley. Oh yes, that would be nice. I

didn't have any lunch. "

"Make yourself at home my dear. I'll be back in a moment."

After Victoria left the room, Kelley took the time to look around the homey sitting room. The tables next to the sofa were piled high with quilting and various craft magazines. On the floor was a large wicker basket filled with knitting yarn and what looked like a half finished shawl in shades of orange and brown. Suddenly, a small furry head popped up out of the basket.

"Oh, don't let me cat, Cleo, startle you," Victoria said as she returned with a tray filled with a tea pot, cups, sugar, cream and a three tiered dish laden with tiny sandwiches and strawberry crumpets.

After they spent a brief time enjoying their tea and sandwiches, Kelley reached down into her briefcase and pulled out a notebook.

"I know that the Commissioner told you I would be helping in the investigation of the loss of your savings."

Victoria hung her head in embarrassment. "Did Andrew tell you that I recently lost my old friend and constant companion, Addie? She was like a sister to me. We lived together for over forty years and I guess that I was so overcome with grief over her death that I was an easy mark."

"I'm so sorry for your loss." Kelley smiled gently. "I read about your case in Scotland Yard's file and I'm going to try to recover your money. Perhaps we could get started on that now."

Victoria refilled Kelley's tea cup and offered her some of the crumpets. "Yes. I'm ready to help you in anyway that I can."

Kelley took a bite of the crumpet. "Delicious." She took a sip of her tea. "I understand that a man bilked you out of your savings. Can you give me a description of him?"

Victoria sat back in her seat. "Let's see. He was a few inches taller than me. Had gray hair. Medium built. Was wearing a business suit."

As she talked on, Kelley realized that she was describing the hundreds of average looking middle-aged men that walked the streets of London and Essex. She was getting nowhere.

Suddenly, Victoria stood up. "And he had the bluest eyes that I have ever seen. And small delicate fingers for a man. And he wore no rings."

Kelley reached into her briefcase once again and pulled out a folder. "I brought along a few playbills of some women who, dressed as men, were in a production at the local theatre some time ago. I'm hoping that maybe you could recognize someone from these."

Victoria studied the photos of several men. "None of these look like the man who came to my house and talked me into giving him my savings."

"Let me show you one more picture," Kelley said as she pulled it from a folder and handed it to Victoria.

"This is a photo of a woman."

"I know, but look it over carefully. Look at the eyes. Does it look anything like the man you met?"

"I'm not sure. The eyes do look like someone I might know."

Kelley put the photos back in the folder, returned it to her briefcase and stood up. "Well, I'll leave you now, Miss Victoria. Thank you for your time." She reached into her pocket, pulled out a small card, wrote on it and handed it to her. "Here's my phone number. If anything comes to your mind, please give me a call. Your brother is most anxious to get this case cleared up."

Just then they heard a knock on the front door. "Are you home Victoria?" a voice called out. "It's Tillie. I need to talk to you about something."

"That's my next door neighbor." Victoria walked over

to the door, opened it and signaled for the silver-haired bent-over woman to enter.

"Hi Tillie." She nodded toward Kelley. "This is my friend, Mrs. Willis."

"How do you do." Tillie acknowledged Kelley, who nodded in return.

"Oh Victoria. I just wanted to tell you that after I picked up my mail from my box by the road, I saw a car stop by your box. The person inside the car, opened your box, pulled out your mail, and rifled through it. When the person saw me watching, he or she quickly threw your mail back inside, closed your box and just raced away down the road."

"Did you recognize the person," Victoria asked. Now, getting very nervous, she began to rub her hands.

"No. I didn't recognize the auto as belonging to anyone around here and I couldn't see inside. But, it looked mighty suspicious so I thought I should tell you."

Victoria patted Tillie on the arm. "Thank you for letting me know."

After Tillie left, Kelley put her arm around Victoria. "I think we should go outside and take a look at your box. This might be related to your theft. We can't let any stone go un-turned."

They walked out to the mailbox. Kelley opened the door to it with her handkerchief and pulled out Victoria's mail. "Someone was interested in your correspondence. Let me take a couple of these advertisements that you won't need, in to Scotland Yard to search for fingerprints. And, if you don't mind, I'll take the door to your box, because we know that prints will be on it for sure."

"Oh dear. Now I'm really starting to get scared," Victoria answered. "Are you sure that this is what Andrew would want you to do?"

"Yes. I'm sure." Kelley answered as she ripped the rusty door off the old mail box. "It looks like you were ready for a new box anyway."

"Yes. This one is quite old. Just like my roof; it leaks too. I'll have my handyman put up a new box." She rifled through the rest of her mail as they headed back into the flat.

"Oh, here is the check from the insurance company from Addie's death."

"Maybe that check is what the thief was looking for." Kelley wrapped the mailbox cover in several sheets of notebook paper and placed it inside her briefcase. "Would you like me to drive you to your bank so that you can deposit it?"

"That won't be necessary dear. I'll be going into town tomorrow anyway and I'll take care of it then," Victoria answered, as her phone rang.

After talking for a few minutes, Victoria concluded the conversation with, "Yes. Four o'clock. Fine. I look forward to seeing you then."

She hung up the phone and turned to Kelley. "I'm selling this old flat and planning to purchase what I think you call a condo. That was the lovely real estate lady that I met at the food market. I told her that I was receiving a large insurance check from the death of my dear friend and that I was considering purchasing a new modern flat with the proceeds.

She said that her aunt is selling her place and is anxious to sell it at a good price. I'm supposed to meet her this afternoon."

"Why don't we sit down and chat for a few moments about this, Victoria. You know, all of this sounds just a little suspicious in view of the fact that you have just been a victim of a swindle already. I'm starting to believe that someone might think that you are quite vulnerable and may be targeting you once again."

Victoria took a seat next to her desk, opened the drawer and pulled out a card. "Here is the real estate lady's card. Her name is Jean McCoy. She's going to pick me up at four this afternoon. Her aunt's flat in 'Paradise Living' is being rented right now. But, the real estate lady said that she could show me the model flat in the building that is almost the same as the aunt's. She might even have a buyer for this old place."

Kelley sat down next to Victoria and took her hands in hers. "I'm sure that your brother will agree that you need to slow down a bit. Why don't you call this lady back and change your plans. Set up the meeting for tomorrow morning at nine. That will give me time to investigate this woman a little."

Victoria thought for a while, nodded, and then picked up the phone and called Jean McCoy. After a brief conversation, she hung up. "She said she would be here promptly at nine tomorrow morning."

"Good. Now I want you to just sit tight. I'm going to head back to Scotland Yard and see if I can get any information on this woman. Also going to take the brochures and the mailbox cover in and see if Commissioner Pope's men can pick up any fingerprints from them. I plan to come back and stay the night with you."

"That's lovely of you my dear. But, do you think that's really necessary?"

"Yes. I want to be here in the morning when this lady picks you up. I plan to monitor your conversation with her and follow you every step of the way."

"I'm confused about what your plans are, my dear young lady. But if Andrew trusts you, so do I."

"Good. Before I leave, I need to ask you something Victoria. Did this Ms. McCoy say anything about money?"

"She mentioned that I could get a better price for the flat if I paid cash. I told her that I would have about twenty thousand pounds for a down payment."

"Okay. I'm going to head to Scotland Yard and fill the Commissioner in on all I have learned. Now lock your door when I leave. I'll be back in a few hours with my overnight bag. Maybe you could have some hot tea ready for me."

"If you're going to stay for dinner, I'll fix us a nice homemade Shepherd's Pie."

Chapter 11

As Kelley headed back toward the city she decided she should talk with James and the Commissioner about what she learned in Essex. If the real estate lady who had contacted Victoria was the thief and was preparing to swindle Victoria once again, definite steps needed to be immediately taken to stop her. That's why Kelley had decided to spend the night at Victoria's and be present when the lady arrived in the morning. She felt certain that it was not safe for Victoria to meet with her alone.

She wound her way through the heavy mid-afternoon traffic in London and approached the tall brick building that James had pointed out as being the temporary location of New Scotland Yard proper.

Oh my gosh. A parking spot right in front, Kelley thought, not believing her good luck. As she jumped out of the car, carrying her briefcase and the door from Victoria's mailbox, she saw Commissioner Pope walking toward the entrance.

She rushed up to him. "Commissioner, I'm so glad that I caught you. I was going inside to look for you."

"Good to see you again, Kelley. How are you doing on my sister's case? James told me that you went out to visit her."

"That's why I was going to look for you. A suspicious

person was rifling through your sister's mailbox this afternoon. I got a couple pieces of Victoria's mail, plus the door from her rusty old mailbox. And I need them checked for fingerprints. And some fast service if possible, because Victoria is planning to meet the suspected thief tomorrow morning."

"Walk with me and fill me in on the way." He headed inside the building with Kelley right behind him.

On the way to the fingerprint lab, Kelley explained all she had uncovered about Victoria's case and its similarities to the cold cases of the past. "I'm hoping that the fingerprints on one of these items will match ones that you have on file."

"One thing at a time," the Commissioner said as they walked into the lab and approached a slender young lady in a white lab coat. "I need a fingerprint check on these items, and now."

Kelley placed her briefcase on the counter and removed the advertisements she had retrieved from Victoria's mailbox. She handed them to the lab technician together with the paper wrapped mail box door.

"Have a seat while see if I can lift some prints." The technician pointed to a couple of chairs placed against the wall. "If I do, I'll run them through several computer programs."

They sat down and Kelley told him everything that had transpired at Victoria's.

"You know sir, our suspect appears to be a very brazen and clever thief," Kelley concluded.

After about a half hour, the lab technician returned. "I picked up a couple of prints that turned out to be from the postman and your sister. All federal employees' prints are on record you know."

"Anything else," the Commissioner asked.

"Yes. The prints of a Ms. Jean McCoy. She has a record for petty theft and one arrest for embezzlement.

She was never tried for that—apparently the victim refused to testify. Here is a photo of her from her arrest." She handed it to the Commissioner.

"Let's compare this with the old photos and playbills that you got in Essex," he said.

Kelley opened her briefcase and pulled out the theatre playbills. After looking through several of them, she exclaimed, "Jackpot. This is the same person. Your sister thought that the eyes of the lady in the playbill looked like those of the man who bilked her of her savings of twenty-five thousand pounds."

The Commissioner placed the arrest photo next to the playbill and looked at them closely. "I think that this lady might be our thief, or she is closely related to him."

Kelley nodded. "This seems to confirm what I suspected. I think that the man who took Victoria's money is really Jean McCoy in disguise. And if I'm right, she's getting ready to cheat Victoria once again."

"You mean to say that we have been wasting our time looking for a man, when we should have been looking for a woman?"

"Yes sir. I think that he is really a she. And she used to perform at the old downtown Essex Theatre."

"Well. Now that we have this bloody criminal in our sights, it's time to put 'Operation Showdown' in action."

"I'll need one of your agents to help me pull off my plan," Kelley replied, as she reached down and thrust the printout of the fingerprints, the playbills and the photos into her briefcase.

"Anyone you need will be at your disposal, Agent Ryan."

"Gee, it's nice to be called Agent Ryan again."

"You did tell James that you liked to be called Agent Ryan?"

"Better to keep my new last name a secret in this line of work."

The Commissioner grinned. "Now tell me what your plans are, Agent."

"I'll be staying overnight with your sister tonight so that I'll be there in the morning when our suspect arrives to pick her up. Also, I'll need one of your agents to meet me at her house early in the morning. Ms. McCoy is scheduled to pick up Victoria about nine. I want to wire Victoria so that we can record her conversation with Ms. McCoy tomorrow. That way we'll have the whole scheme on tape when we apprehend her."

"Good. Agent Wallace is familiar with wiring people. I'll have him meet you there early in the recording van."

Within seconds, the Commissioner was on his phone. He called Agent Wallace and asked him to join Kelley and him in his office immediately.

The Commissioner led Kelley upstairs to his office, where Agent Wallace was already waiting for them.

After they were seated, the Commissioner explained the plan to Wallace. "You are now assigned to Agent Ryan for the duration of this case. She'll fill you in on all the details about Operation Showdown."

Wallace looked at the Commissioner and rubbed his hands in glee. "Just like the old days, Andrew. I'm so glad to be working out in the field once again. Sick to death of all that desk jockey stuff."

"Know the feeling Wallace. But we all have to work where we are most effective." He stood up. "Now, I must excuse myself. A meeting to attend. Keep me posted agents."

After he left, Kelley leaned toward Wallace. "Now, I'll update you on the operation."

After leaving New Scotland Yard, Kelley drove to the Fleming house to pick up her cosmetic bag and pajamas for the overnight stay. She was apprehensive about telling her groom that she planned to spend a night of their honeymoon apart from him.

Entering the house, she discovered that Phil was not there yet.

"Tomorrow is our big day," James said as he and Eva greeted Kelley and led her into the kitchen. "Eva has already packed her bag for the hospital stay."

After they sat down at the table, James turned to Kelley. "And how is your case going, Agent Ryan? I talked to the Commissioner a few minutes ago. I understand that he titled it Operation Showdown. Nice code name. Said it was going to be Agent Ryan's collar. I believe that is what you Americans call it when you catch a bad guy. But, I'm so disappointed that I can't be there."

"You, my friend, need to be with your lady when she delivers."

"I wouldn't miss it for the world. Now, tell me what you have planned for the operation."

Kelley carefully explained her plans to him. "Don't worry about me. I'll do just fine."

"That's what I like about you Yanks. You're so confident."

Kelley smiled briefly; then ran her hand nervously through her hair. Little did he realize how anxious she was about trying to solve this case. "Now, I have to go upstairs and pack a bag. I'm planning on staying with Victoria tonight."

"Wait a minute. Does your husband know about your plans for tonight and tomorrow," Eva asked.

"No. I didn't want to bother him at work. He said he'd call me when he gets ready to leave the office. I plan to tell him then."

"He probably won't be too happy about you putting yourself in danger," James replied.

"I think that he's used to what I do by now. He's always very supportive of whatever I decide to do." She stood up. "I wish you good luck tomorrow. I can't wait to see your two little girls."

As Kelley drove toward Victoria's home, her phone rang. It was her newlywed husband, who was soon to realize that he would be spending the night away from his bride.

After exchanging endearing hellos, Kelley asked him how his day went. He said that everything in the case that he was working on was proceeding according to schedule. "I'm getting ready to leave the office and take the bus back to the Flemings. I've just about wrapped up my work at the firm. The accountant that stole the money has been arrested. Two detectives are taking him back to the States. And the innocent man will be freed. Now, tell me how your day went. Are you back at the house yet? "

"That's what I need to talk to you about dear." She told what had transpired at Victoria Pope's house and that she felt that she needed to stay overnight with her so that she could be there early in the morning.

After her explanation, Phil replied, "I think I can manage for one night without my bride. After dinner with Eva and James, I'll read that book that I brought along on our trip. Never got to it on the ship. But are you sure that you don't need me to help you in catching this woman?"

"No dear. Just sit tight. I'll call you tomorrow and let you know how things went."

"Just be careful. I love you so much. I couldn't stand it if anything happened to you."

"I know. I'll be careful. And I love you too. I'll think of you when I'm all alone tonight."

"Sweet dreams, my brave little agent."

Chapter 12

Early the next morning, Agent Kelley Ryan, fully dressed and having finished eating Victoria's hot porridge for breakfast, stood patiently at the front window of the flat looking for Agent Wallace. She watched him drive into the driveway in a dark older van and get out with a large valise in hand.

She went to the door and opened it. "Good morning, Wallace."

"Didn't know if you were here. I didn't see the car from the Yard that you were driving."

"Victoria's neighbor, Tillie, let me park it in her garage. I didn't want our suspect seeing it. I guess you brought all the necessary equipment to wire Victoria."

He motioned toward the bag. "Got everything we need in here. Is Miss Victoria up for this?"

"Yes. She understands what we plan to do and said that she is ready, willing, and able."

"Good. I thought that maybe this situation would upset her."

"No. On the contrary. I think the idea of being wired and helping to trap a criminal has her quite excited. She said that she couldn't wait to hear what her brother would say about it."

"Let's synchronize our watches then," Wallace said.

"I want to be sure that we're on the same time."

"I have eight fifteen," Kelley responded. "Ms. McCoy is supposed to be here for Victoria at nine."

Wallace reached into the valise, pulled out a gun and a shoulder holster and handed them to Kelley. "Got you the Smith and Wesson that you requested. Had to hunt around the office for a spare holster. But, one of the fellows offered to lend it to you. Most of our equipment is in transit to the remodeled building."

Kelley took off her jacket, put on the holster and looked at the gun. "Ammo?"

"Here are two clips. I must say, Agent Ryan, not only do you look the role, but I heard from Agent Fleming that you're an extremely good shot."

Kelley put her jacket back on as Victoria, dressed in low comfortable shoes and a cotton dress, buttoned down the front, entered the room. She caught herself up sharply as she looked at Wallace. "I take it that you are Andrew's assistant, Agent Wallace. He has mentioned your name often."

"Been working with the Commissioner for years."

"Glad to met you," she smiled sweetly at him.

Wallace grinned, leaned over and pulled the wire equipment from the bag. Kelley led Victoria to the sitting room sofa and motioned for her to sit down. Wallace turned his head away as Kelley unbuttoned Victoria's dress and taped the wire equipment to her. Victoria put on a lightweight jacket over the dress.

"Just speak normally, Victoria," Kelley said. "Don't talk loudly or do anything to make Jean McCoy suspicious." She buttoned Victoria's dress back up. "Now, do you have any questions?"

There was a long pause. "No. I do feel a little strange with these wires on. But, I believe that I understand your instructions. I'll wait for Ms. McCoy to arrive. Then, I'll go along with whatever she wants to do. I know that you and Agent Wallace will be following us and recording everything that we say."

"Correct. Just try to talk in a normal tone of voice. That way we'll be able to record everything," Wallace added.

Victoria clapped her hands. "My, this is so exciting. No wonder Andrew loves working for Scotland Yard."

Kelley looked at Wallace and winked.

The small petite Victoria could hardly contain herself. "Maybe, Andrew will let me help him with his work in the future."

"I love your spirit, Victoria. But, I want you to remember that Jean McCoy could be armed and dangerous," Kelley cautioned. "Your brother would not want you to take any chances with her. But rest assured, Agent Wallace and I will be close at all times and will rush in if we think anything is going wrong."

"I know. I'll just sit down here and wait patiently for Ms. McCoy to arrive." Victoria took a seat on the sitting room sofa and picked up the morning newspaper.

"Try to act in a normal manner," Kelley instructed. "Just go to the bank with her, cash your check and then let her proceed." She patted Victoria on the shoulder. "And remember to stay calm. We will be able to hear everything that is said and will be at your side in a moment's notice if necessary."

Saying nothing, Victoria tried to read the newspaper.

Kelley turned to Wallace, "Operation Showdown is about to begin."

He closed his valise and headed outside to the van, with Kelley close behind him. Wallace started up the van, drove it about a half a block away and parked it on the opposite side of the street.

When they turned on their listening and recording equipment, they heard Victoria. "Testing. Testing. One. Two. Three. Can you hear me?"

Two short toots of the van's horn signaled her that they could and they were ready for action.

At about nine, Jean McCoy drove into Victoria's driveway, parked her car and entered the flat. The two agents in the van could clearly hear the conversation as the ladies greeted each other.

"I see that you're wearing a light jacket, Miss Pope. Good idea. I put on a warm pant suit this morning. A slight nip in the air," Jean was heard to say.

They emerged from the flat, walked slowly to Jean's car and drove away.

Agent Wallace waited for the car to get a short way down the street before he started the van. Staying a good distance behind Jean's car, they followed it to Victoria's bank.

They listened to the conversation when the ladies were in the bank. Over the protest of the bank manager, Victoria cashed her check for twenty thousand pounds and walked out the door with the cash in her handbag.

Next, Jean drove Victoria to the Paradise Living complex. Before they left the car, Jean said, "I've made arrangements for us to look at the model flat that resembles my aunt's."

They exited the car, walked into the main building and approached the reception desk. A man's voice said, "Nice to see you again, Ms. McCoy."

"Thank you. This is Victoria Pope. We are here to look at the model flat. Victoria, this is Claude Smithers, the manager of the building."

"How do you do," Victoria replied softly.

Kelley soon realized that Victoria was a bit nervous about wearing the wire and carrying a lot of cash. She definitely was not her usual chatty self.

Leaving the recording equipment running, Kelley and Agent Wallace both put on ear pieces as they left the van, so that they could continue to monitor the conversation.

When they entered the building, they could see Smithers, a portly gentleman, leading the ladies down the hall to the lift and watched as the sign above indicated that it had stopped at the fourth floor.

"You stay here and watch the front door in case Jean tries to make a run for it later," Kelley said.

Using the stairway, she ran up to the fourth floor. The hall was empty. A door to a flat at the far end of the hall was open. Assuming that was where the three had entered, Kelley ran to a nearby supply closet and slipped inside, leaving the door open a crack so that she could peek out.

Through her earpiece, Kelley could hear the conversation taking place between Victoria, Jean and Smithers as they toured the model flat.

Smithers described the amenities in the flat as he showed the ladies around. "Here is a packet with the rules for our residents. There's a two hundred pound monthly fee for the utilities and the grounds keeping. It also includes a weekly cleaning by our housekeepers and one spot in the underground parking garage which is monitored at all times. Washers and dryers are in the basement.

If you ladies don't have any more questions, I leave you to look around on your own. I'll be downstairs at the desk in case you need me. Just lock the door behind you as you leave and return the key to me."

Kelley looked out of the closet door; she saw the manager leave the flat and walk to the lift. She watched as it descended to the first floor. In her earphone, she could hear Jean McCoy telling Victoria the many extra features that her aunt's flat had that the model one didn't.

Suddenly Kelley saw the door to the flat next to the one that Victoria and Jean were in open. A middle aged woman pushing a cart full of house cleaning supplies emerged and pushed the cart toward the flat across the way.

Through her earpiece Kelley heard Victoria say, "I like what I've seen and I'm ready to purchase your aunt's flat. I'll give you the twenty thousand pounds cash for the down payment now, but, I'll need a receipt."

"Of course. I'll just tuck this cash into my briefcase and give it to you," Jean answered. "I prepared a purchase agreement and a receipt ahead of time when I realized that you were earnest about purchasing the flat and had cash for the down payment. You were fortunate that you could quickly jump on this smashing good deal."

"Where do I sign," Victoria asked.

"Right here," Jean answered. "But wait, we'll need a witness to our signatures to make it legal. Let's see if there's anyone around."

She opened the door to the hall, saw the housekeeper and called her into the room.

Kelley heard Jean instruct Victoria where to sign the agreement. Then, she asked the housekeeper to sign as a witness to both their signatures.

Jean said, "My aunt is out of town, but was anxious to sell. So she gave me power of attorney. Several other people have expressed an interest in purchasing this flat but your cash down payment helped you edge them out. You can plan on moving in soon. And I'll be by your place the first of the week with a couple who might be interested in buying it. Now, I'll return the key to the manager and take you back home."

From her hidden spot, Kelley saw the door to the model flat open and Jean and Victoria step out into the hall. Kelley whispered to Agent Wallace in her mouthpiece, "Our ladies are on the move."

Once in front of the lift, Jean stopped. "Oh my gosh, I forgot my handbag. I'll meet you in the lobby, Victoria."

Victoria nodded as Jean, with her briefcase, headed back into the room. After the door to the room closed, Kelley stepped out from the closet and took Victoria by the hand, "Good job. You kept your cool and we should have everything on tape. We'll arrest Ms. McCoy when she gets back down to the lobby."

Kelley stepped back inside the closet to wait for Jean McCoy to emerge from the room as Victoria entered the lift and headed downstairs.

After several minutes, the room to the model flat opened. A young boy wearing knickers and a baseball cap came out and headed for the stairwell. Kelley stared at him for a moment. Then, she realized that this was probably Jean, in a disguise and trying to escape. Kelley jumped out of the closet and raced down the stairs after her.

Stopping briefly on the third floor, Kelley spoke into her mouthpiece, "Wallace, be on the lookout for a young boy in a baseball cap. It's McCoy."

When Kelley reached the lobby, she found Agent Wallace hanging onto the boy by the back of his shirt.

"I've got him, Agent Willis," Wallace said as he whipped the cap from the boy's head. Jean McCoy's hair tumbled out of the cap. Wallace drew her arms behind her back and calmly said, "You're under arrest, lady."

"You've got nothing on me," Jean yelled out.

Claude Smithers jumped up from his desk and ran over to them. "Just what's going on here?"

Wallace flashed his badge. "I'm Agent Wallace from Scotland Yard and I'm arresting this young man. Excuse me, I mean this woman."

"Not out here, please," Smithers said as he headed toward a door off the lobby. "Follow me. I don't want you to upset our other residents."

Wallace pushed Jean into the office, as Kelley and Victoria Pope followed.

"Okay lady. Hand over the money," Agent Wallace snarled.

"Don't have any money."

"Where's your briefcase and handbag," Kelley demanded.

"Does it look like I have them?" Jean smiled.

Kelley whirled around. "Oh shit. The housekeeper. She never came out of the room."

She glared at Jean. "She's in on this with you. You gave her the briefcase with the money."

"Don't know what you're talking about."

Wallace sighed. "We've been had. Now what do we do?"

Just then, a voice called out. "Hey Kelley, look what I found out back."

Phil walked into the office pushing the housekeeper ahead of him. "I caught this woman coming down the fire escape in the back of the building with a briefcase in her hands. I thought it looked mighty suspicious for a housekeeper to use that escape route when there's no fire."

Kelley ran to him and threw her arms around him. "Thank you, my darling husband. But, how did you know where we were?"

"James had a talk with the Commissioner this morning before he left for the hospital with Eva. The Commissioner filled him in on what you and Agent Wallace had planned. James gave me this address. So I thought I would take a cab over and see if you needed any back up."

Wallace looked at him and grinned. "Seems like we did. Now let's check that briefcase out."

Kelley unzipped it and found Victoria's money inside. She looked at the housekeeper. "I believe that you are about to be arrested too, my dear."

A haze of fury engulfed the woman as she pointed at

Jean McCoy. "It's all her. I'm innocent. She made me do it. She made me do it."

Kelley replied simply, "Just tell that to the Scotland Yard."

She turned to Wallace, "Now, I guess you'll have to handcuff both of these ladies and take them in."

As Wallace started to push the two ladies out of the office, Commissioner Pope walked in.

Startled, Agent Wallace exclaimed. "Good morning Commissioner. What brings you here?"

"You aren't the only one that gets tired sitting in the office, Wallace. Besides I wanted to see if my sister is okay." He turned to Victoria. "And how are you doing, my dear Vicky?"

She clapped her hands. "Just fine. Your agents recorded everything that Ms. McCoy said. I love playing detective. This has been so exciting. Maybe, I could help you in some other cases."

The Commissioner embraced her. "I think that you've had enough excitement."

He turned to his assistant. "Good job, Wallace."

"Thank you sir." He pointed to the briefcase on the floor. "We have your sister's money in there sir."

"Good. We'll need it for evidence." The Commissioner walked over to Kelley and Phil and shook their hands. "Can't thank you people enough. You've brought this long sought after criminal to justice."

"Glad to be of some help sir," Kelley said. "But before my husband and I leave, I want to give you back the firearm from the agency. I'm just glad that I didn't have to use it. And, here's the key to the car I used. It's in Victoria's neighbor's garage. Maybe you could drop us off at the hospital on your way in so we can see how James and Eva are doing."

"Sure. No problem. Wallace, you take these two ladies to the Yard and book them. I'll be in later. Vicky, you can come with us to the hospital. Then I'll take you home."

Kelley whirled around. "Oh, Victoria, I forgot that you still have the wire on. Let's go into the ladies room and I'll remove it."

"Yes. Please."

After the women emerged Kelley walked up to Phil, "Well, it looks like Operation Show Down is over. Now, what's next?"

He grinned at her. "What's next? Well, here's my plan. We're on our honeymoon, remember. From now on, your name is Mrs. Kelley Willis. Say good bye to Agent Ryan once again."

Chapter 13

Before Phil had a chance to say any more, Claude Smithers tapped Kelley on the shoulder. "Here is the tape from the model room. Someone from Scotland Yard came out late yesterday and set up a video camera in the room."

"Thanks." She took the tape and walked over to Agent Wallace. "I called into Scotland Yard yesterday afternoon and asked the Commissioner to have someone put a video camera in the flat when Victoria told me that she was going to be shown the model. Here is the video—you'll probably need it for evidence."

"You don't miss a trick, Agent Ryan. I can see now why Agent Fleming said that you were one bloody good partner." He shook her hand. "You better look me up the next time you are in London. I owe you a fish and chips lunch."

"Thank you. I'll look forward to it, Wallace."

"That lunch includes a pint of Guinness."

Kelley and Phil sat in the back seat of the Commissioner's car and Victoria sat in the front beside him, as he drove back into London. Along the way, they talked about what had transpired that morning. Both the Commissioner and Victoria voiced their gratitude to Kelley.

"Thank you so much for your help, Kelley. Because of you, Jean McCoy and her accomplice will be on their way to prison," the Commissioner said. "And a special thanks to you too, Phil. I understand that you apprehended the housekeeper as she came down the fire escape."

"It's all in a day's work, when you live with my little wife," Phil replied, patting her hand. "But now, I'm anxious to get back to our honeymoon."

Kelley leaned toward him and whispered, "Sleeping at Victoria's house last night was a bummer. I'm used to you next to me."

He whispered back, "So promise me, that there won't be any more nights apart in the weeks and years to come."

"I promise."

The Commissioner looked back over his shoulder. "We're almost at London Bridge Hospital. That's where James said that his wife was going for the delivery of her twins."

Kelley looked at her watch. "It's almost one and they were supposed to deliver the twins this morning. So the girls should be here by now."

"And I've got a surprise for you my dear," Phil said. "Before I left the house, I packed our bags and sent them on ahead to London. We'll be staying tonight at a hotel near the airport."

"Oh, I thought we were going to stay on a few days so that I could give Eva a hand with the girls when they all come home."

"No. I told James that I had a big surprise planned for you and he decided that Eva and he would do okay without us. Besides, I think that just dealing with the twins will be enough for them. They don't need the additional burden of trying to entertain us."

"We never did take them out to dinner the other

night, you know."

"Kelley, getting through the delivery and taking care of the twins are their only concerns right now," he replied.

Just then, Victoria announced, "Oh there's the hospital right ahead, Andrew."

"We'll just drop you off in front and keep on going, if you don't mind," the Commissioner said. "I've already arranged for a large bouquet of flowers from Scotland Yard to be delivered to the new parents. And, I'll call James later in the day to personally congratulate him."

He parked his car in front of the hospital and all four got out. The Commissioner walked around to the boot of the car and took out a package wrapped in brown paper. He shook Kelley's hand and gave her the package. "Here's a little remembrance of your time spent with us at Scotland Yard.

"Can I ask what it is?"

"It's a framed eight by ten photo of the original Scotland Yard," he answered proudly.

"Thank you," Kelley said, "We'll always think of you when we look at it."

"I think it would look fantastic hanging in my office, honey, "Phil added.

"Maybe, you and your wife, Birdie, will take a flight over the pond and visit us sometime," Kelley said to the Commissioner.

He nodded. "I'm sure that she would love to see New York. She's never been to the States you know."

Victoria had tears in her eyes as she hugged Kelley. "I'll never forget how kind you've been to me. It was so good of you to spend the night with me and accompany me on this morning's adventure. I hope that you'll visit me again, when you return to London. Maybe you could join me for high tea."

"You can count on it, Victoria."

The Commissioner and Victoria drove off as Phil and Kelley entered the hospital. Inside, they stopped at the front desk and asked for Mrs. Fleming's room number.

"Room four, twelve. Steps and lift down the hall," the elderly volunteer said.

"What shall we take," Kelley asked.

Phil smiled, "The lift. I think we've had enough exercise already today."

Approaching Eva's room, a voice that Kelley recognized as belonging to James called out, "Wait guys. Don't you want to meet the girls—Celine and Claire? They're all cleaned up and in the nursery now. Just follow me."

They whirled quickly around and followed the proud father as he walked briskly down the hall toward the nursery.

James waved at the nurse inside and motioned for her to bring the twins to the window.

Kelley pulled her camera out of her bag and took several pictures of the girls, both of whom were dressed in little white buntings with pink stocking caps. "Golly, I can't believe how adorable they are."

As they started to leave the nursery window, the nurse came out. "Would you care to have your photo taken with the girls and your guests, Mr. Fleming?"

"Of course. These are our dear friends from the States and they're going to be on their way. So that would be smashing."

The nurse went back into the nursery and came out with the babies. She put the girls, now wrapped in pink receiving blankets in their father's arms. With Kelley and Phil standing on either side of him, she took several photos.

As the nurse started to take the babies back from James, Kelley asked in a pleading voice, "Can I hold them for a moment?"

The nurse looked at James, who answered, "Of,

course."

She put the babies in Kelley's arms as Phil snapped their picture. "Beautiful. You'll make a wonderful mother," he whispered to her.

She smiled. "Someday." And reluctantly handed the babies back to the nurse.

Kelley and Phil followed James toward Eva's room. Along the way, Kelley grabbed James's arm. "Well, I already heard you call the girls Celine and Claire. But, as a woman, I need some more information. How much did they weigh? And how are you going to tell them apart?"

"Don't know. Guess we'll have to keep their name tags on for a while—until we can tell the difference. Celine was born first. She's the biggest—weighed six pounds, two ounces and they put a name tag on her leg right away. A few minutes later, Claire was born. She weighed just less than six pounds. They're both about nineteen inches long. The Doc said that they were quite large for twins. Good thing that Eva had a C-section."

"And speaking of Eva—how did the dear lady do?"

"She was just unbelievable. A little tired afterwards. In fact, she was sleeping a few minutes ago, so let's be quiet," James replied as they got to the door of her room.

He opened the door and looked in. To his surprise, Eva was sitting up in bed brushing her hair. The minute that she saw Kelley and Phil, she smiled and held out her arms for them. "I'm so glad that you came. Did you see my beautiful babies yet?"

Kelley ran to her and embraced her. "Yes. We just saw them. They're just gorgeous. And we love their names, too. Celine and Claire Fleming sounds very distinguished."

"We named the girls after our mothers. James' mom is Celine. And my mother is Claire."

James pulled up a chair for Kelley and they talked for about twenty minutes before a nurse entered the room. "I think that Mrs. Fleming could use some rest now. Before long it will be time to feed the girls and I'll be bringing them in to her."

"Oh nurse, we're leaving today. So could you take a picture of the four of us together," Kelley asked.

After the photos were taken, Eva grabbed Kelley's hands. "I love you guys. I wish you would stay with us a little longer."

"I'm certain that you'll have your hands full caring for the babies," Kelley replied. "But, I'll call you in a few days to see how you and your little ones are getting on."

"Thank you. The girls and I are staying in the hospital for another two days. I just talked to my mum and she insisted on coming here to give us a hand for a week or two."

"Now, I must ask you to leave now so our new mother can get some rest," the nurse said firmly.

James led Kelley and Phil out into the hall, where they said their good byes.

Phil shook James' hand. "I've certainly enjoyed getting to know you and Eva and we can't thank you enough for your hospitality."

"It was a pleasure having you. You must come back and stay longer."

Kelley gave James a kiss on the cheek and a hug. "No. It's your turn to visit us."

"Maybe, when the girls get a wee bit bigger."

"We'll count on it," Phil answered. "We're staying at a hotel near the airport tonight. But right now, I plan to take my wife on one of those famous red bus tours of London if you can tell us how to find one. One last look at Jolly Old England."

"There's a double-decker bus stand right around the corner from the front entrance. You can catch it there. When you're done, just take a cab to your hotel."

"Thanks buddy," Phil said. "Now, I can see why Kelley

and you were such a great team and why Kelley thinks so much of you."

"You are one terrific chap yourself and you're very fortunate to have Kelley as your mate."

"I know that."

Later, as Kelley and Phil took their seats on the top deck of the red tour bus, she turned and said; "Now, I'm anxious to see Buckingham Palace."

"And that you shall, my love."

"So what's our next adventure?"

"You won't believe where I'm about to take you," Phil replied, rubbing his hands and grinning.

Chapter 14

After the bus tour of the city, Kelley and Phil took a taxi to the hotel near the airport, where Phil had their bags sent previously. Sitting in the back of the taxi, Phil looked over at his wife. "Is that a tear in your eye, Kelley?"

"Yes, it is. I'm going to miss the Flemings. Wish we didn't live an ocean apart."

"Well, James said that he hoped to holiday in the States in a couple of years when the girls get older. And we can always return to London and other hot spots in Europe."

Kelley smiled. "I've never been to Paris, you know."

"Now for my second surprise," he added, as the taxi pulled into the hotel. "I'm taking you to a five star restaurant tonight, called, 'The Baltic.' Our reservations are for seven and it's now five."

"So, I have time for a nice leisurely soak in a big bath tub first?"

"Right. But, I want you to wear something snazzy and those diamond earrings that you got last year in Miami from your jeweler friend, Harry Wilson."

"You are just one surprise after another."

"You know Kelley; I want to show you off tonight. We're going to meet Bobbie and Nicky Wilson and help them celebrate their marriage."

Kelley looked at him, astonished. "How and when did you arrange all this?"

"Harry Wilson did say to give him a call if we ever got to London. So I called him the other day while I was at work. He invited us to join him and his wife, Corrine, together with Bobbie and Nicky for dinner. He said for us to bring our appetites. So I want you to look beautiful and to have a fantastic time. Try to put this episode with Scotland Yard behind you. Let's just relax and enjoy life from now on."

"I think I can manage to do that. But what about you?"

"I talked to my law firm in Syracuse and they instructed me to enjoy the rest of our honeymoon."

That evening with the Wilsons proved to be very enjoyable and the three men took turns offering toasts to each other.

Nicky toasted the whole group, who "Looked smashing."

Harry Wilson toasted, "To the newlywed couples. May they enjoy a long and happy life together."

Later, as the orchestra played enchanting music the couples stood up to dance. Phil tapped Kelley on the shoulder and in his broad New York accent asked, "You wanna dance?"

Kelley placed her left hand on his shoulder and put her right one in his after they walked onto the dance floor.

"You see Kell, my dance lessons did pay off," he whispered in her ear. Kelley put her head on his shoulder and shut her eyes. If only this moment could last forever, she thought.

The evening was over much too soon for them. It was time to bid the Wilson family good evening and goodbye once again

After they returned by cab to the hotel, Phil said, "Okay, now it's time for my final surprise for you, to thank you for planning such a beautiful wedding."

"And what is that?"

"Tomorrow morning, we are off to Ireland. We're going to visit your paternal grandmother. The one that you've never seen."

Kelley stared at him in astonishment. "My mother hasn't talked to her in years. So how did you arrange that?"

"I got her address from your mother. I located her phone number in Ireland and called her. She sounded very anxious to finally meet you. We're leaving for Dublin early in the morning and by noon the two of you should be giving each other hugs."

"I doubt that. As I remember, she never seemed very interested in meeting me."

"Maybe now that the old lady is getting nearer to the gates of Heaven, she is ready to meet and greet you."

"I'm overwhelmed with the thought of getting acquainted with her. I lost my father early in life you know. And, I've never heard from her in all these years. In fact, I only saw one picture of her."

"But she is part of the Ryan family tree. And you should meet her since we are nearby."

"Are there any more tricks up your sleeve, Mr. Willis?"

"Not at the present time. We're going to fly into Dublin tomorrow and find a way to get to your grandmother's place. She has a ranch outside of Dublin. Been in the same place for years, she said."

"I can't believe it. I'm finally going to meet Nanna Ryan. Just think, tomorrow, I'll see her."

Chapter 15

The British Airways flight from London to Dublin took less than an hour. After they got off the plane, Phil said, "Maybe we should get something to eat before we pick up a rental car. The continental breakfast at the hotel didn't fill me up."

"Good idea," Kelley said. "Let's find someplace here in the airport for some coffee and donuts."

After a quick stop at a fast food place, Phil took her by the arm. "I'll go get the car and you gather up the bags. I'll meet you at the exit by baggage. But first, I'll call your Nanna and tell her we're in Ireland and check her schedule."

After stopping along the way to call Kelley's grand-mother, Phil headed toward the rental car booth. As he approached, he spotted a fifty something man, wearing a Trafalgar Tours badge and holding up a sign that read, 'Trafalgar Tours.'

The man walked up to Phil. "Are you Mr. Flanagan from Chicago?"

"No. I'm Willis from Syracuse New York."

"Sorry to have stopped you then sir."

"No bother. In fact I have a question for you."

"Ask it lad."

"I'm on my way to rent a car and I need to know how

far we are from the city center of Dublin, and do you know of a good place to catch a two or three hour tour of the city?"

"Laddie, I may have the answer to all your questions." He reached into his jacket pocket and pulled out his mobile phone. "Anna, this is Eddie. Do you have any fare to Dublin now? No. I got an American who needs a ride to Dublin and is looking for a short tour of the city. Are you interested in that?"

He turned back to Phil. "My sister is a licensed Dublin city tour guide as well as a licensed taxi driver. Said she could take care of you if you're interested. She knows more about Dublin than anyone."

"Great. My wife is meeting me with the luggage at the exit by British Airways"

"What's your full name sir?"

"Willis. Phil Willis."

He spoke into is phone, "The bloke's name is Willis. Meet him and his wife at British Airways exit. He's wearing a brown sport coat and he'll be looking for you."

He pocketed the phone. "You can't miss Anna, Mr. Willis. She's built like a brick-you-know-what and has flaming red hair. Drives the only red convertible taxi in Dublin. It's her trademark. Everyone around here knows her. Just ask for Anna Spoto. And enjoy your tour of Dublin. And, be sure to have a pint of Guinness while you're visiting."

Phil shook his hand and headed for the exit by baggage claim. He spotted Kelley pushing a gurney cart loaded with the two checked bags and the two carry-on's piled on top of them.

He walked up to her. "Hi sweet heart. Looks like you've got all the luggage."

"Yes. I was looking for you. I thought you were going to pick up a rental so I was watching for you to pull up in a car."

"Change of plans. I talked to your Nanna. Said she's volunteering at the hospital this morning. Wanted us to come to her place in about three or four hours."

"Oh, what will we do in the meantime?"

"Got that all worked out too. After I talked to her, I ran into a tour guide. Told me his sister drives a cab and she can take us on a private tour of Dublin. We can always pick up a rental car later."

"Boy, you make quick decisions," Kelley replied. Then, looking around at the maze of taxis parked along the curb, she asked. "And just how are we going to find this person?"

"She's supposed to be driving a red convertible and has red hair."

"Sounds very interesting."

Suddenly, a red convertible with a taxi signs on its sides, screeched to a halt near them.

Kelley spotted the buxom forty-year-old woman who climbed over the passenger seat and jumped from the cab.

"I think our ride is here." Kelley said as she waved at her.

The red-head walked quickly over. "Mr. Willis?"

"Yes. Glad to meet you, Anna," Phil shook her outstretched hand and asked, "How much do you charge for a ride into Dublin and a three hour tour of the city?"

"Two hundred Euros. And you'll find that it's worth every penny. I've lived in Dublin almost all me life and know the city like the back of me hand. Not only will I show all the sights but we'll stop for a quick tour inside some of the places.

We'll see St. Patrick's Cathedral, Dublin Castles, and Trinity College, where the book of Kells is stored. Then a walking tour of O'Connell Street, which is about the number one tourist sight in the city. And finally we'll wind up with a tour of the Guinness Brewery and have a pint of the dark brewed beer on me."

Phil looked at Kelley and nodded. "Sounds good to us."

As Anna started to wheel their suitcases to the cab, she stopped for a moment and added, "Only one problem. We'll have to skip the National Art Gallery. It's closed for two days. They're setting up a special exhibit of Van Gogh's paintings."

"Oh, that's a bummer," Kelley said. "I would love to have seen that. I admire his work and have several of his paintings. Not the real ones you know, just prints."

"Perhaps you could come back later in the week," Anna suggested as Phil took the suitcases from her and loaded them into the boot of the small car.

"You sit in the front Kelley and I'll sit in the back with the carry-on bags," he ordered

After she climbed into the passenger side; Anna got in and shut her door. "We're off. So sit back and enjoy yourselves on this nice sunny day. Have your cameras ready and don't be afraid to ask me questions."

As she started off, she looked over at Kelley, "Do, you know what we folks in Ireland call the Queen of England?"

"No what?"

"We call her 'The Hag with the Bag'."

Kelley laughed, "I get it. Cause she always carries her purse wherever she goes."

"You got it girl," Anna whirled out of the airport. "And now, my people, we're off to Dublin."

As Anna stopped at an intersection in O'Connell Street, she pointed out the statue of Molly Malone. "Do you know what we call Molly?"

"No. But, I can't wait to hear."

"Because she took a bath in the local fountain, we call her 'The Floozy in the Jacuzzi'."

As the light turned green and Anna drove onward, both she and Kelley sang a few bars of 'Molly Malone.'

Anna showed them the sights of the city for an hour and a half, then pulled into the parking lot of the Guinness Brewery. "Time out for Dublin's most famous refreshment," she said, as she jumped out of her side of the car, ran around and opened Kelley's door. "Follow me, you two. We'll need to spend at least a half hour here. Me cousin, Gene, works here and will show us around. That way, we won't have to pay the regular admittance fee either."

After a quick tour of the brewery, Phil sampled the regular Guinness beer, while Anna and Kelley choose a lighter pale lager.

As they sipped the slightly tulip shaped pint glasses of beer, Kelley said, "You know I'm really glad that we ran into you, Anna. I've collected a bunch of brochures of the city and I took a lot of photos."

"And I especially love the anecdote that you told about Oscar Wilde, the writer of 'The Picture of Dorian Gray'," Phil said. "I never heard him called 'The Dick with the Stick' before."

"And I loved seeing the statue of him in Merrion Square," Kelley added.

"And now, to wind up the tour, we'll stroll down O'Connell Street and view all the shops. And by the way, did you know that Dublin was named after the mayor—many years ago?"

After they finished their walk, they returned to Anna's cab. "Thank you for a lovely time, Anna," Kelley said. "The tour has been fabulous, hasn't it Phil?"

"Indeed it has. But now, we have to find a rental car so we can drive to Kelley's grandma's ranch near Kilkenny City."

"That's no problem." Anna said, "I'll drive you there."

"But I have to phone and let my grandmother know we're on the way,. "I've never met her, you know."

After she talked briefly with her grandmother, they

climbed back into the red convertible and headed down the road to Kilkenny City.

As they passed through the small town, they spotted a sign that read, 'Ryan's Irish Stud Farm.'

"That's where we're going," Phil shouted to Anna. "That's the name of my wife's grandmother's place."

"It is?" Anna looked over at Kelley. "That's your granny's place? And you've never met her? Boy, you two are in for one big surprise."

Chapter 16

As Anna's taxi pulled up to the large wrought iron gates at the entrance to the ranch, Kelley noticed the metal sign on the stone fence beside the gates read 'Keep Out.'

"Well, that's friendly," she said.

"Not really." Phil pointed toward the rusted wrought iron sign above the gate; 'Ryan's Irish Stud Farm.'

Anna sighed. "This is the place. I'm going to leave you now. Just be careful around that old lady. I heard rumors in town that she's a bit unusual."

She got out of the car and helped Phil unload the bags from the boot. Kelley took the carry-on bags from the back seat and placed them on the ground beside her.

"Here's me card. In case you ever need me."

After Phil shook hands with Anna and pressed a generous tip into her hands, she jumped back into her taxi and with a squeal of the tires and a puff of dust, was off.

Next to the driveway was a narrow walkway with a wooden gate in front of it. Kelley tried to open it. "It's locked."

Phil tried it once, and then looked over the top of it. "It has one of those goofy locks. You have to reach over the top of the gate, and pull the little round knob up to unlock it."

"I've got it," he said as the gate opened with a loud

creak. "Could use some oil on the hinges."

He turned around, grabbed the handle of a suitcase in each hand and pulled them toward the front porch. "Thank God for the wheelies."

Kelley grinned, reached down, put a strap from each of the two carry-ons over her shoulders and followed.

Approaching the house, they heard two loud gun-shots ring out.

"That sounds like it came from the back of the house," Kelley said.

Phil set his bags down on the front steps. "Let's go around and see what's going on."

Kelley dropped her bags and followed Phil.

Standing in front of them was a slim lady about five feet six; dressed in tight fitting jeans, a plaid shirt and fancy cowboy boots. An old suede hat that looked like it had been purchased in the Australian outback was pulled down over her face. In her hands was a shotgun.

Kelley inched her way toward the woman, "Grandma Ryan? It's me, Kelley Ryan, from America. Well, Kelley Willis now. Come to visit you."

Kate carefully put the gun down on a nearby stump, wiped her hands on her jeans, took off her hat and walked over to them. "Well don't just stand there. Give me a big hug," she said with outstretched arms.

She was surprised to see that although her grand-mother had snow white hair, she looked much younger than most women in their sixties. She threw both of her arms around Kate and squeezed tightly.

After a few minutes, Kate took a step back and wiped a couple of tears from her eyes. "Now, that's enough girl. Let me meet that new husband of yours."

She turned to him and put out her hand. "You must be Phillip. I talked to you on the phone."

"Yes, Kate. I'm so glad to meet you."

"Same here. Didn't think you were coming until tomorrow. Never the less, you're both here and you'll not be rushing off too quick. Okay?"

"Okay grandma. But, we hope that we won't be a burden to you."

"Sakes alive. You could never be a burden. But first, please don't call me Grandma or Granny; it's just plain Kate, okay? I'm so glad you're both here."

"What are you doing Kate," Phil asked. "We heard you shooting."

"Been practicing my aim. That's my handyman, Brian, over there. I'm shooting old clay birds."

She pointed to a young man dressed in bib overalls; standing at the side of the yard next to a skeet shooting trap.

Kate yelled out, "Brian, meet my granddaughter, Kelley and her husband, Phil. They're from America."

Brian waved at them and they acknowledged his salute with the same.

Kate nodded toward the gun. "What about you two? Ever do any shooting?"

Phil hesitated for a moment, looked at Kelley and laughed. "Now, that you mention it Kate, my little bride is quite a sharp shooter. Care for a demonstration?"

"Why not. Let's see what the little gal's got. Shoot 'um up." She put a couple of shells in the gun.

"You first Kate," Kelley said.

Kate lifted the gun to her shoulder and yelled, "Pull."

Brian fired off two clay pigeons in rapid succession. Kate pulled the trigger quickly and both pigeons disintegrated in mid air.

"Good shooting, Kate. My turn," Kelley said. She took the shotgun from her, picked up a couple of shells from the stump and loaded the gun. "Nice. A Savage over and under double barrel. Very nice."

"At least you know your guns," Kate said admiringly. "Now, let's see if you have the Ryan eye."

Kelley shouted, "Pull." Two clay pigeons shot into the air. Kelley hit them both.

"Not bad." Kate said. "Let's try again. Only this time, I'll have Brian kick up the speed on the shooting trap." She took the gun from Kelley and loaded it.

Kate hit the next two birds in rapid succession and set the shot gun down. "Now girl, I'll bet you a Guinness that you can't match that."

Kelley grinned. She picked up the shot gun, loaded it and yelled, "Pull." The two clay pigeons crossed in mid air and Kelley knocked them both out of the sky with one shot.

She turned to her grandmother. "I'd like my Guinness cold."

"That's some good shooting," Kate said. "You're a true Ryan. Let's go inside for a snack and a cold drink."

She yelled to Brian, "Clean the shot gun and put it away lad. I think we've had enough shooting for one day. Then, you can bring the luggage in for these young people."

Kate led Kelley and Phil into the kitchen where they both took a seat at the table. After serving lemonade and cookies, she sat down beside them. "Since you're going to be here for a few days, let's not try to tell each other our life stories right now. Let's save that for another time."

After they finished their refreshments, Kate stood up. "Phil, I need you to give me a hand in the parlor if you will."

Kelley and Phil followed her. In front of the stone fireplace that covered the far wall of the room, was a tall step ladder.

"Phil, if you would, I'd like for you to take down the picture of me late husband, Sean, that's above the fireplace mantle. It's been up there these many years, but now it's time for me new love."

Kelley stood there somewhat surprised at Kate's mention of a new love, as Phil climbed the ladder, removed the picture and climbed down with it.

"Now, dear boy, put this picture in its place." Kate reached behind the sofa and pulled a huge picture in a distressed oak frame.

Phil climbed the ladder and slipped the wire on the back of the picture over the large hook in the wall. "Tell me if it's straight," Phil said, leaning back a little.

"It's perfect," Kelley said, looking up at the oil painting of a beautiful chestnut colored horse. "What a beautiful horse."

"That's not just a horse," Kate said gazing up at the painting. "That's my prize mare, 'Celtic Thunder.' You'll meet her later. I had an artist paint that for me from a photograph. Cost me three hundred Euros. But, she's worth it."

They stood and gazed at the painting. "Nanna, she just takes my breath away. She's so majestic."

"Yes. Tall for a mare and sturdy too. But remember—you're to call me Kate, lass."

"Oh, I forgot. I'll try to remember, Kate.

"I'm really younger in spirit than me white hair makes you think." Kate continued. "You know, me late husband, Sean, and me were married for over forty years before he passed last year. It was a very happy marriage, with just a few bumps in the road. Unfortunately, your father, David, was one of those little bumps. You see he was born just a year after we married and both Sean and I were quite young."

"Yes. Mother told me that."

"Well, David grew up to be very independent and stubborn like his Da. The two never got along. So when he was seventeen, David ran off to America. Later we heard he married and had a child—you. Neither he nor your mother would have anything to do with us as long as Sean was alive.

Finally, I wrote last year to tell them that he had died. Your mother sent me a short note back. She said that your father had passed away when you were but a wee lass. Me heart just breaks when I think of all those years wasted in bitterness because those two men were so bull headed."

Kelley gave her a gentle squeeze. "But, that is all in the past, Kate, and we can't change it. We'll talk about it more later. For now, let's just concentrate on our time together."

She hoped that in the days to come, her grandmother would give her more insight into the complicated relationship between her father and her grandfather.

"Thank you me Luv. I hope that you'll stay a while so I can get to know you both. We've got so much to talk about. But, Brian should have your bags in your room by now so you can freshen up. I always go to town for the five o'clock evening mass on Saturday at St. Bridget's. I love me Sunday mornings at home. And you two can sleep in then. After mass, I'll treat you to supper at the local pub."

"That's very kind of you Kate," Phil said. "But I insist that it be my treat."

"I won't argue with you, my boy. I just hope that you two will like your room. This old house only has two bedrooms. But this guest room has a nice soft double bed with a goose down comforter. You newly-weds do sleep together don't you?"

Kelley chuckled. "For almost two weeks now, Kate."

Chapter 17

About a half hour later, Phil and Kelley came back downstairs and walked into the parlor where Kate was sitting by the fireplace reading a book. She looked up at them. "Good, I'm glad you both put on jackets. It gets a little cool when the sun goes down. Especially if it decides to mist a little. We call the mist—Irish Magic."

"We've already discovered that your weather can change quickly," Kelley replied.

"Let's go then. We'll take my jeep." Kate reached into the hall closet for her jacket. "As long as you're staying with me, there's no need to rent a car."

The ride to the church in the open jeep and over dirt roads seemed very adventurous to Kelley and Phil.

"Here we are—St. Bridget's Catholic Church," Kate said as she zipped into a parking space.

Walking up to the front door of the church, they met a priest standing outside. "Evening Kate. Good to see you."

"Father Ted, this is me granddaughter, Kelley, and her husband, Phillip. Visiting me from the States, they are."

He shook hands with them. "Good to meet you. So nice of you to accompany Kate to mass."

After the service was over, Kate led them outside. "Now that we've given some time to thank the good lord for all the blessings, he's bestowed on us; it's time for food and music."

They jumped back into the jeep. Kate drove down the street of the small town of Kilkenny City and pulled into a tavern that had a sign outside, 'McAllister's Pub.'

When they entered the smoke filled pub, Conor McAllister, who Kate introduced as the owner of the establishment, greeted them. Once again, she explained that this was her newly-wed granddaughter and her husband, from America.

"Kate, me darling," McAllister said, "I've got a lovely place for you right near the music." He led them to a table next to the small raised stage.

After they took their seats, Kate said, "Now, I'll treat you two to an authentic Irish meal."

While Kate was ordering, a tall lean man, who appeared to be in his late sixties, walked up to the table. "Good evening, Kate."

"Evening, Mr. Flynn."

"Now Kate, you know the name is Terry. We've been friends and neighbors for many a long time. Don't you think it's time that you called me by my first name?"

"Okay. It's Terry, if you like."

After Kate introduced him to her guests, he pulled a bottle of Paddy Whiskey from behind his back. "Let's toast the visit of these Yanks by treating them to one of the finest whiskeys in Ireland. I just bought it from the bar. May I join you Kate?"

"Sit yourself down Terry." She motioned to the chair beside Phil.

After the four sipped a small glass of the fine whiskey, Kate waved for McAllister to come over with the food menus.

"You have to try the steak and mushroom pie," she told Kelley.

Kelley smiled, and Kate ordered that for both of them.

Phil looked at the menu and said, "I'll have the corned beef and cabbage."

Terry ordered the sausage and potatoes and two pitchers of Guinness.

"We take our time eating in Ireland," Kate instructed. "That's part of the dining experience here. Give the taste buds time to wrap around all the flavors."

As they visited during the meal, Terry leaned over and asked quietly, "And how are you doing with your financial problems Kate?"

"Not quite sure what to do next," she responded. She gestured to him, desperate to change the subject, as Phil and Kelley looked at each other questionably.

After downing a couple glasses of ale with his dinner, Phil leaned back in his chair and sighed.

Terry asked, "How about some dessert, They have a fine whiskey cake here. Topped with fresh cream."

"Think, I'll pass," Phil answered.

"Me too," Kelley chimed in as a young boy walked over to the table. He stopped in front of Kate and bowed. "Evening Miss Kate. Me da is ready to start playing now. He wants to know if your guests have any favorite tunes that they would like to hear."

Kelley looked at the young fellow, dressed in knickers, plaid socks and a plain brown weskit. "And who are you," she asked.

"I'm Cody and that's me da," he pointed to Conor McAllister who was now sitting on the stage with a fiddle in front of him. A white whiskered old gentleman in bib overalls was standing next to him with the drums. A heavy-set lady was sitting at the piano, ready to accompany the two.

"Have your da play me favorite, *Danny Boy*, before he starts the foot stomping stuff," Kate said.

Cody sang along with the music, his fine tenor voice and beautiful rendition of the song brought tears to

Kate's eyes.

After a few more traditional Irish songs, Conor announced, "Now folks, it's time to clap and stomp your feet."

As the trio played the Irish jig, several of the patrons got up and danced. Finally, at Kate's urging, Phil and Kelley joined the group. They danced, laughed, stomped their feet, clapped their hands and sang along with the crowd.

Exhausted after almost a half hour of strenuous dancing, Kelley and Phil returned to their seats beside Kate and Terry. They picked up their glasses of ale and quenched their thirst. Suddenly, Kate stood up, "All this stout beer is going through me. I have to visit the ladies' room. Care to join me Kelley?"

"No thanks. I'm good."

While Kate was in the restroom, Cody approached their table, with his father, Conor, close behind him. "This is me da, Conor McAllister."

Phil stood up. "We met you when we came in sir. Won't you have a seat?"

"Don't mind if I do," Conor said as he slammed down a pitcher of beer and a glass on the table in front of him. "So, you two are on holiday from America?"

"Well sort of," Phil replied.

"Actually we're on our honeymoon," Kelley added. "And my husband brought me here to meet my grandmother, Kate, for the first time."

Conor smiled. "She's one special lady. All the folks 'round here think the world of her. And you've come at a good time, what with, her finally starting to get herself back on her feet after that bastard Sean's death."

Terry Flynn looked up from the beer that he was sipping. "Maybe, you shouldn't go into that Conor. That's Kate's private business and maybe, she doesn't want her granddaughter knowing about it."

Kelley sat up straight in her chair and frowned at the two men. "No. Tell me what you are talking about. I want to know everything about her. Maybe we can help."

Terry Flynn took a sip of his beer and looked quietly at Kelley. "Well, knowing Kate, she probably made light of Sean and his death about a year ago."

"Yes." Kelley answered.

"I think that this young lady should know the truth about her grandfather. It's not right for her to believe him to be a saint like Kate likes to make him out to be," Conor said to Terry.

Terry shrugged. "Maybe you're right."

Phil placed his hand gently over Kelley's and looked directly at the men. "I know that my wife would like to hear everything."

Terry nodded. "Tell them."

Conor leaned back in his chair. "Well Kate seemed to turn a blind eye to some of the things that Sean did over the years. He always was a heavy drinker. Liked to gamble and chase after loose women too. Last year, he was found in an alley in Dublin, with his pockets emptied and his throat cut. So far, they never found the bloke what did it."

Kelley gasped. "Oh, my gosh. Kate never told us that. She made it sound like grandpa just passed away peacefully in his sleep."

"That's not the worst of it," Conor continued. "After his death, Kate learned that Sean had mortgaged the ranch to the hilt. We guess to feed his gambling habits. Kate's been fretting about the ranch ever since she heard that the bank might be getting ready to foreclose."

Kelley looked as though she was ready to cry. "Oh my God, Phil. Kate acts like nothing is wrong. She would probably have never told us about her problems."

Terry nodded. "Well, she is one very proud lady."

"And a mighty fine one, too," Conor added. "But we've

said enough."

Terry looked at the couple and smiled. "You two might just be what Kate needs now. With your support, she'll get through this."

Conor jumped to his feet. "Enough of this serious talk. The next drink is on the house. Please, enjoy yourselves for the rest of the evening." He walked away.

"And don't tell Kate that we had this little talk," Terry whispered, as he saw Kate returning to the table.

The four of them sipped on their beers and chatted for a while. Then, Kate said to Terry, "I think these youngsters have had a long day and it's time for us to leave."

He stood, bent over and took Kate's hand in his. "Bring your granddaughter and her husband to my place tomorrow night for supper. Please, Kate."

She looked at him and smiled. "We'll see Terry. We'll see."

As they exited the pub the sky was very dark and thunder could be heard rumbling off in the far distance. They drove out of town and as the jeep approached the gate to the ranch's entrance, Kate used her remote control to open it. She drove up the driveway and pulled in front of the garage. "You two hop out and go on in. The key to the front door is under the door mat. I'll meet you inside. I've got to check on me children before I come in."

Kelley jumped out of the jeep. "You're talking about your horses aren't you, Kate?"

"Yes. Tomorrow I'll take you out to the horse barn to meet my babies. And by the way Phil, thank you for treating me to supper. It was nice of you to pick up the check."

"It was my pleasure, Kate. It's kind of you to put us up," he responded as he jumped out of the jeep.

"Where else would me family stay?" Kate waved at them as she pulled the jeep forward and into the garage.

Walking up the path to the house, Phil put his arm

around Kelley. "You know your grandmother is some-what of a mystery to me."

"To me also."

Kate met the two in the hall and accompanied them upstairs to the bedrooms

In front of the guest bedroom door, she stopped abruptly. "So there you are. Have you been a bad boy again?"

Phil and Kelley looked at each other with puzzled looks on their faces.

"How's that," Phil asked.

"No. Not you Luv. I'm talking to me dog, Jack," Kate answered.

They stared down at one of the largest dogs they had ever seen. Brownish in color, he appeared to be some kind of immense hound, with long floppy ears, droop-ing jowls and a drooling mouth. He looked up lazily at them.

"This is Jack. He was me husband's dog. An old bachelor fellow, named Jack, played poker with me Sean years ago. When Jack ran out of cash, he bet the dog on his next hand. Sean had a full house and won the dog. The mutt didn't have a name. So Sean just called him Jack—after his former owner."

Kelley reached down to pet the dog.

"Oh no. Don't pet him. Just talk to him until he gets used to you. He's kind of old and set in his ways, just like me. An independent cuss, too."

Kelley leaned over. "Hi there Jack. Good boy."

The dog just looked at her—no response.

Kate opened the door to the guest room. Jack got up, walked slowly into the room and lay down on a crum-pled up comforter that was in a corner.

Kate followed him into the room and pulled back the bedspread on the bed. "This is where you two will sleep. I hope you don't mind but Jack is used to sleeping over there." She gestured toward the dog, who was re-arranging the comforter. Once he had it just so, he flopped down.

"You see, Jack likes to spend his days hunting rabbit and squirrels or sleeping on the back porch. But, he's gotten kind of used to sleeping in here at night."

"He sleeps in here," Phil asked.

Kate shrugged and nodded. "Yup. Hope you don't mind. Sometimes, he snores a little, but that shouldn't bother you too much."

"You mean in here—with us?" Kelley chimed in.

"Oh, don't worry. He never jumps in the bed. Sean never tolerated that. You see, when Sean would come home late, after having a pint or two too much, he would sleep in the guest room so as not to wake me. Well, Jack just got used to sleeping in here with him."

"Oh," Kelley replied weakly.

"After Sean passed on, I didn't have the heart to put Jack out. Now, the dog thinks that this is his room."

"I hope that we won't disturb him," Phil said.

"No. He sleeps soundly. Just leave the door open a crack so that he can get out early in the morning. He won't wake you. He knows enough to come and get me when nature calls."

Phil looked slightly relieved. "Good."

"Well. I'll leave you two to get settled in. Don't forget to leave the door open."

Phil sat down on the bed and looked at Kelley. He looked over at the dog, which now appeared to be sleeping soundly. "God, that's an ugly dog. You'll never see him at Westminster."

Kelley lay back on the bed and started giggling uncontrollably. "Just look at him. He drools in his sleep."

"You know, Jack sort of reminds me of that old dog in that Tom Hanks movie. The one where he was a cop and had that big dog that chewed everything up and drooled all over the place. What was the name of that movie?"

Kelley was now laughing. *"Turner and Hooch."*

Phil rolled off the bed and pulled his pajamas from the nearby suitcase. "Yeah. That's the movie."

After they washed up and changed into their pajamas, they climbed into bed.

Phil reached over and gave Kelley a kiss. "Good night dear."

"Good night Phil."

Once again they started laughing as they said in unison, "Good night, Jack."

As they huddled together in bed, she asked, "Where are we headed after our stay here?"

"We'll see. Just enjoy your stay with your Nanna. We'll be here for a couple of days. We're going to find out what problems she has, and we're going to figure out some way to help her. That's the least we can do."

"Thank you, honey. That's what I love about you. Always ready to help everyone—any time—any place."

She kissed him and turned over to go to sleep. "But it sounds like my Nanna has a really big problem."

Chapter 18

"Phil, Phil, are you awake?" Kelley nudged her husband; lying in bed beside her.

"Yes, dear. I am now."

"I thought that you could smell the freshly made coffee."

"You're right. Where's there's fresh coffee, there's Phil. And your grandmother said she had homemade sweet rolls for this morning's breakfast."

As they entered the kitchen, Kate, dressed in jeans and a plaid shirt was standing in front of the stove. She put the cups she had in her hands down and gave them both a hug. "I can't tell you how pleased I am to have you here. Did ya sleep well?"

"Yes." Phil took a seat at the kitchen table. "I think I heard a heavy rain pass through during the night."

Kate looked out the window over the sink. "Sun is out now. Supposed to be a nice day. Let me fix you some breakfast and then we'll get going. I have so much that I want to show you."

"Just coffee for me," Kelley answered. "And yes, I got the best night's sleep that I've had since the wedding. I'm so happy that we're all together at last. I just wish that mom could be here with us."

Kate just looked at Kelley and said nothing.

Phil realized that the older woman had suddenly become uncomfortable with his wife's comment. So he quickly changed the subject. "Just coffee and some of those sweet rolls that you promised me last night."

Kate poured three cups of coffee, got a pan of freshly baked cinnamon rolls from the oven and placed them on the table.

After breakfast, Kate stood up. "I'm glad to see that both of you put your jeans on. Why don't you go upstairs and put on some old shoes or boots. Mighty muddy outside after last night's rain. If you didn't bring any boots with you, check the hall closet. I have some of Sean's and my old boots in there. You should find what you need."

"Thanks Kate," Kelley said, as she walked to the sink and rinsed the dirty dishes.

"Just leave the dishes there," Kate said. "Meet me in the horse barn."

Minutes later, Phil and Kelley entered the horse barn. Having never been around horse barns, they were amazed at how clean and neat it appeared and how sweet it smelled with the scent of fresh hay.

Kate pointed to the three stalls that had horses enclosed in them. "I want you to meet me other family. This is 'Banner'," she said, walking up to a chestnut colored mare.

At the next stall she said, "And this is me fickle girl, 'Lightning'."

In the third stall, she rubbed the nose of a tall mare. "And this is me prize mare, 'Celtic Thunder'."

"She's beautiful," Kelley said as she patted the horse.

"Do either of you ride?"

"My love is motorcycles. Like to drive them and tinker with them too," Kelley replied. "And Phil loves cars. All kinds of cars."

"Well then Phil, you'll love my late husband's toys.

They're in the garage. Why don't you take a quick look at them? Just back the jeep out of the way. There's an old car. Chevy, I think and there's even an old motorcycle for you Kelley. Maybe, you could see if they both still run. My trainer is off today, so I need to exercise my horses. Be sure to drop your muddy boots outside the kitchen door as you enter the house."

"No problem," Kelley answered.

"Let's head to the garage," Phil said.

"You'll find the keys to the vehicles in the kitchen. On a hook near the back door. See you two later."

Phil returned to the house. He slipped off his muddy boots on the back porch; and stepped over his new sleeping companion, Jack, on his way into the kitchen. He grabbed the keys to the car and motorcycle off the hook.

Kelley and he were heading to the garage when they saw a young man walking up the driveway.

"Kelley, you back the jeep out and I'll see who that is," Phil yelled.

As he got nearer, the young man called out "Hi there. Remember me, Cody McAllister. I live in the farm across the road. We met last night at my da's pub."

"Sure. I remember you. What can I do for you this morning?"

"Well, Kate told me that she had a riding lawn mower for sale. I'm starting up a part time lawn service. Need to save some money for college. Kate told me that I could take a look at it. Also, she said for me to check out her computer while I'm here. Said it wasn't working right."

"Okay. But take off your boots and throw them on the porch before you come in. Kate's fussy about mud on the carpets, you know," Phil said.

He turned to Kelley, "You check out the garage honey. We'll be out in a little while."

She headed for the garage as the men went through

the back porch and into the house.

"Hi Jack," Cody said as he stepped over him.

Jack looked up briefly, waged his tail and put his head back down.

"Let's both take a look at the computer." Phil led the way. "I think I saw it in the parlor. I'm somewhat of a computer guy myself so maybe between the two of us we can figure out what's wrong with it."

Cody followed him into the parlor, where they found an ancient looking Gateway computer on the desk.

Phil sat down. "Let's see if it starts up." He reached down and turned it on. "Looks like Kate has an old dial up system connected to her phone line."

"Here's a sticky note attached to the top of the computer," Cody said. "Her password is 'Lightning'."

"Well, that's convenient. Not very secure though," Phil added. He tinkered with the unit for several minutes and soon had it up and running.

"Looks like you know a lot about computers, Mr. Willis."

"Worked on a few in my day. What Kate needs is a speedier system. I'll call the phone company tomorrow, and see what they can do for her. But, what she really needs is a new computer. Now, let's head out to the garage Cody."

Phil saw that Kelley had already backed the jeep out. She ran over to him and grabbed his arm. "Wait until you see what I discovered under an old canvas—a Corvette."

She led him into the garage where a silver colored Corvette was sitting. Phil took one look at it and shouted. "Holy cow. This isn't just a Corvette, Kell. This is a vintage Corvette. I'm not sure of the year but it could be worth big bucks."

Cody walked up beside them. "Do you think it will run Mr. Willis?"

"I'll know in a minute." Phil opened the hood of the car and looked inside. "Everything looks fine in here. Let's see if I can get this baby started."

He climbed into the driver's seat and after a couple of tries the car started up. He turned the ignition off and got out. "Doesn't have much gas in it right now. After I put some in, I'll give it a run down the road."

Kelley waved for him to follow her to the back of the garage. "Look what I found back here. An old Harley Davidson. I think it's one of the first ones ever made. This could be worth a lot of money too."

Phil grinned. "Well, it seems like Grandpa Sean was a collector of manly toys. Now, Cody, let's take a look at that lawn mower."

They walked over to the riding mower and pushed it out of the garage. Cody jumped on it and after a few coughs, it started.

"It appears like today is our lucky day," Phil said.

"It's turning out to be a nice day. The sun seems to have been drying everything out, so I'll cut Miss Kate's lawn first. It sure needs it and that's the least I can do. Then, I'll head home with this baby. I'll call her later and see how much she wants for it."

"It looks like Kate has a lot of work to do in order to keep this place up," Phil said, looking around.

"That's for sure. Oh, by the way, Mr. Willis, there's a dealer in Dublin for classic cars and a large cycle store too."

"Thanks mate." Phil shook his hand. "Whoops, now I sound like an Englishman."

Kelley looked at him. "Honey, Australians say 'mate' not Englishmen."

As Cody drove off on the lawn mower and started to run up and down the lawn, Phil put his arm around Kelley's shoulders. "Let's go tell your grandmother what treasures we've found."

"She'll be happy to hear that grandpa's toys might be worth some money. I think that she's really having financial trouble. She mentioned that she bounced some checks last week and that the taxes for the ranch are overdue."

Entering the horse barn, they found Kate in the stall with Celtic Thunder. She was bent over, brushing the mare and cooing at her at the same time.

She looked up. "So what have you two discovered?"

"We want to have a serious talk with you," Kelley said.

Kate stood up, walked out of the stall and shut the door. "Well then, let's head into the house. We'll sit down and talk. I had some errands to do in town, but they can wait."

Inside the kitchen, Kate washed her hands, walked to the refrigerator and pulled out a large pitcher. After removing glasses from the cupboard, she sat down at the table. "Okay kids. Sit. Have some iced tea and some small sandwiches. We'll talk."

Phil and Kelley told her about their finds and that they thought that both the car and the cycle might be worth some serious money.

"Next," Kelley said, "we want to spend the rest of the day, trying to help you get your books and finances in order."

At first Kate was reluctant to disclose her troubles; but after some discussion, she led them into the parlor. They sat on the floor with Kate's papers spread out in front of them.

Finally, Kelley said, "First of all, what you need is overdraft protection on your checking account. Tomorrow, we'll go to the bank and see if we can set that up. Then, Phil will go to the dealerships and find out what you can get for selling the car and the cycle. I'll take some pictures of them and see if that will help determine what both are worth. By the way, both seem in good running condition."

"Do you think I'll be able to hang onto the ranch and the horses? I know that me friend, Flynn, wants to buy them real bad."

"One step at a time, Kate," Phil answered. "One step at a time."

As they were finishing going through Kate's papers, the phone rang. Kate jumped up to answer. "My goodness, it's after four already."

"It's Terry Flynn. Hope you and your company haven't eaten supper yet. I've got my grill going and I've got steaks ready to throw on. I hope that you will join me."

Kate relayed the message and Phil nodded. "It appears that my granddaughter and her husband are in need of a good meal. And you got Phil's attention when you mentioned steak. Give us some time to clean up and we'll jump in the jeep and come over. "Kate stood up. "I need a shower. Then, I'll be ready to leave."

"We could use one too," Kelley replied.

"Please don't say anything about me business to Terry."

"We won't breathe a word of it," Phil reassured her. "Now, let's head upstairs and get washed up Kelley. My stomach has been growling ever since I heard the word steak."

After Phil headed upstairs, Kate turned to Kelley and smiled briefly. "That's a mighty nice man that you have for a husband, my dear granddaughter."

"I know."

Chapter 19

The next morning passed quickly for Phil and Kelley as they went into Dublin with Kate to help take care of her business. They knew that soon they would be leaving for their final honeymoon destination and then would be returning to the States and their jobs. They wanted to assist her in getting her problems resolved before they had to leave Ireland.

By noon, things were looking up for Kate. It had taken over an hour at the bank, but now, her checking account overdraft protection was set up so that she would no longer bounce checks.

The next stop was to the electric company office, where Kate presented them with a new check and put her account on a monthly budget plan. The last stop was the phone company. She replaced their bounced check with one that was covered by sufficient funds. Phil helped her change her internet connection for her computer to a higher speed that would make using it a lot easier and faster.

"We've got two more things to take care of Kate," Phil said, "and then we should be done."

They drove to the classic car dealership and motorcycle store to ask about selling the vehicles. Both places were interested in Sean's toy collection and agreed to send someone to the ranch to appraise the vehicles and perhaps purchase them.

After stopping for a quick lunch, Kate said, "Now kids, I'm scheduled to volunteer at St. Joseph's Hospital at one. I know you wanted to see the Van Gogh exhibit at the National Gallery. So why don't I just drop you off there for about three hours. I'll pick you up in front about four thirty. That should give you plenty of time to look around. "

"Thanks. That sounds like a great idea," Phil answered. "It's a once in a lifetime opportunity for Kelley to view the real Van Gogh's."

"After I pick you up, we'll drive back to the hospital. I want you to meet my coworkers."

"Oh, I'd love to meet them," Kelley said. "Exactly, what do you do there?"

"I work four days a week and put in about four to six hours each day. I volunteer on the third floor—Pediatrics. Babies, you know."

Phil looked at Kelley and winked. "My Kell is really into babies these days. Aren't you honey?"

She smiled back.

As Phil stepped up to the ticket window at the gallery to purchase the tickets, a voice rang out. "Mr. Willis. Phil—over here."

Phil looked over to the side of the room where he saw a small group of what appeared to be tourists standing in a cluster. At the front of the group was a red-haired, buxom tour director holding a red umbrella in the air. Phil immediately recognized Anna, who had given them their quick tour of Dublin, when they first arrived in the city.

After yelling out to the group, "Stay here my people,"

Anna walked over to Phil and Kelley.

"Hi folks. Glad to see that you made it back to the museum. But save your money. I had two people cancel out of my tour after I bought the tickets yesterday and you're welcome to them."

Kelley looked at Phil and nodded. "We've love to use the tickets, Anna."

"They close the place at four, so you'll have time to look around. The Van Gogh exhibit is on the third floor. I saw it briefly yesterday when I brought four people in. You'll love it."

"Thanks," Phil replied.

Anna reached into her large red tote bag and pulled out a couple of ear phone sets. "Here, the gallery provides 'whispers' for all the visitors. That way you can press the buttons in the different galleries and get descriptions of the exhibits and paintings without disturbing the other visitors. You can join my group with the local guide or look around on your own, whatever you prefer. See you in the front at closing."

"Let's go on our own," Kelley said. "That way, we can tour most of the gallery quickly and save a lot of time for the Van Gogh exhibit."

After touring the first and second floors, and stopping to listen to their 'whispers' in front of the various paintings, they headed for the third floor. With little success, they tried to push their way to the front of the crowd that was gathered around the original Van Gogh's.

"Oh, my gosh," Kelley exclaimed. "I love Van Gogh. And I did want to get a close look at his paintings. We'll probably never get a chance to view the originals again."

She felt a tap on her shoulder, turned around and saw a young man in his late thirties or early forties, dressed in a navy blue business suit. "I'm Reginald Casey, the curator of the museum and I overheard what you just said. I'll get you up closer."

"Thank you. That's very kind of you," Kelley whispered back.

He looked at her and smiled. "But please, no flash photos. They damage the paintings, you know." He eased his way to the edge of the crowd, and then excused himself as he pushed his way through to the front.

"We're from America. I studied Van Gogh's work in college. In fact, I have several prints of his work at home."

"You sound like quite an authority on him," Mr. Casey whispered.

She smiled, "I like to think so."

"I'll leave you two to enjoy the exhibit," Reginald said, as he walked away.

Phil looked at his watch. "We've got about an hour left, so we can spend the rest of our time in this gallery. Look and admire to your heart's content, my love."

They walked around the exhibit and Kelley pointed out some of the paintings. "This is 'Starry Night', this one is 'Sunflowers', this is 'Poppies' and this one is 'The Potato Eaters'."

About three forty five, as the gallery started to empty out, all the lights suddenly went off. One of the guards standing at the entrance to the gallery announced, "Folks, it is almost closing time and the power seems to have went out. Please follow the lighted exit signs above the doors to exit the gallery."

As they started for the exit, the lights came back on.

"Wonder what the heck happened, Phil?"

"Who knows? We have about fifteen minutes left before the place closes. Do you want to take a final look?"

"Yes. Please. I want to take another look at 'Sunflowers.' That's my favorite. You know the one I have a print of in our bedroom."

She walked over to where the painting was hanging. "That's strange, Phil. This is the spot where 'Sunflowers' was hanging. Now 'Fritillaries Copper' is here. And it looks like just a print of it too."

Phil frowned. "Are you sure? It looks the same to me."

"Of course, I'm sure. 'Sunflowers' was painted in a ceramic vase. And this painting is of flowers in a copper vase. Big difference."

She ran frantically toward the security guard when she saw Reginald Casey entering the gallery.

He walked up to her, "Sorry, it's time to leave. We close in a few minutes."

"Okay. But first, I've got to show you something." She led him over to the paintings. "When did you take 'Sunflowers' down and put a print in its place?"

"What are you talking about? We didn't make any changes in the exhibit."

"Look." Kelley pointed at the painting. "This is where 'Sunflowers' was hanging. Now a print of 'Fritillaries' is there."

Casey walked up to the painting and stared at it in amazement. "You're right, this is not 'Sunflowers' and we didn't remove it. Someone has stolen it and has mistakenly replaced it with a print and an incorrect one at that."

His jaw tensed with anger, he quickly summoned the security guard to his side. "We've been robbed. Someone has taken Van Gogh's 'Sunflowers.' Please notify the head of security and have him call the police."

Kelley tapped Reginald Casey on the shoulder. "My husband and I were formerly private investigators. The lights in here just went off a few moments ago and only for a short time. That may have been when the painting was switched. May I suggest that you lock all the exits to the building and have your security guards check the patrons as they leave."

As soon as Kelley finished her sentence, Mr. Casey was giving orders over his mobile phone. "Lock the premises. Let no one leave until we search their bags."

Looking at the nearby guard, he started barking out more orders. "Go to the security room. Check the film in the surveillance cameras for the Van Gogh gallery. Maybe you can see who switched the paintings."

He turned to Kelley and Phil. "We've never had a theft before. Do you two have any more suggestions on how we should proceed?"

"Make sure that your people check out the storage area and the closets," Kelley said.

"Also the shipping room," Phil added.

"In the meantime, my husband and I will start searching the various restrooms. Phil, you check out the men's rooms on every floor and I'll take care of the ladies. I did see a couple of the people from Anna's tour group standing near the painting just before the lights went out."

"Good idea, Kell. I'll meet you by the front doors on the main floor."

She checked out the ladies rooms on the third floor first, then the second floor.

Finally, she entered the ladies room on the first floor. Hearing a noise coming from one of the stalls, she called out, "Anyone in here?"

The door to one of the cubicles opened and Anna walked out. "Hi there, Kelley. Say what's going on? I had my group assembled in the main lobby, all ready to board the bus when the guards said there was a problem and no one was allowed to leave the building."

Kelley walked slowly down the long line of stalls, opening each door, one by one, and looking in. At the last stall in the line, she spotted an eight by ten gold picture frame sitting on the back of the toilet.

She picked up the picture frame and carried it back to Anna. "There's been a robbery. Someone took a small Van Gogh painting. Probably a woman, since it looks like she came in here and took the painting out of the frame. It's easier to conceal just the rolled up painting."

"You're kidding me. I can't believe that someone had the nerve to steal a famous painting in broad daylight. But, how long are they going to keep us here? My group is scheduled to view the Cathedral in thirty minutes. And we'll lose our tour time if we're not there."

"I think that the gallery's security force is going to check everyone out before they let them leave the building. You might just have a slight delay."

"I'll phone the guide at the Cathedral and tell her we might be a few minutes late. In the meantime, I better return to my group and inform them of our next move before they start to get excited."

Kelley nodded. "I'll walk with you Anna. But tell me— was there anyone from your group using this restroom in the past few minutes?"

"No." Anna paused for a second. "Wait. That grumpy woman."

"What grumpy woman?"

"An elderly couple joined our group at the last minute. They said they heard at their hotel that we were coming to the National Gallery for the exhibit and they wanted to join the tour. She pushes one of those big black walkers with a seat on it. Has an iron canister oxygen tank hooked to the walker. My neighbor has one of those; she smokes too much."

"You said that you just saw her in here?"

"She was leaving the bathroom when I walked in. Most likely she's with the crowd getting ready to go on the bus."

When Kelley and Anna got to the front entrance of the gallery, they discovered that Anna's group had already been screened and had entered the bus.

Kelley walked up to the security guard at the front door, "I'm Mrs. Willis. My husband should be down shortly. He's helping search the building. Would you please tell him that I went outside to the tour bus?"

Anna and Kelley left the building and walked toward the bus. "I need to ask your driver a question," Kelley said.

Anna called out to the driver who was standing next to the open front door. "Hey, Eddie, over here."

"Do we have a problem Sis?"

"Hope not," she answered. "This is Kelley Willis."

Eddie shook her hand. "Yes. I know the lady. I met her husband and her at the Dublin airport. Remember, I called you to set up their private tour."

"Yeah, I remember. Haven't lost my buttons yet. Kelley wants to ask you something."

"Shoot."

"Are all your passengers on the bus?"

"All accounted for. I was just waiting for Anna to hop on. Then, we're off to the Cathedral. I have two extra seats if you and the hubby want to join us."

"No thanks. We've got other plans after this. What about the elderly couple. You know the grumpy lady with the walker and her husband. Are they on the bus?"

"Yes. The last ones to board. When I went to help her load the walker and the oxygen tank, she got all excited. Cursed at me. Said to keep my hands off her things. I'll sure be glad to see the last of those two."

Kelley stopped and thought for a few minutes. "Tell you what, Eddie. I'm going to board the bus now. My husband should be coming out soon. Please tell him to wait outside for me."

"Got it."

"And Eddie, please get on the bus and announce that you are waiting for one more passenger."

Eddie hesitated for a moment and looked at Anna.

"Just do it Eddie," she commanded.

"Okay. You ladies are the boss." He entered the bus, stood at the front and made the announcement.

As Kelley started to get onto the bus, Phil walked up. "Hi girls. Nice to see you again, Anna." Taking Kelley by the hand, he whispered, "What's going on, honey?"

She nodded toward the bus. "I found the frame to the missing painting in the ladies room. Anna and her brother brought a group in to see the gallery and Anna saw one of the women from the tour in the bathroom a short while ago."

"So," Phil asked.

"Well, Anna said that the woman and her husband joined the tour at the last minute, when they found out the group was coming to see the Van Gogh exhibit. Also, they acted kind of suspicious. They're on the bus now."

"I understand," Phil answered. "You're going to go on the bus to check them out. Right?"

"Right. You stand outside by the door, in case they try to make a run for it."

"You're the boss honey. Just be careful." Phil helped her up the steps.

She slowly moved down the aisle, until she reached the back seat of the bus, where the lady with the oxygen tank was sitting next to the window. Her tank was on the aisle seat beside her.

Kelley smiled at the woman, "Hi there. My husband and I are getting a ride back to our hotel with your group. May I take this aisle seat?"

"Hell no," the woman snarled. You can see that I need it for my oxygen tank."

Kelley looked closely at her and noticed that the nasal oxygen tubes were not inserted in the woman's nostrils. She looked closely at the oxygen tank itself. The flow meter to the tank was closed and the pressure gauge read zero. Not only was the tank not turned on; it had no oxygen in it.

She snatched the nasal tube from around the woman's neck, grabbed the oxygen canister and ran to the front of the bus. The woman jumped up, shouted several curse words and yelled to her husband, "Harry that woman just grabbed my oxygen tank."

Without her walker, the woman ran down the aisle after Kelley. Harry was close at her heels.

Kelley jumped off the bus and put the oxygen tank on the ground. When he saw Harry jump off the bus and try to grab the tank, Phil stepped in between Kelley and him. "That's my wife pal. I wouldn't try anything."

Kelley turned the oxygen canister upside down. "Just as I suspected. A false bottom."

She unscrewed the metal cap from the bottom of the tank, reached inside and slipped out the rolled up painting.

She opened it. "Here it is. Our missing painting."

The elderly woman rushed toward Kelley and tried to grab it. "Out of my way you little bitch."

Anna, standing nearby, put out her foot and tripped the woman. Down went the grumpy old lady.

"I think that we've got our thieves Phil," Kelley said as the police, together with Mr. Casey, ran toward the bus.

In a few moments, the police had both of the thieves in handcuffs.

Kelley handed the painting to Mr. Casey. "I believe this belongs to the gallery. That lady had it rolled up and inside her empty oxygen tank."

Casey took the painting from her and tucked it under his arm. "I can't believe how inventive thieves can be. An oxygen tank is one place where I would have never thought of looking. If you hadn't been here, these people would have been long gone with one of the world's most valuable works of art. You know private collectors will pay almost anything for an original Van Gogh."

Phil took Kelley's hand, "Here comes your Grandma Kate." He pointed to the jeep that came to a screeching halt in front of the gallery.

Kate jumped out and walked over to them. "Hi there kids. What's all the commotion?"

Anna stepped in front. "Kelley and Phil just stopped a couple from stealing a famous Van Gogh painting."

Kate just smiled. "That's my grandchildren. Always on the ball. Well, if you're done here, we've just got time to head to the hospital before all my friends leave."

"It was so good to see you two again," Anna said. "If you're ever back in Dublin, I hope you'll look Eddie and me up. Now, give me a big hug."

They both embraced her and shook hands with Eddie and Reginald Casey.

"How can I reach you if the police have any questions," Mr. Casey asked.

Phil pulled a card out of his pocket. "Here's my cell phone number. We'll be staying at Ryan's Irish Stud Farm for a few more days."

"Okay, kids let's get going to the hospital." Kate walked over to the jeep and jumped in.

After Kelley and Phil were settled in the back seat, Kate leaned over her shoulder. "Glad to hear that you two didn't get into any trouble while I was gone."

Kelley grinned. "No just another quiet afternoon."

Getting out of the elevator on the third floor of the hospital, one of the nurses ran up to Kate. "Hi there. Wait until you see the new set of triplets. Redheads—all three of them."

Kate introduced Kelley and Phil to the nurse. As they started to walk down the hall the nurse yelled out, "Oh, Kate. Are you in this week's raffle? First prize is a new Dell computer. Maybe you'll get lucky."

"Yes. I have a couple of tickets. But me, lucky? No."

After a brief tour of the nursery and viewing the triplets, Kate introduced her granddaughter and husband to everyone. "You see ladies, am I or am I not, the lucky one? Isn't me granddaughter lovely? And me new grandson is a lawyer from New York. "

They all nodded.

"Now, let's go kids. Me horses are waiting."

Chapter 20

A nurse's aide came running up. "Kate, come quick. Someone's on the phone for you. Said it was urgent."

"Hold your knickers. You kids wait here," she said to Kelley and Phil.

She walked to the nurse's station and picked up the phone. After a few seconds, they heard her call out, "No. Oh, no."

They ran toward her as she screamed hysterically. "No. Not my barn. Not me horses. Me horses."

Phil grabbed the phone out of Kate's hands, listened for a few moments and answered. "Yes. Yes. We're on the way."

He hung up the phone and turned to his wife. "That was the McAllister kid. Kate's horse barn is on fire."

They raced downstairs and out of the hospital. Kelley put her arm around Kate, who was now shaking, and guided her into the passenger side of the jeep.

Phil jumped into the driver's side and Kelley climbed into the back. With tires squealing, the jeep zipped out of the hospital parking lot and down the road toward the ranch which was about thirty minutes away.

Phil glanced over at Kate, who had her head in her hands and appeared to alternate between praying and saying aloud, "Please God, don't let me horses die."

When they pulled into the driveway of the ranch, they saw the fire trucks next to the smoldering ruins of the barn. Only the smell of burnt wood and ashes remained where Kate's horse barn had once stood. And there was no sign of the horses.

Phil jumped out of the jeep, walked around to the passenger side and helped the trembling Kate out as a fireman approached her. "Sorry Kate. We got here as fast as we could. But it was too late to save the barn."

If Phil had not been holding her up, Kate would have sunk to the ground. She was overcome with grief. "Me horses. Did the fire get me horses?"

"To be honest with you Kate, we never saw the horses. Didn't hear them either. We can only hope that the smoke overcame them before the fire did them in."

"How did the fire get started," Kelley asked.

"It's too soon to tell. We have to inspect the burnt out building before we can determine that," the fireman replied.

Just then a voice called out, "Kate. Kate. Are you all right?"

Terry Flynn walked up and grabbed Kate's hands in his. "I spotted the fire from my house. Called the fire department and rushed right over."

Looking at the shell of the barn, he added, "Sorry, they couldn't save it."

Kate started to sob. "Me horses. Me poor horses. Burned to death."

"No, Kate," Terry answered. "They're fine. My hired hand and I came over with my horse trailer. We got them out and took them over to my place. I knew that they would panic because of the fire and the sirens. But we knew it was too late for us to try to save the barn."

"You mean to say that my prize mare is safe? My babies are safe and all I lost was that old barn?"

"That's what I've been trying to tell you, Kate. All

three horses are safe. And you know, I told you long ago that you needed to replace the ancient wiring in the barn. That probably sparked the fire."

"How can I ever thank you, my dear friend," she sobbed.

"No need to. Now, can we go into the house and sit down and talk," he asked.

"No," Kate answered. "I have to see me horses. I must see if their okay. After that we can talk."

She looked up and saw her dog, Jack, moving toward her. "Thank God, you spend your days on the back porch and not in the barn. I would have hated to lose you, old fellow."

She bent over, scratched his ears; and then headed for the jeep. "Come on kids, hop in. We're going to Terry's place."

As soon as they pulled into Terry Flynn's yard, Kate jumped out of the jeep and raced to his horse barn.

Running up to Celtic Thunder, she threw her arms around her head. "There you are my beauty. You're safe. Kate's gonna build you a new and bigger barn. And you're going to get a special stall with your name above it. You'll see."

After looking the other two horses over, she turned to Terry. "Now, we'll go inside and talk. In fact, I could use a nice hot cup of tea with a double shot of whiskey in it."

Terry, Kelley and Phil laughed. The old Kate that they knew and loved was back, and ready once again for action.

They sat in the kitchen, drank their tea and talked. Phil stood up, "Kelley, why don't we go into Terry's parlor. I want to use my cell phone to call my office."

"And I should give my mother a quick call too." She followed him out of the kitchen.

For the next several minutes, Kate and Terry sat in the kitchen and talked and talked. First, Terry would get up and pace around the room, then, as he sat, Kate would get up and pace as she talked.

Kelley called Ann, her mother first. After Kelley visiting with her, she put her hand over the phone and turned to Phil.

"Everything okay with mom," he asked.

"Everything's fine. She wanted to know how things were with Grandma Kate and was very upset when she heard about the fire. I told her that you were taking care of everything on this end and she said to give you her love. She just said that she would like to talk to Kate for a few minutes."

"Great idea." Phil went to the kitchen and asked Kate to come to the phone and talk to Ann.

As they talked, Kelley and Phil could only hear Kate's end of what sounded like a very emotional conversation.

As Kate said goodbye to Ann and hung up the phone, she wiped tears from her eyes.

She looked up at Kelley. "You know honey, your mum and I should have talked long ago. We've wasted so many years. But, we'll both make it up to you in the future."

Phil grinned. "Now that you ladies are all caught up, I'll call my office and make sure that it's okay to spend a few more days on this well, somewhat strange- honeymoon."

Kate returned to the kitchen and Phil made his call while Kelley sat patiently beside him. After he completed his call, Phil took Kelley hands in his. "Here's the plan Mrs. Willis. I need to report back to the office in the States, starting a week from Monday. So we have a little over a week left on our vacation. And, now, we're going to start our real honeymoon."

"What do you mean, real honeymoon? Where are we headed next?"

His response was a low deep laugh. "You'll see. It's the best surprise of all."

"Oh Phil. Don't keep me in suspense. Tell me please."

"In due time, honey. In due time."

As Kelley prepared to tease the answer out of him, she saw Kate and Terry standing in the doorway of the parlor with their arms around each other.

"We're working our way around Kate's problems," Terry said. "But tonight, I'm going to take you out for dinner. The pub is featuring barbecued ribs and some wild dancing. Let's just relax and enjoy each other's company."

"Morning, Mrs. Willis." Phil tapped his wife on the shoulder. "Time to get up. Lots to do today. But first I want to tell you about our next destination."

Kelley sat upright in the bed. "It's about time. You've had me wondering since yesterday. Is it Rome? Paris? Madrid? Okay, I'll bet its Scotland."

Phil held up his hands, stopping her from guessing further. "We're leaving tomorrow."

"Tell me," she shouted in excitement.

"It's Sicily."

Opening her mouth to speak, she found that no words would emerge.

"Remember, your maid of honor said that she spent a ten-day vacation there. And she showed us those fantastic pictures of the picturesque island. So tomorrow morning, we're flying from Dublin to Palermo, Sicily. We need a real honeymoon. So get your appetite ready, dear. It may be pasta every night."

Kelley threw her arms around him. "I love you. So how many days in Sicily?"

"About a week. We'll rent a car in Palermo and see the sights. I have some pamphlets here that I ordered before we left home. You can look through them and pick out the highlights. Also, you better brush up on your Italian."

Still in their robes, they went down to the kitchen. On the table, they found a note from Kate, stating that she went to work for several hours at the hospital.

"It seems like we have the house to ourselves for a while dear," Kelley said. "Want some breakfast?"

"Just juice and toast."

After breakfast, Kelley rinsed the dishes. "I'm going to go to our room and gather up the dirty clothes. I want to do our laundry so I can pack later in the day. What time do we leave tomorrow morning?"

"Plane leaves at ten, so we need to be at the airport by eight. Kate said that the airport here shouldn't be too busy that early so we'll probably leave here about seven."

"That sounds great," Kelley said as they heard a knock at the kitchen door.

Phil opened it and saw Cody McAllister standing in front of him.

"Come on in, Cody."

He left his muddy boots on the mat outside and stumbled over Jack and entered the kitchen. "Morning Mr. Willis. Ms. Kate called me from the hospital. Said that she won the drawing for the new computer. It's a Dell. She asked me to pick it up and bring it back so you could help me get it set up today. Said that you and the missus were leaving tomorrow. You got a few minutes to work on it now?"

"That's no problem. I didn't have anything planned for this morning," Phil answered.

"Ms. Kate said that I could have the old computer too. I rebuild them as a hobby."

"I have to go upstairs and get dressed. Then I'll be ready to give you a hand with the computer. Why don't you bring it in the house and get it unpacked. Put it in the parlor where Kate has the old one."

The phone on the kitchen wall rang. Phil walked over

and answered it. He talked for a while, said "yes" a couple of times and hung up.

Turning to Kelley, he rubbed his hands together. "Yes. Oh yeah, yes. That was the car dealer in town. He said he talked to Kate earlier this morning and they agreed on a price for the vintage car. He's going to send someone over with a tow truck to pick it up."

The phone rang again and Phil answered. "Hi, Kate. Yes, we know. You sold the car. And the cycle too. You got how much for them? My God girl, that's fantastic."

After he hung up, he told Kelley what Kate had gotten for the two vehicles.

She chuckled, "Negotiating seems to be Kate's strong point."

"That's what I said to her." And she answered, "No Phil, it's me blue eyes that gets these men all the time."

The rest of the morning passed quickly as Kelley took care of the laundry while Phil and Cody worked on the computer. The grandfather clock in the hall struck the noon hour as Kelley entered the parlor to see if the men were ready for some lunch.

"Computer's up and running," Phil said as they heard the front door open.

Kate appeared in the parlor doorway, her arms filled with boxes from various dress shops. They stared at her speechless. It was a new Kate that stood in front of them. Her white hair had been dyed a light auburn, streaked and cut short. The new hairdo made her look much younger.

"Kate Ryan, what have you done to yourself," Kelley exclaimed as she ran over and threw her arms around her.

"I decided to cut my hair short and spend some time and money on myself," Kate replied. "First, I went to the beauty shop in Dublin; had a do over and then I went shopping on Grafton Street for some new female duds.

Today's me birthday and the staff gave me a card with some cash in it."

Phil took the boxes from her arms. "Why Kate, I do believe that you're looking to catch a man. Do I see you training those blue eyes on Terry Flynn these days?" he teased.

She laughed. "Who knows? Who knows? Now, let me get you young people some lunch. Then, you can show me how to operate my new computer."

As they finished lunch, Kate said, "After I see you off in the morning, Terry is coming over with a couple of men to clean up the rubble from the barn."

"Oh, it's Terry now, is it Kate?" Phil teased.

"Well, why not. I'm still a young woman and he plans to help me build a new barn for me horses. In the meantime, he'll keep me babies at his place and I'll go over there every day to care for them."

"Sounds like you'll be seeing a lot of Terry in the future, Kate," Kelley said.

"Seems like it. That's why I decided to spruce myself up a bit. Oh, I have to tell you. Terry and I are going to breed a race horse. His stallion has racing stock and we're going to put him in with Celtic Thunder and see what happens."

"Your future seems to be looking up, Kate," Phil put his arms around her.

"Well, I can't tell you how much happiness you have given me for my birthday by bringing me granddaughter here. I know that God sent the both of you."

"We didn't know that today was your birthday, Kate. I feel bad because we didn't get you anything. Maybe we can take you out to dinner tonight to celebrate," Kelley said.

"Not necessary darling. You're my present. And I brought home some fish and chips for our supper."

That night, before she turned over to go to sleep, Kelley said, "Thank you my darling for bringing me here. I'm so grateful that I got to know my Grandma Kate."

"She's quite a woman, isn't she? And so is her grand-daughter. Now, I hope you're prepared for our next adventure."

"I'm ready to sit back and enjoy Sicily. Nothing but peace and quiet for the next week."

"I hope so dear. And I'll even let you pick our future adventures."

"In Sicily, I plan to do nothing but sight-see and sample the good foods. I think our adventures are over for now."

"With you my dear, Kelley Ryan Willis, there's bound to be more of them. But now, it's time for Sicilian pasta and pizza."

Chapter 21

The morning flight from Dublin to Palermo, Sicily, was a bit bumpy and neither Kelley nor Phil could manage to doze off. But the hour flew by quickly as they reminisced about their happy memories of Ireland. Once again, she thanked him for all that he had done to straighten out Kate's finances.

"It looks to me like Jerry Flynn will take care of Kate from now on," Phil said.

"Yes. And Kate mentioned that she hoped that they'd start traveling together. I told her that a visit to the States and us has to be one of their top priorities."

Phil leaned over and kissed her on the cheek. "Let's not fuss about other people for the next few days. It's time for us to act like tourists on their honeymoon."

"Speaking of tourists. Did you charge up the video camera?"

"Yes. And I've got about five hundred still shots on the digital from our visits to London and Ireland. It's going to take me forever to go through them when we get home."

"We want to be sure to send some photos to the Flemings and Grandma Kate when we get back."

Phil reached over and fastened his seat belt as the plane prepared to land in Palermo.

"I just hope that your grandma remembers all that I taught her about her new computer. She said that she never downloaded photos before."

Kelley pushed her bag further under the seat, preparing for landing. "Well, at least, she's got Cody McAllister to give her a hand with it."

"Yeah. That kid is pretty sharp."

After the plane landed, they disembarked and headed for the baggage department. "Please don't let our luggage be lost," Kelley said.

"Honey, how could they lose it? It was a straight flight with no connections."

"Well, they could have forgotten to put it on the plane."

"If they did, they would just send it over on the next flight. You did put the name and address of our hotel on both bags didn't you?"

"Yes. You put me in charge of the luggage and I took care of it. Our entire itinerary is in one of the zipped pockets, so they would know our plans."

"Good," he said. "Now let's collect the luggage, pick up the rental car and head for the hotel. Afterwards, maybe we can act like real Sicilians and find an authentic Sicilian pizza place to stop for lunch."

"Say, this Sicilian adventure is really starting to grow on me," Kelley replied.

She grabbed Phil's arm and pointed, "Look, there's our luggage. The big ones with the red straps around them."

He ran over to the conveyor belt and lifted the two pieces of luggage off. "Why, do these things keep getting heavier?"

"Oh, Kate sent a couple of things home with me to give to Mom."

With her tote bag and purse in hand, Kelley grabbed one of the roll about suitcases by the handle, and started across the room to the rental car desk. Phil was right behind her with the other suitcases.

At the desk, Phil soon learned that the only car that was available was the 'Smart Car.'

"That car's kind of small isn't it," he asked. "We have two rather large suitcases."

The rental clerk looked at the suitcases and assured him that they would fit behind the seats in the car. Phil agreed to rent it knowing that it would save him on the high price of gasoline on the island of Sicily.

After the shuttle bus drove them to the rental car lot, they discovered that the clerk was terribly optimistic. It took a great deal of determination and shoving before their suitcases fit in behind the seats.

Kelley put her carry-on bag at her feet in the passenger side of the car and broke into laughter once they were settled in. "I feel like we're riding in one of those goofy cars like the clowns all pile into at a circus."

Phil grinned. "Well, I'll bet that none of them had very long legs. Just think of this as another adventure."

"Be careful of all those motorcycles and vespas scooting around us," she said as they left the airport and headed toward their hotel.

"Yes dear. I'll just go with the flow."

Phil easily maneuvered the tiny car through the narrow and busy streets of Palermo, the capital of Sicily, located in the center of the island. They looked around at the mountains covered with lush vegetation that surrounded the city.

After stopping to ask directions only once, Phil found their hotel, The Astoria. It was a sixteen-story brown building with a circular driveway and iron gates at its entrance.

He pulled the little Smart Car up to the front doors and both of them climbed out.

A valet approached them and after confirming that they were staying at the hotel, he pulled their luggage from the back. "Tight fit," he said in English.

"That's all they had, my good man," Phil replied before he and Kelley headed inside to the reception desk.

After announcing who they were, Phil presented his passport and credit card to the clerk, who in return, gave him a large key. "Room 1510. Nice view of the city. Pool and exercise room on the top floor. And a computer room with free internet access just off the lobby."

Heading toward the elevators, Phil gazed at the huge key in his hand, "Guess they haven't converted to the new card entry system for the rooms yet."

A short while later, their luggage was delivered to their room and Kelley unpacked them and hung their clothes in the closet. "I think that most of the wrinkles will hang out of your suit, Phil."

He flopped on the bed and turned on the television. "I hope I won't need it here. I plan to live in casual clothes the rest of this vacation. In any case, welcome to Palermo, my love."

He gave her a kiss and hug as she sat down beside him. "Looks like only two television channels are in English here. Guess we should have brushed up more on our Italian."

After changing into shorts, an open necked shirt and good walking shoes, he put the camera strap on his shoulder. "Let's get a bite of lunch first and then drive around the city.

"Sounds like a good plan," she said.

Phil looked at himself in the mirror on the wall and grinned. "This is as close to looking like a tourist that I can get. Are you ready to tour the city, lady?"

Dressed in shorts, a T-top and sandals, Kelley nodded. "Ready. Let's try and get some pictures, with us in them, in front of the different attractions."

After getting directions from the desk clerk, they found a small Sicilian restaurant, just around the corner.

"You got your Italian book ready, pal," Kelley asked as they took a seat in the back of the ristoranto.

"You just watch this," he replied as the waiter approached them.

"Good afternoon," the waiter said.

Phil opened his little translation book, flipped through the book and replied, "Buon pomeriggio."

"And what can I get you two this lovely afternoon," the waiter replied in English, but with a distinctive accent.

After fanning through his booklet briefly, Phil decided that it would be easier to just reply in English. "A pizza and a bottle of your red house wine, please."

The waiter wrote the order on his pad. "I'll get the wine now. The pizza will be ready in about twenty minutes." He bowed and left.

"Great job on the Italian," Kelley said. "Now I wonder where the ladies' room is."

Phil looked around and pointed to the back wall where a picture of a man and a woman was posted beside the lavatory doors. "Over there."

After they finished their lunch, he said, "Time to get the car and start our tour. But first, let's get a photo of us with our waiter."

"Yes. And I must have a postcard or a photo of the restaurant itself."

After taking several pictures, she looked at her guide book. "We should see Palermo's most visited site-the beautiful Cappella Palatina Cathedral in Monreale. It's a short drive from here. Everyone said that it's the one thing in Sicily you must see."

They walked back to the hotel, had the attendant get their car from the underground parking garage and headed to the Cathedral.

With the instructions he had received from the hotel attendant, Phil had no trouble finding it. The parking lot was full but luckily a car was pulling out and he swung the Smart Car into the space.

Kelley exited the car and was soon busy taking pictures. "Phil, I want to get a photo of you standing in front of that sign that gives the name of the Cathedral."

She snapped several more shots. "There's music coming from the church. Let's hurry in."

Inside, they gazed in amazement at the magnificent and austere Cathedral, said to be one of the loveliest creations of the Norman period in Sicily. The church was filled with well dressed people and they could see a young couple kneeling in front of the altar. A wedding was in progress.

"Let's stay for the ceremony," she whispered.

"Sure. Why not. A nice way to start our tour of Sicily. And I know that you love weddings," he answered as they slipped into the last pew.

She quietly took a couple of photos of the ceremony, making sure that the flash on the camera was off.

After the ceremony ended they waited for the church to empty, and then proceeded to walk around viewing the majesty of the gold mosaic work that was on the ceiling and the walls. Kelley was snapping pictures as fast as she could.

From behind them, they heard a voice say quietly. "You seem to love my church. I'm Father Demetrius and if you have a few minutes I would be delighted to give you a private tour."

"Thank you Father. We would love it," Kelley answered.

"And you young people are?"

"We're the Willis's from America. This is my new bride, Kelley, and I'm Phil."

The priest shook hands with them. "Glad to meet you. Now let me tell you the history of this beautiful place. It was founded by Roger II in 1132. The Capella is in a basilica plan with central nave and two aisles separated by arches resting on ornately decorated columns. It has a splendid Moorish style wooden ceiling."

Taking pictures with his video camera, Phil looked up at the mosaic covered ceiling, then down on the floor. "It even has magnificent mosaics on the floor."

"Yes. And all the gold you see in them is real," the priest said proudly. He pointed to the altar. "That is a mosaic of Christ the Pantocrator surrounded by the Archangels with open wings."

"It's absolutely stunning." Kelley gazed upward.

The priest led them through the Sacristy and to the two naves explaining the scenes that were depicted in the exquisite mosaics.

After about a half hour, the priest had filled their heads with so many facts that they were getting overwhelmed.

"I'll have to get a book with pictures of the Cathedral and all these details because I'll never remember them all for my travel album," Kelley said.

"Enough for now. Most of the shops have colorful and informative books that you can purchase," the priest said leading them to the front doors.

"Thank you so much Father, for the private tour," Phil said, shaking his hand.

"Yes, thank you. I'll always remember this marvelous place," Kelley added.

The priest reached into his pocket. "Before you leave, I have a small gift for you."

He presented each of them with a gold medal. "These blessed medals are of Saint Rosalie. She is the patron saint of Palermo. I suggest that you go visit her church and grotto before you leave the capital. It's one of our most popular tourist sites and is just outside the city, high in the mountains. It's well worth your time."

"Thank you Father. We'll be sure to see it," she said.

"There are road signs, in both English and Italian, directing you to the church and grotto. Now bless you my children and enjoy the rest of your vacation," the priest added.

As they headed back to the car, Kelley took Phil by the arm. "I'm so anxious to see more. But first, I need something cold to drink. It's getting warmer." She pointed to a row of small shops and cafes at the edge of the parking lot.

Outside of one of the shops, Kelley saw a rack filled with post cards. She stopped, looked through it and selected a folder filled with about twenty photos of the church and Palermo. "I'm going to buy this. It'll help me identify all my photos and give me some information about the different attractions."

Phil rifled through a stack of books. "Add this to your purchase. It's a book on Sicily and it's in English. That should help you too."

After paying for their items, they headed for the car "How are the Euro's working out Phil?"

"I should have enough for the trip. I'm using the credit card whenever I can and saving the Euro's for small stuff."

Inside the car, she leaned over and gave her husband a kiss. "You saved the best part of the trip for last. Thank you for bringing me to Sicily. I love you and this country."

"Ditto. And by the way, since we arrived here, I noticed you admiring a few of these good looking Italian men."

"Not me. I'm very satisfied with my handsome husband."

"Good. Now, let's explore the rest of Palermo. I'm sure we can find a place for dinner with some excellent wine and yes, some pasta."

"Pasta, dear?"

"Yes. Homemade Sicilian pasta. And, by the way, how are your feet holding up, Kelley?"

"Okay."

"Well, my legs are a little stiff. Damn, Smart Car. Next time we need to rent from Hertz. Hey, I may even try to get an upgrade."

Chapter 22

With the help of the list of tourist brochures and the map that the concierge at the hotel had provided, Phil and Kelley toured the city of Palermo. They drove through its center, called 'Quatto Canti' because the four corners of the intersection each had a Baroque building decorated with fountains and statues.

They stopped at several churches, the public garden, 'Villa Bonanno' and 'Palazzo de Normanni' behind which was the 'Chiesa di San Giovanni degli Eremit' with its pretty cloisters, interior gardens and exotic red domes. Finally, Phil headed out of the city proper and up the mountain to the Shrine of St. Rosalie.

Kelley purchased a candle at a stand outside of the church as she had observed the other tourists doing. They climbed the many steps to the church, taking pictures along the way.

Inside the church, they entered the grotto with its lovely blue illuminated altar. They lit the candle, placed it in the rack and knelt down and said a brief prayer.

Back outside the front of the church again, they shopped in the colorful vendor tents which were filled with an extensive variety of souvenirs.

Kelley purchased several medals, while Phil bought a book that described the history of the shrine. A tent, at the end of the row, featured T-shirts and sweat shirts. Phil purchased two sweat shirts with the word, 'Sicily' embroidered on the front and the red and yellow flag of Sicily on the sleeve; a large one for himself and a medium sized one for Kelley.

As the afternoon heat started to get intense, she suggested that they return to the hotel and rest before going out for their evening dinner and a short walk.

"Remind me to recharge my video camera when we get back to the room," Phil said.

"Yes. And the clerk said that they had a computer and internet access in the lobby. So I want to email Mom a note, if I can. No sense in sending postcards to people. We'll get home before they would arrive."

"Good idea. And I think that I'll email my folks and my secretary and tell them that we saw that beautiful Cathedral with all the gold mosaics this morning. My secretary raved about it and boy, was she ever right."

As they drove back to the hotel, Phil said, "We should lay out some good walking shoes for tomorrow. I'm planning on driving a couple of hours to an ancient town, called Savoca in the morning, where they filmed the movie, *The Godfather, Part I*. I heard that there's a lot of walking uphill on cobblestone streets there. In the afternoon, we'll drive up to see Mt. Etna. That's going to be a lot of walking in rough terrain. Also could be kind of cold, so we should take warm jackets."

"Boy. Sounds like you've got our day all planned. You should open your own travel agency."

"Good idea. The concierge told me of a good place to eat tonight. It's called 'Gabry Auto.' I know it sounds like a car dealership but it's supposed to be a restaurant and disco with authentic Sicilian food."

"Can't wait," Kelley replied. "Boy, this traffic is so slow. It seems like it's taking us forever to get back to the hotel."

"The guy in front of me is all over the road. I can't get around him. First, he stopped. Then, he speeded up. Now he's stopped again. I wonder if they have to take a driving test before they get a license here."

She waved her hand, interrupting him. "Did you see that? The guy in the car in the outside lane is driving crazy. Now, he just slowed down. Oh my gosh! He just pushed a girl out of the car and drove off! Look, she's lying on the sidewalk. And my God, it looks like she's pregnant!"

"You're kidding."

"No. Stop. Let me out. I've got to go and help her."

He pulled over to the curb and she jumped out of the car.

He leaned out of the car and yelled, "You stay here and help her, Kell. I'm going to follow that car and find out who that asshole is." He pulled the passenger side car door shut and drove off.

Kelley ran over to the young woman lying on the sidewalk. "Are you okay miss?"

Phil raced after the car from which the woman had been thrown. Down one street, up another narrow side street; the car sped with Phil in the little Smart Car close behind. Suddenly, the first car came to a screeching halt. The driver's door was thrown open; a young man jumped out and ran down an adjoining alley.

Phil pulled his car over, jumped out, and without hesitation, took off running after the man. Halfway down the alley, Phil caught up to him, tackled him from behind and knocked him to the ground.

The man started screaming in Italian, what Phil assumed were curse words.

"Calm down, buddy," Phil said in English. "You're not going anywhere."

He whipped the man's hands behind his back and looked for something to tie them with. Not seeing anything that he could use, Phil just lay across the man's back, holding him to the ground.

People streamed out of the nearby shops and gathered near them, pointing at them and talking loudly in Italian.

Phil looked up at them and shouted, "Police. Get the police."

Suddenly a mid-size, white car marked "Polizia" pulled up and two uniformed Sicilian policemen got out.

"This man just pushed a woman out of a moving car," Phil shouted to them.

One of the policemen shouted something to Phil in Italian. Phil looked around, bewildered.

"I'm American. I don't understand Italian. Can someone here help me?"

A woman stepped forward from the crowd. "I speak both English and Italian. The policeman asked you for identification."

Still lying on top of the man, Phil reached into his jacket, pulled his U.S. passport from his pocket and handed it to the officer.

In English, Phil told her that he and his wife had just witnessed this man push a young pregnant girl from a moving automobile.

While the woman was translating this to the police officers, the man managed to roll out from under Phil. He jumped to his feet and ran down the alley. One officer drew his gun and shouted, "Termine. Termine."

But the man didn't stop.

As he neared the end of the alley, a couple of young lads standing nearby tackled him and held him to the ground. The police officers, Phil, and the woman who had been translating ran up to them.

While the police officers dragged the man to his feet, pulled his arms behind him and hand cuffed him, Phil said to the woman, "It's so good of you to translate for me. What's your name?"

"Gina Martin. I'm from the U.S. But I live and work in Palermo."

"I'm Phil Willis. An attorney from Syracuse, New York. My wife and I are here on our honeymoon. And, like I said before, we just saw this fellow push a pregnant woman out of his car a couple of streets back."

She nodded and translated this to the police officers, who in turn, started to interrogate the man.

He answered the police rapidly in Italian.

Gina whispered in Phil's ear. "He says that he doesn't know what you're talking about. Says it wasn't him."

Then the officer looked at both of them and said in broken English, "Take us to the girl he pushed out of the car."

Phil thanked Gina for her help and followed the officer to the police car. The officer gestured for Phil to get in the front seat.

The other policeman shoved the man into the back seat and jumped in beside him.

When they arrived back at the place where the young girl and Kelley had been, they saw an emergency crew placing the girl on a stretcher.

Phil and the driver got out of the car and ran over. The second police officer yanked the man from the back seat and pushed him ahead of him toward the group.

Kelley grabbed Phil by the arm. "They're getting ready to take the girl to the hospital. I'm going with her. The paramedics think that she is about ready to have her baby."

The officer who spoke English walked up and tapped Phil on the shoulder.

"We're taking the signore to see if the signorina can identify him."

Kelley and Phil watched as the two officers dragged the man to the open back door of the ambulance.

A short while later, the officer walked back to Kelley and Phil. "The signorina said it was him. We're arresting him and we'll get her statement later. Looks like she has something more important to do now. The bambino is on its way."

Kelley started toward the ambulance. "And I'm going with her."

Phil reached into his pocket; pulled out a card and handed it to the policeman. "Here is the name and address of the hotel where my wife and I are staying. You can contact me there if you need my statement. Now, if you will take me back to pick up my auto I would appreciate it."

"Si Signore. We'll drop you back off there before we take this fellow to the jail."

"Thanks. And I'll need you to give me directions to the hospital where the ladies are going so I can join my wife. I think that young lady can use all the support that she can get."

Chapter 23

Phil rushed into the lobby of the Palermo Hospital and looked around for Kelley. Before he could ask anyone where she might be, he spotted her sitting in the admittance office just off the front lobby.

He knocked briefly and walked in. She spun around in her chair. "Oh, this is my husband, Phil Willis," she said to the elderly female volunteer seated behind the desk.

"Are you okay, honey," Phil asked.

"Yes. They took the girl in through the emergency entrance, she's up in a delivery room. This lady wanted to know who she is and I told her that all I knew was that her name was Maria. She told me that on the way here. However, I did find her purse on the sidewalk and brought it along. We were just about to go through it and see if we could discover something more about her."

Phil sat down in the chair next to Kelley. "Well. The police took the guy who threw her out of the car to the police station. But, he wasn't very co-operative. Kept saying that he didn't do it."

"Well, the girl said he did. I heard her say that. Right now, we're just trying to find out who she is."

Kelley opened the purse, pulled out a billfold and rifled through it. "Here's her Italian driver's license, says her name is Maria Rossi."

With a lightning reflex, the woman behind the desk jumped up. "Rossi? You said Maria Rossi?" She grabbed the driver's license from Kelley's hands.

Startled at her sudden outburst; Kelley and Phil stared at her.

"Yes. Maria Rossi," Kelley answered.

The woman looked carefully at the driver's license, and slowly sat down. She picked up the phone, dialed a number and talked rapidly in Italian.

Within moments, a woman wearing a navy blue business suit, a white lacy blouse and fashionable high heels ran into the office. She identified herself as Theresa Costello, the hospital administrator and asked Kelley and Phil how they knew Maria Rossi.

"My name is Kelley Willis and this is my husband, Phil. We're visiting from America."

Kelley spent the next several minutes relating how they had seen Maria pushed out of a car, and how Phil had chased and apprehended her assailant. She explained that she had accompanied Maria to the hospital in the ambulance.

"So, that's everything that we know up to this point," Kelley said.

"Have you heard how the young lady is doing," Phil asked.

"I'm going to call the delivery room now and see," Mrs. Costello responded. She picked up the phone, asked several questions in Italian and snapped out a couple of commands. The only thing that Kelley and Phil understood was a couple of "Si-si's."

She hung up the phone. "Maria has delivered a beautiful bambina. It's a healthy baby girl. They were just preparing to put Maria into a ward; however, I ordered them to place her in a private room. Her father, Mario Rossi would be most upset if I put his only daughter into a ward with other patients. I know that he will demand only the best of care for his daughter and granddaughter."

"Mario Rossi?" Kelley questioned.

"Yes. Signore Rossi is very prominent in Palermo. He would be extremely insulted if we did not treat his family with the utmost care. And the nurse upstairs just told me that Senorina Rossi is asking for the lady that accompanied her to the hospital."

"Now, would you please follow me upstairs? I'll take you to Maria."

Mrs. Costello led them to the elevators. Kelley sucked in her breath and hesitated for just a moment before entering. Mrs. Costello looked at her. "Something wrong Mrs. Willis. You look apprehensive."

She laughed. "Oh, I had a bad experience with a lift in London recently."

"Well, I can assure you that this one is quite safe. We have it inspected monthly."

Kelley took Phil's arm and whispered, "I think that's what they said about the other one."

He patted her arm reassuringly.

Mrs. Costello continued, "As you can see we are completely redoing the hospital—from top to bottom, as you Americans say. Now, let's go see Ms. Rossi. I still have a few questions for her."

As the elevator opened on the maternity floor they saw men in white painter's clothes standing nearby. When they saw Mrs. Costello emerge from the elevator, they walked up to her and started talking rapidly.

The only thing that Kelley and Phil could understand was when the men said "painting the room" and pointed down the hall.

Mrs. Costello answered the men in English. "I'll be with you shortly." Then, she turned to Kelley and Phil. "Please follow me to Maria's room."

Entering the room, they saw Maria sitting up in bed, dressed in a hospital gown. She had a black and blue bruise on her forehead and looked very tired. Sitting in a chair next to her was a middle-aged man, dressed in police uniform.

Kelley rushed over to her, sat down on the edge of the bed and gave her a hug. "Maria, I'm glad to see that you are looking better."

"Yes. And thanks to you, I have a healthy baby girl."

"Maria, this is my husband, Phil," she said as she motioned for him to come closer.

"You're the American who chased Maria's assailant, aren't you," the police officer asked.

"Yes, I'm Phil Willis."

The policeman stood and shook Phil's hand, "I'm Police Chief Greco, head of the police here in Palermo. When we interviewed the young man at the police station, he informed us that this young lady was none other than Maria Rossi. I realized that her father would be very concerned when he heard about this so I decided to personally handle this incident."

Kelley and Phil stared at him as they started to realize that Signor Rossi must be someone tremendously important because everyone seemed to jump at the very mention of his name.

The Chief continued, "I've been interviewing Maria about the incident. She said that it was her old boyfriend, Georgio, who pushed her out of the car and she doesn't want to press charges against him. However, I'll need a signed statement from each of you if she does decide to do so."

Phil leveled a calm gaze at him. "Let my wife talk to her alone about it. Maybe she can persuade her to press charges."

The men moved toward the door as Kelley sat on the edge of the bed and proceeded to calmly talk to Maria.

After a few moments, Maria cried out, "No! No! Georgio didn't realize what he was doing. He didn't mean to hurt me. He was just so upset when he saw that I was going to have someone else's baby."

Kelley looked up at the Chief. "Well, I guess you've got your answer. Right now, let's let Maria enjoy her new baby."

He shrugged his shoulders, motioned for Phil to follow him out of the room and led him to a private conference room at the end of the hall.

"Mr. Willis, I have a favor to ask of you and your wife. Would you both go to the Rossi home and gently explain to Signore Rossi what has happened. I'm afraid that if I call him and relate this incident to him over the phone that he'll fly off the handle as you Americans say. He might order his associates to harm Georgio. I'll keep Georgio in jail overnight for his own safety or until I hear from you."

Phil looked concerned. "It sounds like Mr. Rossi could be a violent man."

"He is of the old school and can be very vindictive if he so chooses. He is part of an old powerful Sicilian family. Even has his own security people guarding his estate. So, I'm hoping that you and your wife can assure him that Maria and the baby are well and safe so that he doesn't seek revenge on Georgio."

"We'll try our very best to handle the situation. I have my car outside so I just need you to give me directions to the Rossi home."

"By the way, Signore Rossi fancies himself to be quite a ladies man. It might be best if your wife does most of the talking."

After giving Phil directions to the Rossi home, Chief Greco walked toward the elevators.

As Phil entered Maria's room, he saw that beautiful young woman of about twenty with long black hair, flowing about her shoulders and deep blue eyes sitting up in bed. She was holding a small baby, wrapped in a pink receiving blanket.

Kelley walked over to Phil, took him by the hand and led him to the bed, where they both gazed at the little one.

She leaned over and grasped one of the baby's tiny hands in hers. "Look, isn't she beautiful. She weighed over seven pounds."

Looking at the baby's black hair and dark eyes, he said, "She looks like a miniature Sicilian."

"That's what she is," Maria said. "She's the very image of her father."

Kelley and Phil looked at each other. Then she asked, "Oh, is Georgio the father?"

"No. Georgio is my old boyfriend. I broke up with him over a year ago and he took it very hard. We ran into each other today and he got very upset when he saw that I was pregnant with someone else's baby. We took a ride to talk things over. Suddenly, he got very angry, cursed at me and pushed me out of the car."

"And who is the father," Phil asked.

"Rosario. He works at my father's vineyard."

Kelley looked at her with deep concern. "And how will your father feel about Rosario being the father of your child?"

Maria hung her head in shame. "He will be very angry with Rosario and very disappointed in me. You see I am his only daughter. I have an older brother, Antonio, who my father expects to follow in his footsteps and take over the estate and winery.

My mother said that from the moment that I was born, I was my father's little 'principessa' or 'princess', as you say in English. He always spoiled me. My exquisite pink bedroom had a four poster canopy bed and a sign on the door that read, 'Daddy's Little Princess.' I always had designer clothes.

"Whatever I asked my father for- he gave me. For my fifth birthday, I received a pony. When I fell off the pony and got hurt, he became so angry that he sold the pony. When I went to the city to attend Palermo University, he bought me a one bedroom apartment a block from the school. My mother said that he vowed that he would never let anyone or anything harm me."

Kelley nodded. "He must love you very much."

Maria's eyes filled with tears. "Yes. But now, he will be very ashamed of me. He wanted me to graduate from University and marry someone from a very prominent family. He will be very angry that I had a baby with Rosario."

"And why is that?"

"Because Rosario has not yet graduated from the University. And he just works in the vineyard for my father."

Phil looked down at her. "I understand from the Chief that your father has a strong personality and perhaps an even stronger temper."

Maria hung her head, as tears came to her eyes. "That is true. That's why I never told him that I was expecting. As you can see I am naturally a big girl and I always wore baggy tops when I went home. So my father doesn't know about the baby. I think my mother suspected but she would never dare to tell him. She knows how angry he would be about me being an unwed mother. That is not acceptable in our rigid Sicilian society."

"You understand, Maria," Kelley said, "that now that the baby is here, you cannot put this off any longer. He must be told about the little one."

Just then the nurse came into the room and noticed that Maria was crying. "I have to ask you people to leave now. We cannot have our new mother getting upset. It is not good for her milk supply and it is time for the first feeding. And then, both mother and baby must rest."

Kelley stood up. "We'll leave you now, Maria, and go talk to your father. We'll try to gently break the news of your accident and the birth of your daughter to him."

Maria reached out and grabbed her hand. "Please Signora Kelley, make my father understand. I don't want him to be angry with Rosario and me. And I don't want Georgio arrested. I just want this to be over so that we all can get on with our lives."

"We'll do our very best," she answered, leaning over to kissed her.

"Try not to worry," Phil added. "Your top priority is to care for your beautiful daughter."

In the hall, Phil said, "The Chief gave me directions to the Rossi Vineyard. Let's go there right away and see if we can help ease this situation for Maria. She certainly needs all the support from her family that she can get."

"This may not be an easy task," Kelley said as they left the hospital. "It sounds like Signor Rossi is very set in his ways. We'll have to deal with him carefully. But, we'll just tell him Maria's story and hope that he can deal gracefully with the situation. "

He looked at her with a thoughtful expression. "Maybe, then we can proceed with our Sicilian honeymoon."

Chapter 24

Following the police chief's directions, it took Phil and Kelley about twenty minutes to arrive at the Rossi vineyard and estate.

"Seems strange that everyone wanted us to inform Signor Rossi about both Maria's accident and the birth of her baby," Kelley said as they drove up a dirt road that wound up the mountain.

"Yes. I got the impression that both the Chief and the hospital administrator like to stay clear of him."

"You don't suppose that he's part of the Mafia do you," she whispered.

He shook his head. "I was told that the Mafia doesn't exist in Sicily anymore. However, everyone seems to treat Signor Rossi like the Godfather. I get the impression that he has both wealth and power."

They pulled up in front of the closed iron gates, parked the car and got out. A tall muscular man, dressed in dirty overalls and a soiled white shirt, exited the nearby bushes. As he approached them, they could see he had a sawed off shotgun in his hands—and it was pointed directly at them. They automatically threw their hands up in the air.

Before the man could say anything, Kelley stammered, "We've come in peace. Do you speak English?"

"Some," he answered. "What is your business here?"

"We're here to see Signor Rossi."

"I'm one of his guards. Signore Rossi sees no one without an appointment. No one."

"He'll see us." Kelley said.

"The Palermo Police Chief sent us here to talk to Signor Rossi about his daughter, Maria. It's very important," Phil added calmly.

"Wait here." The guard pulled out his mobile phone and walked a short distance away, all the time keeping his gun trained on them.

After a short conversation on the phone, he walked to the gate, punched a couple of buttons on the security panel and opened it. "Get back in your car and follow me. I'll take you to Signore Rossi."

Phil started the engine and slowly followed the guard as he walked up the drive, lined with cypress trees, to the house at the top of a hill.

Kelley looked out at the vast vineyards that seemed to stretch to the horizon on both sides of the road that led up to the villa. A second floor porch covered the width of the villa and was flanked on each end by tall columns.

"Some spread," Phil said.

"Look at these acres and acres of vineyards," Kelley said as she gazed in awe at the vine-clad hills.

As they approached the front of the house, Phil added, "Signor Rossi must be worth a fortune. Just take a gander at the well-manicured gardens."

The guard stopped and motioned for Phil to pull into a gravel parking space just off the main driveway.

They exited the car and followed the guard toward the front entrance. The guard asked, "You gotta a name?"

"Willis. Mr. and Mrs. Phil Willis from America. I told you that Chief Greco sent us."

Kelley heard a voice call out in Italian, what sounded like cuss words. Then the voice said in English, "I hate this bike."

Directly in front of them, a young husky boy, who appeared to be about ten years old, with dark hair and deep blue eyes was standing next to a small motor scooter. After uttering a few more cuss words in Italian, he kicked the bike's tires a couple of times.

Phil walked up to him. "Hey there kid. No need to do that. What's the problem?"

"My scooter-no start."

"My wife knows bikes. Mind, if she takes a look at it?"

Kelley knelt down in front of the scooter and tinkered with it for a few minutes. "I just need a screw driver to adjust it."

The young boy reached into a pouch on the back of the scooter, pulled out a couple of tools and handed them to her.

While the others watched, she made a few adjustments and then tried to start the scooter. It sputtered a few times and then stopped.

"See Signora. Told ya. Dumb bike—don't go."

She worked on it a bit more as a thirty-something man, dressed in casual tan slacks and an open necked white shirt approached.

"Good afternoon, Signora. I'm Antonio. This young man's father. And you are?"

She stood up and brushed the hair out of her eyes. "I'm Kelley Ryan. I mean Kelley Willis. And this is my husband, Phil. We're here to see Signor Rossi about his daughter, Maria."

"Chief Greco sent us," Phil added.

"Maria is my sister and this frustrated young man, is my son, Michael. You say that the Chief sent you about my sister?" Antonio tensed, somewhat alarmed. "Is she alright?"

"She's fine now," Kelley answered. "But, we prefer to discuss the situation directly with your father."

"I'll take you to him then."

Kelley knelt back down by the scooter. "Just give me a minute more and I'll have this thing purring like a kitten."

She made a few more adjustments to the scooter and stood up. "Now try it," she said to the young boy.

He jumped on the scooter and it started right up.

"Look, Papa. The pretty lady fix. Grazie. Grazie." He waved his hand as he drove off down the driveway.

"Slow down," Antonio yelled.

Antonia took Kelley's hand. "Thank you for fixing my son's scooter, Signora. Please accept my apologies for him. Not all Sicilians are so impatient."

"It goes with the age," Kelley replied.

"You say that you have news about my sister?" Antonio turned to Phil.

"Yes. Very important and private news."

"Follow me. I'll take you to my father. You can explain to both of us why you are here."

"Grazie Signore," Phil replied.

"Please, speak English. I spent a number of years in the States, going to college. I speak four languages and my parents speak English as well."

Following Antonio up the front steps to the double doors, Kelley stared around in wonder. "How big is this villa, Antonio?"

"Four floors. Eight bedrooms with adjoining baths. A great room, dining room, library and a wine cellar. Also the cellar has an antique wood burning oven that is still in use."

Kelley looked at the stone lined walls as they entered. "It appears to be quite old."

"It has been in my family for generations. But, of course, it has been completely restored to suit our modern lifestyle. However, the original frescoes are still here." He pointed to the walls of the hallway as they walked through.

"They add to the old world charm of the villa," Kelley said.

Antonio looked down the hallway. "I can see that the door to my father's study is open. He's usually in there working on the books at this time of day. This vineyard is his life. Please follow."

They entered the dark study with its paneled walls and ceiling. The only light in the room was provided by a small lamp on the desk, with the outline of a large man seated behind it.

Antonio approached the man. "Good afternoon father. These people have come to talk to you."

The man slowly got to his feet. In his late sixties, Marco Rossi was about six feet tall and had a full head of black hair, with streaks of white along the temples. He was very muscular. Kelley decided that this was probably a result of working all his life in the vineyards.

Wearing dark slacks, a smoking jacket and a colorful scarf around his neck, Marco fit the image of a Sicilian vineyard owner. In perfect English, Marco asked his son. "Who are these people? And why are they here?"

"I'm Kelley Willis," she stepped forward, "and this is my husband, Phil. We're from America."

"What. He can't speak for himself," the old man demanded.

"You would be amazed at what he can do, sir," she responded quickly.

"State your business, Mr. Willis. I've got a vineyard to run."

Antonio put up his hand. "Papa, they have news about Maria."

Marco Rossi stiffened slightly; then sat back down in his chair.

Kelley had the feeling that he was preparing himself for bad news. Before they could speak, the old man asked quietly, "Has harm come to my Maria?"

Now, it was Kelley's turn to put her hand in the air. "First sir, may we sit down."

"Of course. 'Sedere'." Then realizing that he had spoken in Italian, in English, he added, "Sit."

Kelley and Phil took a seat in front of the desk as Antonio stood anxiously beside his father.

Kelley took a deep breath. "Well, it's like this Signor Rossi."

She told him how she and Phil had seen Maria pushed from the moving automobile and how she had accompanied her in the ambulance to the hospital.

Then, Phil related how he had chased Maria's assailant and that the man was now in jail. Finally, he told Marco that the Palermo Police Chief had asked them to personally drive out to the estate and tell the story to him.

After they concluded the tale, Signore Rossi sat back in his chair, sighed and thought for several minutes. Then he abruptly got up, slammed his fist on the desk and ordered. "Antonio, I want you to go to the jail. Bring the man that harmed my Maria to me."

Kelley jumped to her feet. "Wait Mr. Rossi. It was Maria's old boy friend, Georgio, who assaulted her and she said that he didn't intend to hurt her. She just has a small bruise on her forehead."

Marco slammed his fist on the desk in a haze of fury and snarled, "You heard me Antonio. Go get this Georgio fellow. We will show these American's what Sicilian justice is."

After hearing his father's order, Antonio turned on his heel and ran from the room.

Now somewhat calmer, Marco leaned back in his chair. "You said that Maria wasn't hurt. Now tell me how she is."

Kelley sighed. "I think Maria's mother should hear

the rest of the story. Is she home? Can you get her?"

Marco jumped impatiently to his feet. "You want my wife. I'll bring her here." He rushed out of the room.

Kelley looked at Phil. "Now comes the hard part. How do we tell Mr. and Mrs. Rossi that their unmarried daughter is the mother of a beautiful little girl?"

"Remember the police chief said it would be better if you tell them gently," Phil said.

Kelley gulped. "Yes. But how?"

Chapter 25

Minutes later, Marco returned to the library. He was arm in arm with a tall slender lady, her silver colored hair drawn back in a large elegant chignon. She was dressed in a simple lilac colored silk pantsuit with diamond studs in her ears and a large diamond studded cross around her neck.

Kelley had seen many attractive looking older Italian women, but she thought that this lady was the most stunning and classiest that she had ever seen.

Marco drew the woman close to his side. "This is my lovely wife, Isabella. Next month, we will celebrate our forty-fifth wedding anniversary. And, we are one tough team. Isabella, this is Mr. and Mrs. Willis from America. They have news of Maria."

Kelley stepped forward and shook her hand, admiring the beautiful lilac colored cashmere sweater that was draped over Isabella's shoulders. Her casual, yet elegant ensemble looked like it came straight from one of Milan's most expensive boutiques.

"Please, call me Kelley. Very glad to meet you," she said as she extended her hand.

"Bentornato," Isabella responded.

"That means welcome," Marco added. "Isabella, please speak English to our guests."

Phil stepped forward and extended his hands to Isabella. "And I'm her husband, Phil. We've only been married a couple of weeks. But we plan to someday equal your record." Turning her hand over, he gently kissed it.

"Very glad to meet you Phil," Isabella responded in English, but with a lovely Italian accent. "Marco said that you had news about our Maria. We have not heard from her lately."

"Let's have these people sit down so that we can talk," Marco said, as he walked toward a large brown leather sofa. An immense marble table was in front of it and two matching leather chairs were on either side.

Kelley and Isabella sat down on the leather sofa and Marco and Phil sat in the chairs.

"Maybe we should offer our visitors some wine," Isabella suggested.

"Time for that later," an impatient Marco responded. "They said that Chief Greco sent them to talk to us about Maria. So, I am anxious to hear all that they have to say."

At the mention of the police chief's name, Isabella sat upright, now somewhat alarmed. "Chief Greco sent you? What is it about Maria? She is okay?"

Kelley smiled gently and took Isabella's hands in hers. "Maria had a slight accident and the paramedics took her to the hospital as a precaution. She only had slight bruises and is fine."

"Then why is she in the hospital? And why did the police chief send you to tell us this," Isabella asked.

Kelley hesitated. "I guess that there is no easy way to tell you this. Your Maria was pregnant and the accident triggered the birth of the baby, but both are doing fine. You are grandparents to a beautiful baby girl. "

Marco shot to his feet. "No. My Maria is not married."

Phil stood up and put his hand on Marco's arm. "Sir, I understand your concerns. But right now, you need to know that Maria has had a lovely baby girl and that both of them are doing fine."

Marco scowled and looked at Isabella. "We didn't even know that she was expecting, Did we?"

Isabella hung her head. "I suspected."

"And you didn't tell me," Marco roared.

Isabella started to sob. Marco looked down at her, paused for a few minutes, then sat down beside her and sighed. "Tell us all the details."

Kelley and Phil could see that the next few minutes were difficult for both Mr. and Mrs. Rossi as they told the entire story of what had happened to their daughter. From time to time, Marco would stand up and pace, intense with emotion. Then, he would sit back down and take Isabella's hands in his as she gently wept.

"Maria is now in Palermo Hospital," Kelley said, "and both she and the baby are well and healthy. She said that she didn't want her old friend, Georgio arrested. She just wants to get on with life. She hopes that this can be a time for joy, not sadness."

Marco jumped to his feet again, walked behind his desk and took out a phone book. He dialed the hospital's number, asked for the administrator and quizzed her about Maria. "I'm sending two of my men over to the hospital. Please post them outside of Maria's room at once. I'll instruct them to call me night or day, if any problem occurs with Maria or the child."

He hung up the phone, walked over to Isabella and put his arms around her. "Don't worry. Everything will be all right. You'll see. I'll take care of everything as I always do."

She dried her tears. "But why would this Georgio fellow hurt Maria?"

"Apparently, he got upset when he discovered she was pregnant, with another man's child," Kelley answered.

"And where is this Georgio now," Isabella asked.

"Chief Greco is holding him in jail at the present time," Phil said.

"Jail. That will be too easy for that bastard," Marco roared.

Kelley looked at him and sighed. "Maria did say that she didn't want him arrested. She said she won't press charges against him."

Marco picked up the phone and called one of his security men into the room. "I want you to take two of your men to the Palermo hospital. My daughter Maria is there. Post one man inside her room and one outside the door. Instruct them that if anything happens to my loved ones, they will pay dearly."

After the man left the room, Marco turned to Isabella. "I have ordered Antonio to bring this Georgio to me. I will deal with him when he arrives."

Kelley and Phil started to protest.

"You won't harm him, will you," she asked

Marco waved his hand. "No, my friends do not worry. I will take care of him in an appropriate Sicilian manner. Now you must relax. You are our honored guests and you must dine with us tonight. We will go to the hospital in the morning to pick up Maria and the baby."

Isabella was now wringing her hands. Marco put his arms around her. "Don't despair, my dove. Now, go and get a bottle of wine. I will take our American guests into the great room where we can chat. We must make them feel at home. They came to the aid of our beloved Maria, when she most needed it."

Marco led Kelley and Phil into the immense great room with floor to ceiling windows overlooking the pool and the vineyards. He instructed them to have a seat on one of the two loves eats that flanked the large floor to ceiling stone fireplace.

Isabella returned, followed by a maid who carried a tray with a large decanter of wine with four glasses on it. She placed the tray on the coffee table in front of the loves eats and poured wine for each.

After she left the room, Isabella sat down and took Kelley's hands with tears in her eyes. "I like how you Americans take charge of things. I want to hear all about you two."

Sipping the wine and talking for a short while, Kelley suggested, "Maybe, we should concentrate on bringing Maria and the baby home tomorrow. You might wish to order a few things for the baby's room. You'll need a crib, diapers, and a changing table right away. I can help you make up a list of things you'll need to order."

"There is nothing that you don't think of Senora Kelley," Isabella answered.

Marco laughed, "See Momma, this beautiful young lady has found more work for you to do. You two take your wine and go to Maria's room. Make up a list of what you think we will need for the little one. Then, call the furniture store, order what you want and have them deliver it tomorrow morning. We will be ready for Maria and her bambina."

After the women left the room, Marco refilled Phil's glass. "Now, it is time that you and I get better acquainted, Senore Willis."

"Please, call me Phil."

"You'll dine with us and then stay the night?"

"We would be honored sir. How can I turn down such an offer?"

"I hope that you wouldn't."

As they talked, Marco was amazed at how different Kelley and Phil were from his two children, Antonio and Maria. After growing up on the Rossi estate, Antonio had gone on to college in the United States and Maria had pursued her education at the university in Palermo, living off campus. This was why, Marco explained, they had seen little of Maria lately. "These modern children want to be so independent."

Marco was amazed to learn that after Kelley and Phil had graduated from college, they had gone on to private investigative work. And he was shocked to hear that Kelley had eventually become a secret service agent.

"You two have experienced much in life for your young age. Do you carry a gun now?"

Phil was somewhat startled at this abrupt question. "I have a permit to carry one; however, I didn't bring it. Can't carry a weapon through airport security these days."

"Does your wife have a permit too? "

"Yes. Her days as a private eye and undercover investigator required it," Phil answered, looking up as Kelley and Isabella entered the room.

"We ordered the furniture and all the items that we'll need for the baby," Isabella said. "I'll have the men paint the room next to Maria's pink for the little one. The baby furniture is set for delivery at nine tomorrow morning. They'll set up the bed, the dresser and the changing table. We also ordered diapers and baby clothes. So, we'll be all ready to welcome our new little princess when she comes home with her mother."

"Good," Marco replied. "Did you tell the cook that we will have guests for dinner tonight?"

"Yes, Marco, I took care of it. She's planning on having veal cacciatore." She looked at Phil. "I hope you like that."

"That sounds delicious."

They heard the sound of the front door opening. Then footsteps could be heard in the hallway leading to the great room. They looked up as Antonio and the man who Phil recognized as Maria's assailant entered. Behind them was Palermo Police Chief Greco.

"Father, after some persuasion, Georgio has accepted your invitation to visit you," Antonio announced.

"Now, hold your temper, Marco," Isabella whispered.

Marco jumped to his feet and walked over to Georgio, "You are Georgio, Maria's old boyfriend?"

"Yes sir," Georgio replied softly.

Marco stood eye to eye in front of him and said calmly, "I heard that you hurt my Maria."

Georgio fell to his knees and clasped his hands together, as if in prayer. "Perdono. Perdono."

"English. Speak English so my American friends can understand you, swine."

"Forgive me. Forgive me. I beg of you Signore Rossi. I acted in anger when I saw that my beloved Maria was pregnant with another man's baby."

"Never the less. You deserve Sicilian Justice," Marco growled.

Chief Greco stepped forward. "Do you wish me to arrest and charge this man, Signore Rossi?"

Isabella stepped forward, grabbed Marco's arm and pleaded. "Please, let it go Poppa. Senora Kelley said that Maria did not want him arrested. We don't need any more trouble. It should be a happy time when we bring Maria and the little one home."

Marco shrugged his shoulders. "Take him away Greco. I never want to see him again."

He turned to Georgio. "If you ever come near Maria or her baby again, I'll...."

"No. No. I promise I will never bother them," Georgio staggered to his feet. He knew only too well that Marco Rossi was granting him mercy only because of his daughter's wishes.

The Chief grabbed Georgio by his collar and dragged him from the room.

"Better to keep the peace, than to seek revenge," Isabella said calmly as she touched Marco on the arm. "Now, it's time that we went into the dining room. Mario, you escort Senora Willis in."

Marco took Kelley by the arm and started for the door. Isabella took Phil's arm and Antonio followed behind them. Suddenly, Kelley stopped. "Wait. Before we eat. I have one more thing I must tell you."

Everyone stood still and waited for her statement.

She paused and took a deep breath. "Maria did tell us who the father of her baby is."

They waited for her to continue.

"His name is Rosario."

Chapter 26

"Rosario? Not Rosario Gianetti?" Marco cried out. "You must be mistaken."

"No, that was the name that Maria gave me," Kelley answered.

"That bastardo works for me," he roared.

"Rosario Gianetti is Marco's Operations Manager. He meets with Marco on a daily basis to discuss the running of the vineyard and the winery," Isabella explained.

Rosario was born to struggling Sicilian peasants and had worked in a winery run by his mother's brother. Rosario's father had always suffered from poor health and worked only part of the time as a clerk in hardware in a nearby small town.

As an only child, Rosario had been forced to work in the vineyards at an early age to help support the family. His mother got him a job working in her brother's vineyard and winery. Rosario soon discovered that he loved the work; he talked to the vines as though they were his friends. His uncle taught him everything that he knew about raising grapes and making vine.

Rosario's only other passion was reading and his mother made sure that he got a good high school education. Unfortunately, there was no money to send Rosario to college, nor could he get a scholarship to the University. He decided to work hard, save his money, obtain a college degree and some day, buy his uncle's vineyard.

As he was about to graduate from high school, Rosario learned that his uncle was planning to sell his vineyards to his neighbor, Marco Rossi. Rosario was devastated at this news.

Marco was in the process of buying up all the small vineyards surrounding his land and would establish one of the largest estates and winery in Palermo.

"I am meeting with Signore Rossi and his son, Antonio, this afternoon to finalize the sale of the vineyard," his uncle told Rosario one spring morning. "You must meet with him too. He wants to hire you to work in his vineyard. And the first thing that you must learn about Signore Rossi is that he always gets what he wants."

"So how long have you worked for your uncle," Marco asked Rosario later in the meeting.

"Since I was a very young boy. I love the vines."

"Yes. And according to your uncle, they love you. He says that you are the reason that his vines produced such an abundant harvest these past years. And that is why I want you to work for me."

"But I'm planning to go to the University and get a degree in agriculture and to one day own my own vineyard."

"Why not work for my father during the day and go to college at night," Antonio suggested.

Rosario thought for a few moments, thrust a hand through his hair and agreed to work for Marco Rossi.

For the next three years, Rosario toiled daily in the vineyards and attended the University of Palermo at night. It was a good life, he decided and he was quite content with it until Christmas last year when Maria Rossi came home from college for the holidays. Prior to that Rosario had seen her briefly from time to time as she came home for occasional visits.

Last year, Marco Rossi had thrown a big party for all the vineyard helpers and the winery staff. When Rosario looked across the room at Maria, dressed in a red velvet dress, with her long black hair flowing over her shoulders, he fell in love immediately.

After they talked and danced together, Maria was equally smitten with Rosario, who was no longer the skinny young man she had noticed previously working in the fields.

He was now over six feet tall, tanned and muscular with dark brown hair that had been streaked with highlights by his days in the sun.

"You're Rosario. I've seen you working in my father's fields," she said.

"And you're his little girl, Maria—now all grown up."

She smiled and put her finger to Rosario's lips. "You like?"

"Yes. I like."

In the next few months, the two were texting each other daily and secretly meeting almost nightly in Maria's apartment after Rosario's evening classes.

All of this, without the knowledge of Marco and Isabella Rossi.

"Rosario Gianetti? You're sure it's Rosario?" Isabella asked. "Marco treats him like a son."

Kelley took her by the hand. "Yes, I'm sure. Rosario Gianetti. Maria told me at the hospital that he was the father of her baby."

"I can't believe that bastardo was sneaking around with my daughter." Marco shouted.

"No. No," Isabella shook her head. "Maria and Rosario would not do this to us."

"I'm afraid it's true," Phil said calmly.

Marco whirled around and grabbed his son Antonio by the shoulder. "Rosario should be out in the west fields. Bring him to me at once."

"Yes, Poppa." Antonio turned, ran down the hallway; the front door slammed shut behind him.

Kelley sighed and gently approached Marco. "You cannot run your children's lives Signor Rossi. Maria is an adult. Like it or not—you must accept Rosario as the father's baby and try to make the best of the situation. If only for Maria's and the baby's sake."

Marco put his hands behind his back and started to pace across the room, while Kelley, Phil and Isabella stared at him.

"What must I do now?" He walked up to Isabella. "Was I wrong in the way I raised my children?"

"You did just fine, Marco. We are now being tested on whether to keep the family bond. You should give Rosario, Maria and the baby a chance to become part of our family. Remember we were young once too. Now, let's all sit down and wait calmly for Antonio and Rosario to arrive."

A short while later, Antonio hurriedly entered the library. "Rosario is gone. Apparently, Maria called him and he went to the hospital to see her. He told one of the men that he would be back soon. I told the field crew to tell him to come to the house directly."

"I sit. We wait." Marco ordered. Looking at Phil and Kelley, he pleaded, "Help an old man decide what he should do. My head is spinning."

"Well, if you really want our opinion," Kelley answered slowly.

"We do." Isabella replied without hesitation.

"Well, first of all, I think you must accept Rosario into your home and your family. Maria apparently loves him and the baby will need a father. They should come into a home filled with love."

Marco grimaced. "That will be difficult for me. Maria and Rosario are not married. The baby is..."

"Stop," Isabella ordered.

He looked at her and frowned. "Isabella, you of all people should realize how difficult this is for me."

He turned to Kelley and Phil. "For generations, we Sicilians had believed in revenge when we are humiliated and deceived. And this deceit has cut into my very heart."

The attorney side of Phil kicked in. "Let me suggest a possible solution, sir. No one need ever know that Maria and Rosario were not married. There's a little chapel in the hospital. You can call your priest in to marry them. Then, you can tell everyone that they were married in secret last year."

"And you could have the priest baptize the little one at the same time," Kelley added.

Isabella sat forward in her seat. "That's a wonderful idea Marco. This could be the right start for the three of them. Later, you can sit down with Maria and Rosario and help them decide what they want to do with their future."

Antonio nodded. "Listen to these people and to Momma, Poppa. They are right. Now is the time for peace, not anger."

Marco sat back and thought for a few moments. "Perhaps, you all are right." He stood up. "Momma, take our guests for a short tour of the house and then we shall dine. And tell the cook to wait dinner and set an extra place at the dinner table for Rosario. We will discuss this situation with him over some good food and wine. Antonio and I will join you shortly. Right now, I need time alone to think."

Isabella was in her glory as she led Kelley and Phil to the kitchen, where a chef and a couple of women were busy working. "This is Chef Donatto," she said. "He runs a successful restaurant in Palermo, but comes here two days a week when his restaurant is closed. These are our new friends, Mr. and Mrs. Willis from America."

The Chef wiped his hands on his apron, and then shook hands. "This lovely villa is my refuge from the hectic pace of the restaurant business. The Rossi and Donatto families go back many years."

He proudly showed an eight burner gas range, floor to ceiling refrigerators and freezers. And granite tops everywhere.

He turned to Isabella, "I assume that you wish me to feed young Michael in the kitchen as usual?"

"No. Tonight, he needs to be part of the family. Please put an extra place setting for him also."

Isabella then led Kelley and Phil out of the kitchen, passing through the massive hallway with its Murano crystal chandelier and into the dining room. "Marco takes great pride in both the house and his family. Both are very precious to him. His family is one of the most admired in all of Palermo. So, you can see, any hint of disgrace would be very hurtful to him."

Kelley stood and stared in amazement at an immense oak dining table that appeared to have about twenty chairs around it. On the wall in back of the table was a large hand painted mural of the villa with the pool and the vineyards in the background. Two immense crystal chandeliers hung above the table. One end of the table was set with lace place mats, china and gold flatware.

"We only use one end of the table, when we have a small group," Isabella explained as she led them back out into the main hallway.

"Most of the villa still has the original tile and terrazzo," she said as they walked down to the billiard room, a beautifully paneled room filled with a massive billiard table. In front of the floor to ceiling windows, stood a large game table with matching chairs. Through the windows, was the pool set in the midst of olive trees. Next to the pool, was a furnished shady gazebo. And beyond that, the tennis court.

Isabella pointed to the beamed ceiling. "The ceiling and the paneled walls are also original. Marco's great grandfather built this house, generations ago, and it has been remodeled and upgraded in the years since. His father modernized all the plumbing and electrical work. Marco put in the new kitchen that you just saw. He redid most of the rooms trying to keep as much of the original features that he could. He also had wireless and internet connections and a state of the art security system installed."

Isabella then led them up the large hand carved wooden stairway to the upper floor. The wall next to the stairway was covered with large old tapestries.

"These must be priceless," Kelley said as she stopped to examine them closely.

Isabella stopped for a moment. "Yes. These were purchased by Marco's ancestors. This one came from Rome. Those two from Belgium. Of course, they have all been restored over the years." Isabella showed them two of the bedrooms, with their adjoining bathrooms, each room decorated in a different style, décor and color.

At the end of the hall she opened double doors leading into the master suite, which had his and her closets, an immense bathroom and a small office adjoining it.

"Marco uses this small office to make phone calls at night. He uses his main office downstairs to do all the paper work for the estate."

"Now, before I take you to your guest room, I must show you Maria's room and the baby's." As she opened the doors to the rooms, they could see that a crew was already preparing it. The floors were covered with canvas. Cans of paint and several ladders were ready for the expected transformation of the rooms.

"You remind me of my mother," Kelley said. "She always gets the job done in a hurry."

"By the time we bring Maria and the baby home tomorrow, her room will be like a fairyland. Marco's men will have this room ready first thing in the morning."

"I'm certain that Maria will just love it."

"I hope so. Maybe, she and Rosario will decide to stay on with us indefinitely with the baby. Or at least until they can afford their own home."

Finally, Isabella led them up to the third floor of the villa. It was one immense room, with a gold and white marble floor, gold and white plaster work on the walls and four immense crystal chandeliers hanging from the ceiling.

"This used to be the Grand Salon. I call it the ballroom and we use it only for large parties." She walked through the room and opened the French doors that led out onto a large raised terrace with columned stone balustrades. "From here, you can see most of the vineyards."

"Now, let me take you back downstairs to the guest room so that you can freshen up before dinner. I'll have your luggage brought up to you."

"But, our luggage is back at the hotel," Phil said.

"My son made arrangements with your hotel to bring your luggage to us. We would like for you to stay with us at least overnight so we can show you true Sicilian hospitality."

"Thank you. That's very kind of you," Kelley replied as they followed her to the guest suite.

Isabella paused outside the door. "It's the least that we can do for all the kindness that you have shown our family."

She pulled them close to her and enclosed them in a group hug. Then, she stepped back and wiped the tears from her eyes.

"Thank you. This is very kind of you," Phil said.

"Freshen up. We'll wait for you in the dining room."

Chapter 27

Later, Isabella knocked on the door of Kelley and Phil's room. "Are you ready," she asked when Kelley opened the door.

"Yes. I didn't know if your family dressed for dinner, so I put on something casual, yet dressy."

Isabella glanced at Kelley's lovely peach colored silk pant suit. "You are just perfect my dear." She looked at Phil as he walked up. "And your attractive husband looks very handsome."

Phil, dressed in white linen pants and a light blue open necked shirt, stepped out of the room.

They followed Isabella down the stairway and through the hall to the dining room. As they entered, Kelley could see that the table was set for seven people.

"Antonio's son, Michael, has decided that this is a special occasion—having you for dinner, and he's looking forward to eating with us. He's such a bright child and he misses his mother. She's in the Lake Como region of Italy, visiting her sick mother."

Marco and a tall handsome young man, in his early twenties, tanned and muscular, entered the room. "Ah, my guests of honor have arrived. I would like you to meet Rosario. Rosario, these are the Americans who helped Maria after her accident and took her to the hospital."

"Yes, Maria told me how you both came to her aid. I am most grateful to you."

Kelley and Phil were astonished to see that Marco was now being very gracious to the young man who he had been so angry with earlier.

Phil stepped forward to shake Rosario's hand. "Nice to meet you."

"No. It is my pleasure. And once again, thank you so much for taking care of my Maria."

Kelley clasped Rosario's outstretched hand. "Maria had so many nice things to say about you. I'm sure that you've already met your new daughter."

"Yes. She is just beautiful. After all, her mother is the loveliest senorina in all of Sicily."

Nodding, Marco beamed at the compliment that Rosario had given his daughter. "Now, we must all be seated."

"I can smell some delicious odors coming from the kitchen," Phil replied, as he walked to the table.

Marco took his place at the head of the table and waved to Kelley and Phil. "Please sit on either side of me. You are our honored guests."

Phil pulled the chair out on Marco's right side for Kelley. Then, as he went around to Marco's left side, he pulled the chair next to him out for Isabella.

"Thank you," Isabella said. "Rosario, you sit on the other side of Senora Willis. Michael will sit next to me and Antonio can sit on the other side of Rosario."

"I hope that you two are famished," she smiled. "We will have a proper Sicilian feast in your honor. Five courses."

"We never rush our dinner. It is our family time," Marco added as Antonio and his son, Michael, entered the room.

"Sorry we are late, Momma," Antonio said as she gestured toward the seat where she expected him to sit.

"Michael wanted to dress up for dinner and it took him a while to decide what to wear."

Everyone looked at Michael, who was dressed in white linen pants with a pink open collared shirt. He looked very elegant and very Italian Kelley thought.

Michael scurried to the table, leaned down and gave Isabella a kiss on the cheek, before he took his seat beside her.

"We are very proud of our Michael," Isabella said. "Already he speaks three languages; Sicilian, English and Italian. He is also learning French and German. Such a bright boy."

She put her arms around him, gave him a big hug and added, "Before we eat, we must pray. Everyone take hold of hands please. Michael, will you say grace?"

They joined hands and bowed their heads as Michael recited the prayer.

Marco stood up. "This moment is the start of our new family and soon Maria and the little one will join us. So let's offer a toast with some vino from our vineyards. Antonio, would you be kind enough to pour?"

Antonio reached for the decanter of wine sitting in front of him. Everyone passed their glass to him. "This is the sweet wine that is produced from the vineyard after the first frost. A toast to our new American friends and to Maria, Rosario and the new bambina."

Everyone held their glass in the air and shouted, "Salute."

Kelley took a sip of the wine. "Delicious."

"You like," Marco asked.

"Yes. One of the finest that I have ever had," she answered.

As they sat back in their chairs enjoying the wine, Marco said, "Now, my plans for tomorrow. In the morning, we'll go to the hospital to get Maria and the baby. The baby's room will be ready by then, won't it Isabella?"

"Yes. The men are painting it right now. And the furniture will be delivered early tomorrow morning."

Now pleased at the way things were progressing, Marco asked, "Please Senore and Senora Willis, will you accompany us to the hospital to fetch Maria and the little one?"

"Yes, Signor Rossi," Kelley replied. "We would be delighted."

He picked up her hand and kissed it. "You are so much like my Maria. You have a gentle heart."

He turned to Phil. "And you are very strong and determined."

Phil raised his glass to him. "Thank you, Signor Rossi."

"Marco. I insist that you call me Marco. Rosario and I have talked things over and have decided that I shall call the church and have the priest arrange both a wedding and a baptism for Saturday."

Chef Donatto walked into the dining room, holding a silver tray high above his head.

Marco looked up. "Ah, Donatto is here with the first course."

Donatto walked around the table, serving the antipasto as Marco continued talking, "Donatto is from Siracusa Sicily. Our families go way back."

Donatto served Kelley, "Mrs. Willis, at Signora Rossi's request I have prepared a souvenir menu that you may take back to the states as a remembrance of this dinner. It lists all the courses that I'm planning to serve. We will start with the antipastos—imported Parma prosciutto, asparagus vinaigrette, cocktail di vongole, which is a fresh clam cocktail. And finally, 'mozzarella e pomodoro', which is simply fresh mozzarella and tomatoes."

"This looks scrumptious," Kelley said, as he filled her plate with the appetizers.

Donatto worked his way around the table serving the

antipastos.

"What's next," Michael asked as he chewed.

Isabella touched his arm. "Don't talk with your mouth full Michael."

Everyone smiled as Chef Donatto continued, "Then, we will have the pasta's—'Rigatoni Bolognese' and 'Fettuccine ala Romana'."

"That's fettuccine in cream sauce, right?" Michael added grinning.

"That's correct. Following the pasta course, I have a nice 'Insalata'—that's baby greens tossed in herb vinaigrette and topped with fresh shaved parmesan cheese."

"That's my favorite salad," Antonio chimed in.

Donatto looked at him, smiled and continued. "For your main entrees, I have prepared broiled veal chop, fried calamari and broiled lobster tail."

"All that sounds very delicious and filling. I hope that I'll have room for it," Kelley said.

"We'll eat slowly and leave time between courses for lots of wine and conversation. When you get back home you can tell all your friends that you ate a dinner in true Sicilian style," Antonio said.

Kelley reached into her pocket and pulled out her camera. Showing it to Marco, she asked, "Would you mind if I took a few photos of the food and your family? I'd like to show them to my mother and friends back in the US."

Marco nodded in approval as Kelley stood up, walked around the table and took several pictures.

When she returned to her seat, Isabella smiled at her. "As Marco said, you'll see that we take our time when we dine so that we can truly enjoy the food and each other's company. Also, we clear the palate with the salad after the antipasto and the pasta."

"Now, relax. And enjoy the true Sicilian dining experience," Marco said.

From somewhere in the background, Kelley could hear soft Italian music playing. She looked around.

"You like," Michael asked.

She nodded, "Yes. Very much so."

As the meal progressed, and Chef Donatto served the various courses, Antonio refilled everyone's glasses.

When the main entrees arrived, he switched to the rich red wines from their vineyards. Accompanying the meal was an assortment of homemade breads and rolls.

While they ate, they talked quietly about several different subjects—the Willis's life in the United States, Rosario's position at the vineyard and his future plans for his young family. They even entered into a lively conversation with Kelley and young Michael, about motorcycles.

Finally, Donatto cleared the table of the dirty dishes and brought in coffee and dessert.

Phil sat back in his chair and stared at the Tiramisu and a layered a homemade rum cake topped with frosting and pecans. Kelley eyed the bowl of fresh strawberries, peaches and melons.

"I think I've managed to save a little room," Phil said. When the Chef asked what dessert he would prefer, Phil replied, "I'll try a little of each."

After the meal, Marco leaned over to Phil, "Isabella and I would like for you and your wife to stay on with us for a few days."

"I'm sorry sir, but we have already made plans for the rest of our time in Sicily. We'll accompany you to the hospital, so that we can say good-bye to Maria and then we must bid you farewell."

"I understand. But tonight you stay with us. I want to show you my vineyard and where we produce the wines. But first, if you would be kind enough to wait for me in my study, there is something I must tell you."

Marco turned to his wife. "Please take our guests to

the study and then you can retire for the night. I'll be up later." She kissed him, nodded and led Kelley and Phil out of the dining room and to the study.

After they left the room, Marco looked at Rosario and Antonio. "I'll say good night to you both now. Plan on meeting us in the dining room at seven thirty tomorrow morning. We'll have a quick breakfast and then drive to the hospital."

Both men agreed to his plans and left the room. Marco walked over to Michael and put his arm around the boy's shoulder. "Thank you Michael. You are getting to be quite the man. You were very gracious to our guests tonight and I appreciate that. See you in the morning."

Michael gave him a kiss and hug. "Good night Grand Poppa."

Marco walked down the hall to the study, where Kelley and Phil were sitting on the leather sofa waiting for him.

He walked across the room and stood in front of them. "I'm sorry to be so secretive. But I have a serious problem and I think I might need your help."

Kelley and Phil sat upright. "Of course, if there is anything that we can do to help you, we're willing," Phil responded.

Marco sighed. "You both are familiar with firearms, are you not?"

"Of course," Kelley answered. "Why, are you in danger?"

"Maybe. I have two of my security guards watching Maria and the baby as we speak. But, I might need some additional help tomorrow and I was hoping that I could count on you two."

His expression was now one of deep concern. "Let's take a walk in the vineyards where I can talk to you in confidence."

Chapter 28

"Walk with me," Marco said. The full moon illuminated the path to the vineyards.

"I have acres and acres of grapes that will be ready for harvesting in September. That is our busy time of the year and Rosario will have to bring in many extra hands." He led them through the fields.

"My God, row after row of grapes. I can't believe how vast your vineyards are," Kelley said, as her eyes tried to take in the immense span of the Rossi estate.

"We've been producing the finest of wines here for about three centuries. I am extremely proud of our excellent wines that are shipped throughout the world to only specially selected shops and restaurants."

As they walked along, he pointed to a large brick building at the side of the path. "That's where we press the grapes and store it in barrels. Next year, I plan to build an even larger facility for this process. When the wine is aged, we transport the barrels to the other building over there, where it is bottled, labeled and shipped. I'm very particular who I sell my wines to."

He stopped walking and took Phil by the arm. "You must come back and visit us again so that I can show you the entire process. In the meantime, I'll ship an assortment of our wines to your home in the States. You must give me your address before you leave."

"Thank you Marco. I would appreciate that. My step-father is quite a wine connoisseur."

"Then he has probably heard of our label, 'Rossi & Company, Fine Sicilian Wines.' The bottles have my great grandfather's picture on the front. Now, follow me to the house. We'll see my wine cellar."

As they entered the room under the villa, Phil and Kelley could see hundreds of bottles of wine, placed in stone racks.

"These limestone racks were installed by my great grandfather years ago. It is original limestone excavated from the famous Comblanchien Quarries in Burgundy, France, and is known throughout the world for keeping the wine at the proper temperature. Of course the room is well insulated and over the years we have installed modern means for controlling the climate in the room."

"This is amazing," Phil said.

"Would you mind if I took some pictures," Kelley asked.

"Only if you use them for your personal enjoyment or to show your family and friends. I never release information about this wine cellar to the public."

"Of course, I understand." She walked around the room taking photos of the many wines, some of which appeared to be over a hundred years old. "These must be priceless."

Marco nodded. "Yes. This, of course, is our family's private collection. And eventually, my son, Antonio, and then his son, Michael, will be running the business. I have talked with Rosario, and as my son-in-law, he will take complete charge of growing of the grapes and the care of the vineyards in the future."

"That is very generous of you. I'm certain that your acceptance of Rosario into the family will make Maria very happy," Kelley replied.

"I hope so. And you must return to us in a few years and see how our vineyards continue to thrive with all the love surrounding them. It takes a great passion to run a successful winery. Now, I have something very important that I must speak to you about. Please sit."
He pointed to a couple of stools sitting in front of a large wooden cask that was turned upside down to make a table.

Phil pulled out the stools for Kelley and himself and they sat down.

"We will have a little of my special brandy while we are talking." Marco went to one of the racks, pulled out a dusty bottle, brought it to the table and wiped it off. "This is a hundred-year-old brandy that I have been saving. Now, I feel is a good time to open it."

"If you don't mind sir, I feel like I've had enough wine already. Why not save that brandy to celebrate your daughter's wedding," Kelley suggested.

"Once again you are right Kelley." Marco stood silently for a few minutes.

Before he could speak any further, she said, "Somehow I've got the feeling that you have something very serious to discuss with us Marco."

"Yes. The look on your face, and the fact that you asked if we were used to handling guns leads me to believe that you think that your family might be in some imminent danger," Phil said with a frown.

Marco pulled up a keg and sat down. "Several years ago, Antonio and I attended a local town meeting. After the meeting, we were talking with one of the local men when the man's son-in-law, Salvatore Amoto, entered the building.

Without warning, he walked up to his father-in-law; shot and killed him. When Salvatore started to run away, Antonio chased him, tackled him and held him until the local police arrived. Later, at the trial, both of us, as eye witnesses, testified against Salvatore. He was convicted of course and sentenced to life in prison. As he left the courtroom, he vowed that he would get revenge against the judge and both of us."

"But, if he is in prison, you have no reason to fear him," Kelley said.

Marco sighed, thrusting a hand through his hair. "That is the problem. Two days ago, I received word from the judge that Salvatore had escaped from prison. I believe that he might come here and attempt to hurt my family. When you said that someone had attacked Maria in the city, I thought that possibly it had been Salvatore. But it wasn't and he is still on the loose."

"I understand why you were so concerned," Phil said.

"The Palermo police chief has his men searching locally for Salvatore. And I have sent a couple of my men to guard Maria and the baby at the hospital. Also, I have several guards posted around the perimeter of the villa and at the entrance gate."

Kelley sat on the edge of her stool. "What can we do to help?"

"I'm sorry to ask you to get involved in this dangerous situation. Perhaps it would be best if you just returned to Palermo and continued on your way in the morning."

Phil shook his head. "No sir. We want to escort your family to the hospital and make sure that your family is safe before we leave."

"You Americans are marvelous," Marco said as he stood up. "Now, I want to show you the real reason why I brought you into my wine cellar." He walked to one of the floor to ceiling wine racks, pulled it away from the wall, revealing a secret door behind it.

"Come with me," he said as he opened the door and walked into a small room. He reached up and pulled a chain on an overhead light. Phil and Kelley saw a small arsenal of weapons in glass enclosed cases.

"Many years ago, Sicily was a country racked with wars between neighbors. My great grandfather always kept weapons on hand in case they were needed to protect his vineyards and family. Over the years, the wars have ceased, but we have continued to update our arsenal and keep modern guns on hand."

"It looks like you could easily fight a huge war with some of these," Kelley observed.

"One of my men cleans and checks these weapons regularly. Your husband told me that you are familiar with fire arms. I would like you both to pick out a weapon that you are comfortable using and wear it to the hospital."

Kelley walked to the cases. "We're both used to Smith and Wesson's. But, I'm not sure if our license to carry a concealed weapon is good in this country."

Marco opened the case, took out two Smith and Wesson's and handed one to each of them. Then, he opened a drawer underneath the case and pulled out ammunition and two shoulder holsters.

"I called Chief Greco earlier and told him of my plans to arm you. He said that he would have temporary permits for you on file in his office in case you had to use the weapons. Which of course, we hope that you won't. Even though I have a couple of my men stationed outside of Maria's room, I want you to carry guns as extra protection. I'm concerned about your safety too, you know."

Kelley and Phil each put on a shoulder holster, picked up the guns, looked them over, loaded them and placed them in the holsters. After grabbing a handful of extra bullets, Phil looked at Kelley and grinned. "Just like being a couple of private investigators again, isn't it?"

Marco put his hand on Phil's shoulder. "Now, you're sure that you want to go through with this? As I said before, you could just leave in the morning and not get involved any further."

"No sir. With a murderer on the loose, we want to be certain that you get Maria and the baby home safely."

"Okay. If you're both comfortable with this, let's head back to the house. Breakfast is at seven thirty. Tomorrow will be an important day in the lives of the Rossi family."

As they walked up the path to the house, Kelley linked her arm through Phil's. "Another adventure. Just like old times dear."

Chapter 29

As he awoke the next morning, Phil looked at the fancy Rolex watch that Kelley had given him as a wedding present. He noticed that it was six thirty in the morning in Sicily and twelve thirty in the evening back in Syracuse.

He rolled over in the bed, put his arm around Kelley and whispered, "Time to wake up sleepy head. We have to shower and pack before we head downstairs for breakfast."

She opened her eyes, yawned and sat upright in bed. "I didn't sleep much last night. How about you?"

"Not much. I think a hot shower will do us a lot of good." He slowly climbed out of the nice warm bed. "I'll shave and shower first, and then the bathroom's yours."

She looked at the two shoulder holsters with guns in them, draped over the nearby chair. "Today may be a very interesting."

While Phil used the bathroom, Kelley made the bed, laid out their clothes, and started to pack their suitcases.

He exited the bathroom and looked at the clothes she had laid out for him. "Black again, I see. You always seem to want to dress in black when you sense upcoming danger."

"Yes. I have the feeling that we should be on guard today. Signor Rossi seems to think that Salvatore guy is desperate for revenge against his family."

She picked up her cosmetic bag and walked into the bathroom. After showering, getting dressed and applying her makeup, Kelley was ready for the big day.

As they walked into the kitchen, they saw that Isabella, Marco and Antonio had arrived downstairs before them.

"Pour our guests some hot coffee," Marco instructed Isabella. He motioned for Kelley and Phil to take a seat at the granite topped kitchen counter. On it was an assortment of pastries and fresh fruit.

Isabella handed each of them a cup of coffee. "Cream and sugar are right there," she pointed. "And please help yourself to the fruit and sweet rolls. We aren't having our usual big breakfast today. My husband is in a hurry."

Marco frowned at her. "We'll need to leave in about fifteen minutes. Isabella and I will go with our driver in the first car. Antonio is going to follow in the Hummer with Rosario and you can follow in your car. If it's agreeable with you, I would like all of us to attend mass before we head to the hospital. I want to talk with the priest about the arrangements for the marriage and baptism on Saturday."

"Of course," Phil said. "We're at your disposal this morning. By the way, where is Rosario?"

"He'll meet us outside. He's giving the men in the vineyards their work orders for the day. We'll take the back roads into the city."

After the mass in the side chapel of the beautiful Monreale Cathedral, Antonio ushered Kelley and Phil to the back of the church while Marco, Isabella and Rosario met with the priest in the sacristy to discuss the wedding and baptism plans.

As Antonio talked with Kelley and Phil, his phone rang. He stepped outside of the church and talked for a short time. When he returned inside, he saw that his parents and Rosario had joined Kelley and Phil.

Antonio walked up to his father. "Chief Greco just called me. He is on his way to the hospital with a couple of his men. Said he would meet us there. So far no sign of Salvatore Amoto."

Marco frowned, his dark brows drawn together. "Maybe, he decided to hide out in the hills until things quiet down. Now, let's drive to the hospital and pick up our beautiful daughter and her baby. Momma is anxious to see that little bambina."

Inside the hospital, they found the police chief and his two men in the lobby talking with Mrs. Costello, the hospital administrator.

"Nice to see you again," Kelley said as she walked up.

Seeming unusually nervous, Mrs. Costello replied, "We'll take the service elevator in the back, up to the fourth floor. I put Maria in a private room there, Signore Rossi, when I got your phone call. Your two men have been taking turns staying outside of her room all night."

Marco smiled briefly. "Good."

When the elevator reached the fourth floor, the administrator stepped out first. "Follow me. It's the last room on the left."

Marco walked ahead of the group and greeted his security man who was stationed outside Maria's room. He exchanged a few words with him and then knocked briefly on the door.

"Entrare," Maria called out in Italian.

Rosario rushed into the room with the others close behind. He went to the bed, fell on his knees and kissed Maria's hands. She motioned for him to stand up. He sat on the edge of the bed and hugged and kissed her. "You look terrific my love."

Maria smiled and pointed to the crib that was on the other side of her bed. "Rosario, say good morning to your daughter."

He got up, walked slowly over to the crib and peered down at the baby who was sleeping quietly. He leaned over, picked up the baby and kissed her forehead. "You're just as beautiful as your mother. My little bambina."

Maria noticed her parents, her brother and Kelley and Phil, who were standing patiently inside the doorway. She reached out her arms to her mother. Isabella ran to her daughter's side with Marco close behind.

"Momma. Poppa," Maria cried out. "Forgive Rosario and me for deceiving you. Please just love the three of us."

"There is nothing to forgive my sweet. And we do love you. We have so much to tell you. But, first let's get you and the little one home," Isabella said, as she hugged her daughter.

"Yes. Now, it's time for me to hold my new little principessa," Marco said as he walked around the bed to the crib.

He took the baby from Rosario's arms and brought her over to where Isabella was standing. Looking lovingly down at the baby, he said, "Look Isabella, she has my eyes."

"That's exactly what you said about Michael when he was born," his wife replied as she took the baby from him and cradled her in her arms.

The door to the hospital room opened and a doctor and a nurse entered the room. The doctor walked over to Maria and handed her a couple of sheets of paper. "Maria, I have signed the release so that you and your daughter can go home now. Here is a list of instructions that you should follow for the next few days.

"If you have any problems please contact me. This is

my assistant, Jenna. She will help you and the infant get ready to leave. Now, if the rest of you would be kind enough to step out of the room for a while, Jenna will take over."

Isabella handed the baby to the nurse as Marco and Rosario both shook the doctor's hand and thanked him.

As they went into the hall, Marco once again took charge of things. "Antonio and the guard will accompany you to the car, Momma. Rosario, you'll stay here with me and Mr. and Mrs. Willis. We'll see that Maria and the little one get downstairs safely."

As they stood outside of Maria's door waiting for the nurse to emerge with Maria and the baby, Kelley noticed something unusual at the back end of the hall. "Phil, I thought the administrator said that Maria's room was the only occupied one on this floor. Why would there be a food cart down by the service elevator there if Maria's going home and no one else is on this floor?"

Startled by this question, Marco and Phil both drew their weapons. Phil started to walk down the hall. "Back me up, Kell. I'll check it out."

She quickly pulled her gun from her shoulder holster and followed closely behind Phil as Marco and Rosario stood watch outside of Maria's door.

As Phil approached the metal food cart, the service elevator door opened and a woman, dressed in a hospital dietary uniform stepped out, grabbed the food cart and pulled it inside the elevator.

Phil stepped into the elevator beside her, put his finger to his lips and indicated for her to remain silent. He opened the doors on the bottom of the cart. It contained nothing but empty dirty dishes.

"Sorry for startling you madam," he said.

Puzzled, she looked at him, and shrugged her shoulders. "Sorry, wrong floor. Going to basement Signore?"

Phil decided to accompany her to the basement and

take a quick look around. "Si."

Meanwhile Kelley walked back down the hall to Maria's room just as the nurse Jenna exited. "Maria and the baby are dressed and ready to leave. I have to get a wheelchair from the store room to take her downstairs."

She walked across the hall to a supply room.

Kelley heard a noise coming from the room next to Maria's. "Who's in that room," she asked Jenna.

"Oh, it's probably just a painter. The administrator put Maria on this floor because it was empty. They're ready to paint all the rooms including Maria's, which they'll do after she leaves."

Kelley turned to Signor Rossi and Rosario, "Wonder where my husband is? Guess he ran off with the kitchen help. You go inside with Jenna and get Maria and the baby. I'll wait here."

Kelley stood patiently outside the door to Maria's room as Marco, Rosario and Jenna went inside.

Suddenly the door to the adjoining room opened and a man wearing white painter's clothes came out. He took one look at Kelley and darted back inside, slamming the door shut.

She jumped forward, yelling, "Hey you. Stop."

Holding her gun in a ready position in front of her, she threw open the door to the room and rushed inside. The painter was standing at one end of the room with two ladders, a drop cloth and open five gallon paint can beside him.

Seeing Kelley with her gun drawn, he backed into the corner, waving a paint brush.

"Do you speak English," she yelled. "Have you seen anyone suspicious on this floor?'

"No. No. Signora. Only me."

Kelley saw him reach into his bulging pocket of his pants. As he pulled out a gun, she acted instantly. She rushed forward and with a swift karate kick, knocked him to the floor. She kicked his gun across the room, out of his reach. Dropping to the floor beside him, she pulled his arms behind him. "I'll bet you're Signor Amoto. You're not going anywhere, until we check you out, pal."

At that second, Phil rushed into the room. He walked calmly over and looked down at them. "Is this the famous Salvatore Amoto?"

"I think so. And that's his gun over there. Let's get Marco or the Chief for a positive ID."

The man got slowly to his feet, exclaiming loudly in Sicilian, what Kelley assumed were cuss words.

"Now. Now. That's no way to talk to my wife," Phil admonished, as he kept his gun pointed at him.

Kelley got to her feet, walked across the room and picked up the gun as Marco and Chief Greco rushed into the room.

"Is this Amoto," Kelley asked.

"That's him alright. Salvatore Amoto," Chief Greco replied.

"Thank God you found this bastard," Marco exclaimed. "If I had the chance, I would have killed him."

"Calm down Marco," the Chief said as he walked over to Amoto, pulled his hands in back of him and cuffed him. "It's over. Back to jail for you."

Chapter 30

As the police hauled Amoto away, Kelley, Phil and Marco walked back into Maria's room. "We have good news," Phil announced to Maria and Rosario. "Salvatore Amoto has been captured."

"How—when—where," Maria asked.

"While you were in your room getting ready to leave, I discovered him in the next room, dressed as a painter." Kelley answered.

Phil grimaced. "Probably waiting to kill you or your father."

Kelley put her arm around Maria. "When I went into the room, he pulled a gun on me. Anyway, I subdued him. Chief Greco and his men took him away a few moments ago. You and your family are safe now."

Marco patted Phil on the shoulder. "God bless the two of you. I'll always be in your debt."

Kelley nodded toward the nurse and Rosario, who were standing next to the wheelchair where Maria sat with the baby cradled in her arms. "Let's take Maria and the baby downstairs to the lobby in the main elevator. The police were taking Amoto down in the service elevator."

Downstairs, they stood near the front door, waiting for the parking lot attendant to drive their cars up. Chief

Greco ran up to them. He pulled Kelley, Phil and Signore Rossi aside. "I just received word that Salvatore Amoto is dead. He slipped out of the handcuffs and overtook one of my men as they tried to put him into the police van to drive him to jail. He grabbed the officer's gun.

"The other officer ordered him to put it down. Amoto screamed, 'I'm not going back to prison.' Then he raised the weapon and pointed it at the officer. So my man had to shoot him in self defense. End of the story."

Kelley sighed. "What a sad ending."

Greco shrugged his shoulders. "Not for everyone. Amoto chose death over prison. Now, he's on his way to the morgue."

"And I must say that our family is the better for it. The cold hearted bastard," Marco said.

Antonio walked in through the double doors of the lobby. "Father, Mother is in the car. We're waiting for you."

After they exited the hospital, Kelley tapped Marco on the shoulder. "Please Signor Rossi, would you take your family over to that tree? I would like to take some photos of all of you before we bid you good-bye."

He walked over to the car, where Isabella was sitting. After a few words, she got out of the car and followed him. The family quickly lined up under the tree with Maria, who was sitting in the wheelchair holding the baby. Rosario knelt down beside the wheelchair as Kelley snapped several photos of the family.

Then, Marco said, "Mr. and Mrs. Willis you must join in the family photo. We'll have the nurse take the picture of all of us together."

Kelley showed the nurse how to use the camera. After everyone finally lined up, the nurse said, "Say Sicilian cheese," and quickly took several shots.

"Antonio gave me his email address, so I'll send you a copy of the photos once I get back." Kelley said as she put the camera in her bag.

As the Rossi family approached the waiting two cars, Signor Rossi asked Kelley and Phil to come back to the house with them and stay for the wedding and the baptism.

"Antonio has already put our luggage in our car. It's time for us to resume our honeymoon and then return to the States." Phil said. "Our next stop is Savoca. We never did get there the other day."

"Besides, your family will need time alone to get acquainted with your new granddaughter," Kelley added.

Isabella took Kelley's hands in hers. "I'll never forget what you have done for my Maria and the little one."

Signor Rossi shook hands with Phil, then hugged him and kissed him on both cheeks. "I have your address. Be sure to look for the wine that I'm sending."

"And I've made arrangements with a special boutique in Milan to send Kelley one of their fabulous handbags and a lovely scarf to go with it," Isabella said.

"Thank you." Kelley answered with tears in her eyes.

"You have been most kind to our family," Antonio said as he shook hands with them.

Rosario with Maria and the baby walked up to Kelley and Phil.

"I too am grateful for your kindness to my Maria and the bambina," Rosario said.

"You have a wonderful life together," Phil said as he shook hands with Rosario.

Kelley hugged Maria and kissed the baby gently on the cheek. They walked toward their waiting cars. Before Maria could get into the car, Kelley grabbed her by the arm. "Wait Maria, you and Rosario never did tell us what you're going to name the baby."

Maria looked at Rosario. When he nodded, she smiled. "You told me that your mother's name was Ann. So, we are going to call the baby—Isabella Ann—after my Momma and yours."

    "Now, we must go Phil. I know, I'm gonna cry."

Chapter 31

Once they arrived back at the Hotel Astoria, Kelley and Phil went up to their room. They decided to order room service for lunch and take a short nap before starting out once again to explore the city.

After their nap, new life came back into Phil's weary body. He reached over for his wife.

"We've had so much excitement that I almost forgot that we're on our honeymoon," she said.

"I didn't. Why do you think I suggested that we take a nap," he said, as he kissed her slowly.

After some time, Phil slipped out of bed. "Why don't we take a nice soak in the tub before we dress?" He walked to the bathroom and looked at the deep European bathtub. "It's big enough for two."

She laughed. "Sorry dear. I like to stretch out and you have mighty long legs."

"But, we're on our honeymoon," he protested as she drew a nice hot bath.

"Come on in then, there's room."

A half hour later Kelley was still lounging in the tub as Phil stepped out.

"Time to get out." He reached for a big fluffy towel and wrapped it around her as she stepped out.

He grinned. "But, we do have time for another nap if

you wish."

"No we don't. I'm getting hungry. And it's supposed to be getting cooler outside. I think I'll put on my warm up suit. Do you want me to get yours out of the suitcase?"

"Good idea."

Later, they entered the lobby and approached the concierge.

"We're looking for a couple of trips outside the city tomorrow. Do you have any suggestions," Phil asked.

A small Sicilian man, standing nearby overheard the conversation and approached them. He was wearing a cap that read, 'Tito's Tours.'

"Excuse me Signore and Signora. May I have a minute of your time?"

"I guess so," Kelley replied.

"What can we do for you," Phil asked.

"I am Tito. He pointed to his cap. "Tito of Tito's Tours. And I need five minutes of your time. Can you follow me outside?"

Tito pointed to a small bus parked outside the hotel. "That is my double-decker mini bus. It holds five passengers on the bottom and six people on the top. I'm in need of two people to fill my tour for tomorrow morning and thought that you might be interested in joining my group. Special rate for honeymooners."

Kelley and Phil looked at each other. "Maybe. Tell us more," Phil answered.

"I've scheduled a family of five from a hotel down the street to fill the bottom of the bus. From this hotel, I have booked four Australians for the top deck. If you would care to join us, I have room for you up there. That is, of course, the best way to see the sights when the weather is nice. No rain scheduled for tomorrow."

"And where are you going," Kelley asked.

"I pick up the people at this hotel at seven thirty in the morning and we will be going directly to Savoca, where they filmed the movie, *The Godfather*."

"That's just where we planned to go tomorrow," Phil said.

"Good. After Savoca, we stop for lunch. Then, we'll go on to Mt. Etna, our active volcano, and we'll end the tour by traveling to Taormina. That's a lovely city, where we'll enjoy a Sicilian pizza party before driving back. I expect to get you back to your hotel by ten at night."

Kelley, now getting quite excited, gave Phil a nudge and whispered, "That sounds like it includes all the sights that we wanted to see."

Phil sighed and asked, "Okay pal. What's the cost?"

"For you and the lovely lady, one hundred fifty Euros each for the day. That includes the dinner at night. Of course, I will expect a small tip if you are satisfied at the end of the day."

"Sounds reasonable to me," Phil answered.

"It's mano then? Or a deal, as you Americans say?"

Kelley and Phil looked at each other. "It's mano, Tito," Phil said.

"I take credit cards or Euros. And bring cameras. We visit lots of souvenir shops."

"Okay. We'll meet you here in the lobby at seven thirty," Kelley said.

Tito took her hands in his and gently kissed them. "Thank you, Signora. Please wear good walking shoes. Also you should bring a warm jacket since it will be cold at the top of Mt. Etna. Plan on buying your own lunch, but dinner at night is included. I'll see you in the morning then, Signore and Signora."

They watched as Tito climbed into his bus and drove off.

Kelley took Phil by the arm, "This sounds like the perfect way to wind up our honeymoon."

"Yes. But, I'm sad to realize that it will be our last full day in Sicily. The next morning, we're off to the States. A plane from Palermo to Rome and then on to New York. And finally home to Syracuse."

"It has been a lovely honeymoon though," Kelley added. "But now, I'm ready for a short walk and a nice supper."

They walked for several blocks before finally finding a quiet small restaurant. After sharing pasta, they sat at the table outside, sipping their wine and watching people pass by.

"I love people watching." She sat back in her chair, and sighed with contentment. "I could easily get used to this life." Reaching over, she took Phil's hands in hers. "Thank you for a lovely honeymoon. You're very special."

He leaned over and gave her a kiss. "No it's you who are special. And I know that we'll have many more trips in our future. But, let's hope that we won't need our shoulder holsters and guns anymore."

Kelley laughed and nodded. "I do feel a lot lighter without them."

"Well, if you're done with your wine. Let's head back to the hotel. Tito's picking us up early and we have a lot to see and do tomorrow."

The following morning, after having eaten breakfast in the hotel restaurant, they arrived at the lobby about seven fifteen.

Standing beside the entrance doors, was Tito. He waved them over and led them outside to the bus and introduced them to their traveling companions. After they entered the bus, he collected payment for the tour from his passengers.

When they were ready to depart, Tito announced, "Savoca, is 160 kilometers east of Palermo, so it will take us a couple of hours to get there."

"How far is one hundred sixty kilometers?" Kelley whispered to Phil.

"Let's see a kilometer is about six tenths of a mile." He figured quickly in his head. "That's about one hundred and five miles."

"Oh, you are so smart," she replied.

"We'll stop for a 'Smiley Room' break and a cup of cappuccino before we get there," Tito added.

"What's a 'Smiley Room'," one of the Australian passengers asked.

"The restroom. I call it that because everyone smiles when they leave it," he replied, as he passed out cards. "But, before we leave, I want everyone to fill this card with your general information and cell phone numbers. And I'll give you my cell phone number to write down. Keep my number with you at all times in case we get separated."

Tito picked up the cards. "Now a final check. I hope everyone has their cameras ready. Also, you should have on good walking shoes and brought a jacket and a hat, especially those of you who are going to sit on the top of the bus."

"How cold will it be at Mt. Etna," a lady standing next to Kelley asked.

"It will get a little chilly at the top of the volcano. Today is supposed to be about 25 Celsius, that's 77 Fahrenheit for you Americans. And no rain in sight. Perfect weather for Sicily."

"Wonderful," the lady exclaimed.

Tito passed out some small note pads. "Here is a pad to write down notes about Tito's Tour. As we drive along, I'll talk over the speaker system, point out the sights and tell you why I love Sicily. Plan on having a lot of fun. Now, you are Tito's troop."

Everyone clapped.

"Our driver is Nicholas. He will sing for you."

Nicholas burst into song.

When he finished, Tito announced, "Everyone take their seats and use your seat belt. We'll be traveling up some winding roads that lead high into the mountains."

As Tito's mini tour bus pulled away from their hotel, Kelley clasped Phil's arm. "What a nice way to end our honeymoon."

On the way from Palermo to Savoca, Tito talked over the speaker system giving the group facts about Savoca.

"This village was chosen to stand in for the less photogenic town of Corleone, for the *Godfather I* movie because of its peaceful atmosphere and stunning views of the sea from the piazza. Also this town was chosen because the real Mafia was none too keen on Coppola's project in the first place. As we near the village you'll see a picturesque scene in the distance. This was what Michael and his two companions saw as they walked through the hills."

As they drove along, Phil kept pivoting in his seat, trying to take videos of the scenery on both sides of the bus.

After they traveled up the winding road to the small town on top of the mountain, Nicholas parked the bus in the piazza and Tito took the group on a walking tour of the town. He led them to Vitelli's Bar in the piazza, where the wedding party reception in *Godfather* had taken place.

As they walked around the inside of the bar, they could see the many items that were left after the film was finished. It was filled with old empty grocery boxes lining the shelves and a dilapidated cane sofa with a rug flung over it. Since they were discouraged from taking photos inside the bar, a group picture was taken outside. "After we get to Taormina, I'll have them ready for you to purchase."

Tito then led them up the paved street to the church. "When the film was made here, all the streets were dirt. The town was paved with stones as a gift from the film production company. And, as you can see, the old buildings are now slipping down the hillside."

As he guided them to the church where Michael and his Sicilian bride, Apollonia, were married, Tito said, "The only problems that the movie people had with the wedding was that the priest would not allow them to film inside the church. So the wedding pictures were taken outside.

"Now you may look inside the church and wander through the town. There are several shops open for you to buy souvenirs and sample the local vino. Please meet me back at the bus in forty-five minutes. We still have a lot to see today."

Kelley and Phil took pictures outside the church and then wandered through the town, stopping here and there for photos. In a small shop, Phil bought several T-shirts and a barbeque apron for his stepfather, all with Marlon Brando's picture on them. "Have to buy some *Godfather* souvenirs," he said.

Sitting at a small café, in the piazza, they both enjoyed a cup of cappuccino before they returned to the bus.

"We are off to Mt. Etna," Tito said as Nicholas started up the bus. After traveling back down the winding road, the bus entered the modern highway that crosses Sicily.

As they approached the mountains once again, Kelley and Phil put on their jackets and hats. "I can feel it getting colder the higher up we go," he said.

"Yes. But the views are spectacular." She took continuous photos of the small villages surrounded by vineyards and fields of vegetables."

"The soil from Mt. Etna is very fertile," Tito told them. "This is one of the best regions in Sicily for growing vegetables and fruits. Of course, they must wait about one hundred years after a lava flow to use the ground."

As Nicholas pulled the bus into the parking lot, Tito said, "Mt. Etna is a kind volcano and her neighbors love her. She always gives lots of warning before she gently erupts. A few years ago, this parking lot was covered in lava. Now, I'll give you two hours to explore, take photos and get a bit of lunch. Please be back at the bus promptly. Set your watches, we leave at three."

Phil and Kelley wandered all around the volcano and stopped at a little food stand in the middle of the parking lot to sample the many varieties of honey that came from the region.

Finally, they went into a small café and had lunch.

"Remember, we were told by Tito. No pizza. We're having it tonight." Kelley said.

Before they went back on the bus, they took one last climb back up to the top of the mountain, where the views were breath-taking.

"The day is flying by my happy little band of travelers," Tito said after everyone was back on the bus. "But, I have saved the best for last. We are on to Taormina. There is much to see. So no napping. You can sleep when you get home. Also take pictures with your eyes so you can remember my lovely country."

"We gotta come back here, Phil," Kelley said.

Phil's cell phone rang as the bus traveled down the highway once again. "Yes. Yes. We're right on schedule, Dad. We just got back down from the top of the world, Mt. Etna. Leaving Palermo tomorrow. Should be home right on schedule if everything goes according to plan. See you soon."

The bus stopped. "Everyone out. You're at the famous Liperus Winery. We'll enjoy a short tour of the winery and then we sit down for a special Sicilian pizza with all the vino you can drink."

Tito led them inside the winery where they met the owner who had glasses of sherry waiting for his guests.

The guests were given a brief explanation of the history of the winery, and then were led into the kitchen with its large open stone ovens. The tourists were seated in a circle in front of a table behind which two ladies clad in white uniforms were standing.

After a demonstration on how mozzarella was made, the ladies threw scraps of dough to a small terrier that was patiently waiting nearby. One of the ladies said that the dog was called 'Mozzarella' because she had developed such a fondness for the cheese.

The woman asked for volunteers from the audience to help make the pizza. Kelley and one of the ladies from Australia stood up as did two of the men.

All four volunteers were given aprons. The men's were quite risqué as was the Australian lady's. Phil laughed and took a picture of Kelley as she stood there in her apron that said 'Red Hot Mamma.'

"Our kids will cherish this photo someday," he whispered to Tito.

After the volunteers put on chef's hats, they were shown how to throw the pizza dough in the air to stretch it to the size of the pizza pans. Next, they spooned pizza sauce onto the pizza crust and topped it with lots of shredded mozzarella cheese.

After a quick demonstration on how to do it, the volunteers put the pizzas on the wooden paddles and threw them into the brick ovens. While the pizzas baked, the tour group was led out to the dining room, where they were served antipasto and salads.

"Man, that was really good. Now I'm ready for some of that Sicilian pizza you prepared, Kell." Phil looked up and saw a young man, dressed in a white jacket and a chef's hat approach the group. Behind him, were several waitresses carrying large platters of pizza.

"Good evening," the man said. "My name is Eric Li-perus and my father owns this winery. I wish to thank those of you who volunteered to make our pizza for this evening's meal. Also, I wanted to inform you that while you were learning to be Sicilian chefs, my staff took several photos of you. You may purchase one of these colorful photos of your memorable experience for only ten Euros.

As Kelley and Phil were looking over the pictures, the elderly gentleman, seated across from them, suddenly keeled over in his chair.

A startled Eric walked quickly over to the man. As Eric gently lowered the man to the floor, Kelley and Phil ran around to the other side of the table to assist.

"Phil, isn't this one of the Australians that were on the bus with us?"

"Yes."

The woman that was seated beside him started to cry, "That's Mr. Henderson. He's staying in our hotel and came by himself on tour. Said he was an Aussie from Sidney. He's what you American's would call 'a loner'."

Suddenly Mr. Henderson began to shake.

"My God, Phil. I think he's having a seizure."

"Someone call an ambulance," Eric calmly directed the staff, as he bent over the man.

Kelley leaned down and saw that the man had a medical alert bracelet on his wrist, just above his watch.

"Look! This is a Diabetic Alert ID Bracelet. Even has his address engraved on it."

As the man wavered in and out of consciousness, Eric gently sat him up against the near-by wall.

"I've had some medical training. I think this man is suffering from hypoglycemia. We need to get some sugar in him quickly."

He ordered one of the waitresses to get a glass of orange juice from the kitchen.

Kelley knelt down beside the man and helped him to sip some of it. After a few minutes, the man gasped. "Glucose tablets in my bag. On the bus."

"How can we find your bag," Phil asked.

"On the bus. Call my cell phone."

"His ID bracelet had a phone number on it," Kelley said. She grabbed a napkin, copied the number and handed the napkin to Phil. "Call that number!"

"What?"

"Just go to the bus and call that number," she said as the waitress walked up to Eric.

"The ambulance is on the way," she whispered as the rest of the tourists sat calmly in their chairs, looking on in disbelief at the scene unfolding in front of them.

Phil jumped up, ran out of the restaurant and to the bus parked outside with the driver standing beside it.

"Quick. Open the bus," Phil shouted, as he dialed the man's cell phone.

As soon as he entered the bus, he could hear a phone ringing. It was playing 'Waltzing Matilda.' He ran up to the top deck, where the four Australian tourists had been sitting, and found the ringing phone, sitting atop a black canvas bag.

"That's it." Phil grabbed the bag, raced down the steps, out of the bus and into the restaurant.

"Here's what we need. "He thrust the bag into Eric's hands.

Eric opened it, looked inside and took out a bottle of capsules. After reading the directions on the bottle, he gave Henderson two of them with more orange juice.

"One of my friends used to go into diabetic shock in school," he said quietly to Kelley and Phil.

Moments later, Henderson seemed to regain both his strength and some color in his face.

"Boy, that was close," Phil whispered to Kelley as the paramedics entered the restaurant pushing a gurney in front of them. After taking the man's blood pressure and vital signs, they gently placed him on the gurney.

"They'll check him over, adjust his meds and probably release him in a couple of hours," one of the paramedics said

The woman who had been sitting beside Henderson said, "My husband and I will go with him to the hospital."

She turned to Kelley and Phil, "We leave for home tomorrow. We're on the same flight."

Henderson looked at her with tears in his eyes, "Thank you."

Before the paramedics wheeled him out of the restaurant, Mr. Henderson thanked Eric, Kelley and Phil for their help.

"Sorry folks," Eric said, "for the unforeseen interruption. But now, it's time to sit back and enjoy your pizza and dessert."

After the pizza, he had the waitresses bring out coffee and lemon chiffon cake topped with fresh cream.

As Tito's tour group left the restaurant, Eric walked up to Kelley, "Miss, I have a gift for you. It's one of the aprons that we sell in our shop—has a picture of the winery on it.

"And by the way, the photos that you wanted to purchase are free. Bet you never expected an adventure like this on your tour of Sicily."

Kelley smiled. "You're right."

Thanks to the summer month, it didn't get dark until the bus was well on its way back to Palermo. Seated on the top deck of the bus, Phil and Kelley were cuddled together under one of the warm blankets.

"Aren't the stars just wonderful here," Kelley asked, looking up. "This country seems like a dream come true."

He gave her a squeeze. "I almost hate to return to the States and the rat race."

"I know. This has been my kind of day. And this country has been a fabulous adventure."

Phil grinned at her, "Yes, but I sure hope that I can get a good night's sleep tonight. I was getting used to Jack's snoring. Kind of miss it."

Chapter 32

Early the next morning, Kelley and Phil got off Delta Flight 1381 from Palermo to Rome and boarded the airport shuttle train that would take them to Airside E for international flights.

"I'm glad that we don't have to go through security again before we board our connecting flight," Phil placed the straps of the carry-on bags over his shoulders.

"I can take one of those," Kelley said.

"No problem. I'm evenly balanced with one on each shoulder."

After they got comfortably seated at their gate, Phil went to the nearby café and got two coffees and a couple of donuts.

She was reading one of her magazines and he was reading USA Today, when they heard the attendant at their gate announce in English, "May I have your attention, please. Will Mr. and Mrs. Phillip Willis please come up to the counter?"

They picked up their carry-on bags, walked up to the attendant and identified themselves.

"You are Mr. and Mrs. Willis?"

"Yes. Is there a problem," Phil asked.

"Just a small one and we're hoping that you could help us out."

"What can we do," Kelley asked, placing magazines on the floor, next to her carry-on.

"You have seats next to each other and are flying first class on our flight to JFK, in New York."

"Yes, here are our boarding passes. Our checked luggage has probably already been put on the plane," Phil said.

"That's not the problem. Mr. Donafaro from our front office wishes to speak to you in private." She nodded her head toward the tall thin middle aged man, dressed in a navy blue business suit, standing beside her.

The name tag attached to his suit, read "Anthony Donafaro, Operations Manager, Delta Airlines."

"Would you please follow me into our private lounge," he asked them.

Somewhat puzzled, Phil picked up their carry-ons, while Kelley grabbed her purse and magazines. They followed Mr. Donafaro down the hall and into Delta's Executive Lounge. He shut the door and offered them a seat at a nearby table.

"What's the problem," Phil asked as he threw the carry-on's on the floor beside him.

"Yes. Tell us. We don't want to miss the boarding call for our flight."

Anthony Donafaro sighed. "To put the problem quite simply. We need two adjoining seats in first class on this flight. Cardinal Recker of New York and his secretary must get on this particular flight. They were suddenly called back from the Vatican to the States. There's a very important meeting scheduled in New York in the morning and they not only need seats; but the seats must be together. They have confidential paperwork that they must go over together during the flight."

"So you want us to give up our seats for the Cardinal," Kelley asked, somewhat stunned.

"Precisely. Unfortunately this is our only flight leaving for New York this morning. And all the other airlines couldn't accommodate the Cardinal and his secretary."

"What happens to us, if we give up our seats," Phil asked.

"We would of course, compensate you generously for your change of plans."

Donafaro was starting to get Kelley's attention. "And how would you do that?"

"We would put you up overnight and then book you on tomorrow morning's flight. You would arrive at JFK at the same time, only one day later."

Phil started to shake his head no.

"But wait, Mr. Willis," Donafaro continued. "We would of course reimburse you for all your meals today. And,we'll give you each a voucher for a future round-trip ticket anywhere in the U.S.—good for one year."

"Anywhere in the U.S., good for one year?" Kelley repeated, as her eyes lit up. "Even Hawaii?"

"But, we wouldn't get home until Sunday night and I have to be back to work on Monday," Phil protested.

"But just think, we would have time to look around Rome. I've always wanted to see this city," Kelley said. "Please Honey, let's do it."

The door to the lounge opened and a short heavy set man, dressed in a black suit and wearing a black Fedora entered. Behind him were two young men, dressed in black slacks, black shirts and wearing clerical collars.

Donafaro jumped to his feet. "Cardinal Recker. Welcome. May I introduce Kelley and Phil Willis to you?"

They walked over to the Cardinal, dropped to their knees and kissed his ring.

The Cardinal helped Kelley to her feet.

"And may I introduce, Monsignor Alton, my secretary, and Father Schaefer, my driver."

"Glad to meet you," they said as they shook hands.

"This is the young couple from Syracuse, New York

that I told you about, Cardinal," Mr. Donafaro said.

"It's so kind of you to give up your seats to us," the Cardinal said, beaming at them.

"Well, your Eminence," Phil replied, "we haven't actually made that decision yet."

Kelley gave him a poke in the ribs. "Well, actually, we have. We would be delighted to accept your offer Mr. Donafaro. And it is an honor to be of assistance to you, Cardinal."

Phil just looked at his wife. He knew when he was defeated.

"Thank you," the Cardinal replied. "I'll have Father Schaefer take you and your baggage back to my hotel suite, where you'll be my guest for the night. You can rest for a while and then spend the day seeing the city. Father Schaefer will try to accommodate you in every way."

Phil nodded his acceptance. Mr. Donafaro grabbed his hand and shook it vigorously. "Thank you so much, Mr. Willis. We'll get you out on tomorrow morning's flight. And here are the vouchers for your free round trip tickets."

"And even though you are only staying one day, you'll have the chance to get the taste and feel of Rome," Monsignor Alton added. "You will, of course, want to return someday for an extended visit."

Donafaro turned to the Cardinal. "I spoke to baggage department just a short time ago. Your bags are already being put on the plane, Your Eminence. We'll be boarding first class in just a few minutes."

Turning to Kelley and Phil, he added, "And your bags are waiting for you at baggage claim."

The Cardinal shook Donafaro's hand. "I can't tell you how much I appreciate your efforts."

"My pleasure."

Turning to Kelley and Phil, he added, "And I am extremely grateful to you for giving your seats up for us. This is a difficult time for our diocese and I must be at that meeting in the morning."

"It's our pleasure," Phil said, extending his hand.

"Now, I want you to go with Father Schaefer, my driver. He'll help you fetch your luggage and then take you to my hotel."

Fr. Schaefer led them to the baggage claim department, where their tagged luggage was waiting. He helped them wheel it outside and led them to the curb where a large black car with an official Vatican license plate was waiting.

Fr. Schaefer opened the back door of the car and helped Kelley and Phil climb inside. After loading the luggage into the trunk, he climbed into the driver's seat and pulled away from the Leonardo De Vinci airport.

Leaning over his shoulder, Fr. Schaefer asked, "Are you in any hurry?"

"Not now," Phil quipped.

"Okay. Then I'll give you a quick tour of my favorite city before I drop you off at the Roman Holiday Hotel. It is one of our newer hotels and the Cardinal loves it because it is in the heart of the archaeological wonders of this eternal city. By the way, I guess you can tell from the tone of my voice that I'm originally from Boston. Only been assigned to the Vatican for the last few years."

Kelley laughed. "You'll never lose that Boston accent."

As he zipped through the busy streets of Rome, dodging the tourist buses and the impatient young people driving small motor scooters, the priest called out the names of the sites as he passed by.

"The glamorous 'Via Veneto' famed as the setting for La Dolce Vita. The Forum and the Coliseum. The Bridge and Castle St. Angel on the banks of the river Tiber. The Roman Baths. St. Paul's Cathedral."

By the time, Fr. Schaefer pulled up in front of the

hotel, Kelley's head was spinning.

"Oh my gosh, I can't take in all of this," she said as they got out of the car.

"You'll never see all of Rome in a day," Fr. Schaefer replied. "I've been here for four years now and I'm still discovering new places and things. Right now, I suggest that you check into your room and freshen up. The clerk at the desk is expecting you. She knows that you will be spending the evening in the Cardinal's suite. Right now, I have a quick errand to run. I'll return for you in an hour and take you to the Sistine Chapel. When we get done there, I can direct you to a tour bus and you can take the rest of the afternoon to see the city on your own."

He got their bags out of the trunk. They wheeled them inside to the check-in desk, where they learned that the Cardinal's room had been freshened up and was ready for them.

An hour later, after having showered and changed clothes, they got a call from the front desk that Fr. Schaefer was downstairs waiting for them.

He drove the car into an underground garage near the Vatican Center and guided them through the Vatican Museums, where they admired the artistic masterpieces collected and commissioned by the Popes. They walked through the Tapestry Gallery and the Gallery of the Maps and finally were led into the Sistine Chapel.

As they entered the room, they were amazed at the vibrant colors of the paintings on the ceiling. Fr. Schaefer whispered to them that Michelangelo had spent eleven years in the preparation of the vault and altar wall and that the paintings had been painstakingly restored a couple of years previous.

The guard at the front of the chapel barked out orders loudly in Italian.

"What's he saying," Kelley quietly asked the priest.

"He's instructing the people to talk quietly and to not take any photographs."

"Well, he's not very quiet. But, I'll keep my camera in my purse."

Both Phil and she were astonished at the layout and size of the chapel itself.

"From all the pictures that I have seen, I always thought that the Sistine Chapel had a high ceiling—like in a Cathedral," Phil said.

"It's good that it's not that high. We can see the paintings better, honey."

After, Fr. Schaefer gave them a quick tour of the Gardens of the Vatican, he said. "Unfortunately, the rest of my afternoon has already been scheduled; but, I will take you around the corner where you can catch a tour bus. I suggest that you get a brochure from the driver. It will list the various sites that the bus stops. One of the things that you shouldn't miss is the Coliseum."

"Oh, I definitely want to see that," Phil said.

"You did mention that this was your first visit to Rome," the priest continued. "I must caution you about having your picture taken with the gladiators at the Coliseum. It will cost you ten or fifteen Euros. And be careful of the pick pockets. They work in pairs and are everywhere in Rome. And they aren't necessarily scruffy looking people; some of the time they are very well dressed."

"Thank you. We'll keep an eye out for them," Phil said, as they approached the corner, where a sign indicated it was a tour bus stop.

"And Mrs. Willis, you might want to have a couple of coins ready when you visit the Trevi Fountain. Legend has it that if you throw two coins in, you'll return safely to visit Rome again."

"We'll be sure to do that. And thank you for all your time." Kelley said.

Phil shook hands with the priest, "Yes. Thank you."

"You're entirely welcome. Ask the tour driver what exit you should get off at to return to your hotel. It is only around the corner from St. Peter's. Please meet me in the lobby with your luggage tomorrow morning at five a.m. We'll go to St. Peters for early morning mass and an audience with the Pope. After the mass, we'll have breakfast in Vatican City somewhere and I'll drive you to the airport in plenty of time to catch your flight to New York. Sunday is not so busy. It is a day of rest for most Romans."

"Oh my goodness. An audience with the Pope," Kelley exclaimed excitedly. "That's a once in a lifetime experience. How can we thank you?"

"Don't thank me. Cardinal Recker personally arranged it for you. He was extremely grateful that you gave up seats for him and his secretary. Now enjoy your tour of my Roma."

After the priest walked away, Phil went over to the kiosk that serviced the double decker hop-on, hop-off Viator bus. He paid for two tickets for the day and got a couple of the brochures that listed the seventeen stops that the bus made.

They enjoyed the afternoon riding the bus and stopping at the various sites. They visited the Spanish Steps, Piazza Navona with its many pavement cafes and trattorias, the Forum, Circus Massino and many of the sites that ancient Rome had to offer.

Stopping at the Trevi Fountain, Nicola Salvi's astonishing 18th Century Fountain, Phil asked, "Do you have your coins ready?"

"Got them right here, in my pocket."

"Then, throw them over your left shoulder with your right hand. That means you will return safely to the Eternal City again."

Late in the afternoon, and now, somewhat exhausted, they walked from the bus stop to the Coliseum.

"Isn't it funny, Phil, I've seen pictures of this in the movies and on television, but somehow, it's more majestic that I ever imagined."

"That line for tickets doesn't look too long. Let's purchase them and look around inside. I want to see where they kept the wild animals and how they brought the gladiators in," he said.

"Speaking of gladiators. There they are," she pointed to two men dressed in the ancient costumes and carrying big swords. "It would be nice to have my picture taken with them."

Phil sighed. "I guess ten or fifteen Euros is worth it for your photo album. Go stand beside them."

She started to walk toward the gladiators, and suddenly, stopped in her tracks. "Did you see that Phil?"

"What?"

"I think that well-dressed young man is following that tourist in the Yankee's baseball cap. He looks like he's sizing him up. Remember what Fr. Schaefer said about the pick-pockets."

"I sense that the undercover cop in you is jumping to conclusions."

She gritted her teeth. "I'm not kidding Phil. And, you heard Fr. Schaefer say that pick-pockets in Rome work in pairs. Now look, the suspicious looking guy is talking to that girl carrying the large red tote bag. And he's gesturing to the Yankee tourist."

"Are you sure that your imagination isn't working overtime, Kell?"

"No. Watch them. It's our American duty to help one of our own."

Suddenly, the suspected pick-pocket went into action. He brushed against the torist, reached into his side pocket, grabbed a brown leather wallet, walked calmly over to the girl and slipped the wallet into her tote bag.

"You take the girl.," Phil said, "I'll get the fellow."

When he saw Phil approaching him, the pick-pocket took off running.

Kelley walked up to the girl and grabbed her by the arm.

As the girl struggled to get out of Kelley's grip, Phil approached them.

He grabbed the tote bag from the girl's hand, reached into it and drew out the brown leather wallet. "I don't think that this is yours honey."

"Bastardo," she snarled. She twisted out of Kelley's hold, grabbed the tote bag and ran off through the crowd.

When he saw that Kelley was contemplating running after the girl, Phil stopped her. "Let her go Kell. Let's give the Yankee his wallet back."

They walked over to him, explained what had happened and returned his wallet.

"Now. Let's go see the inside the Coliseum. You can get your picture taken with the gladiators when we come out."

As Phil and Kelley walked through the Rome airport the next morning, she said, "Well done dear. You brought me to Rome if only for a day. And it was a memorable experience. I can't believe all that we saw in such a short time."

"And the mass and audience with the Pope was something that I'll never forget," he added.

"Me neither. I can't wait to see how our pictures of that turn out. And we have to be sure to send a thank you to Cardinal Recker for arranging it."

"And one to Fr. Schaefer for being our personal driver. I felt just like a VIP when he drove us around in that Vatican car."

"The day in Rome was the topping on the cake as they say. What a way to end a fabulous honeymoon. And

I'm so glad that we had the chance to buy medals and a book on the Vatican in the shop outside St. Peters."

"And, I promise you Mrs. Willis, that we'll return to Rome again. After all, we did throw two coins into the Trevi Fountain."

"I'm going to hold you to that promise, Mr. Willis. But right now, let's get a quick coffee before we head to our gate.

"Sounds good to me," he replied as he looked around for a couple of empty seats in the food court.

Phil walked up to one of the counters, purchased a couple of cups of coffee and returned to where his wife was sitting. As they sat there sipping the hot coffee, Phil noticed a black bag on the chair next to him.

"Where are our carry-ons, Kelley?"

"On the floor by my feet. Why do you ask?"

"Because there's a black carry-on bag on the chair next to me, and it looks like one of ours."

Phil picked up the bag, and put it on his lap. "Someone must have left it behind."

Kelley reached over. "Here's a tag on it. The name says Gio Tortini." Maybe we should turn it in at the desk."

"Good idea," he responded and then stared in amazement as he saw his wife undo the zipper on the bag.

"My God, Kelley. What are you doing?"

"I'm going to see what's in it. Who knows it could be a bomb."

"Once an undercover agent. Always an undercover agent," Phil mumbled shaking his head.

"Holy moley. Or should I say holy money. This bag is filled with money," Kelley whispered as she quickly zipped it shut. "Who would leave a bag of money just sitting here?"

"We are in Rome, Kell. Maybe it's mafia money."

As Kelley looked up she saw two tall heavy set men hurrying toward them. Nodding her head toward them, she whispered, "I have a feeling that this bag may belong to them. What should we do?"

Phil said calmly, "Just get up and walk away Kelley. Leave the bag behind. We didn't see anything."

"You're right." She jumped to her feet and took Phil's arm. "Grab our bags. Let's head for our gate. Personally, I've had enough adventures for a lifetime. From now on, you can take the spotlight, Mr. Attorney. You can call your adventure, 'Justice 4 Willis'."

Phil winked. "Love that title."

Articles and Short Stories by Raymond Weaver

"A Star is Born" published in *Chicken Soup for the Soul-Inspirations* for the Young at Heart; August 2011; a story about Ray's appearance in a play at the local theater.

"The Cell Phone" published in *Chicken Soup for the Soul-Inspirations* for the Young at Heart; August 2011; a story about Ray's first experience with carrying a cell phone.

"The Past Sixty Years" published in *Chicken Soup for the Soul: Twins and More*, March 2009; a story about Ray and his twin brother, Ed.

"A Grandfather's Dream", "The Wieliczka Salt Mines", "Ground Zero in New York", "So this is Canada, Eh", "Ray and Ellie visit Lourdes"; among articles published in the *Safety Harbor* Florida, newspaper, *The Tropical Breeze*.

"So this is Sterling" published in the Dunedin Florida's newspaper, *The Highlander*.

"Make your Memories" published in the "Seniority Section" of the *St. Petersburg Times*.

Second place in "June Times Remember Section" of the *St. Petersburg Times* with a story about his granddaughter.

Story about Grandpa Weaver's 1902 Grocery Store, published in *Bend of the River Magazine*.

Numerous articles published in the *Suncoast Hospice* newsletter.

Author Bio

Ray Weaver is a resident of Clearwater, Florida. He and his wife, Ellie, have been married for over fifty-three years and have two children and six grandchildren. Ray has been writing for nine years and has numerous short stories and articles published in major magazines and newspapers.

He is very proud of the three stories that he has had published in the *Chicken Soup for the Soul* books.

His first novel, "Tightrope to Justice" was published in 2010 and his second novel, "Miami Justice" was published in August 2011. This novel, "European Justice" is the third and final of the series featuring Kelley Ryan Willis. He is now putting Kelley's adventures to the side and concentrating on those of her attorney husband, Phil.

Ray is now working on his next novel, "Justice 4 Willis."

Ray loves to hear from his readers
You may contact him at raymondellie@aol.com

www.ingramcontent.com/pod-product-compliance
Lightning Source LLC
Chambersburg PA
CBHW070333260626
47160CB00003B/1028

9 780981 943282